INNO
VOICES

GUARDIANS OF GRACE BOOK 2

JULIE BONN BLANK

INNOCENT VOICES

Copyright © 2022 by Julie Bonn Blank
North Beach Books
Cover by milbart
All rights reserved.
ISBN: 979-8-9854548-7-1

INNOCENT VOICES

NOTE

This is Book 2 in the "Guardians of Grace" series. Although It can be read independently, readers will have the best experience with first reading Book 1, "Innocent Lives".

DEDICATION

For my mom - my forever cheerleader, encourager and master of hospitality. Love you!

HEADS UP

Recommended for ages fourteen and up.
This book is not for everyone.
Please note that although it ends positively, content is suggestive of violence, substance abuse, prostitution, rape and trafficking **in the effort to raise awareness and elicit change.**

If you are a survivor or domestic abuse, sexual assault or trafficking, please proceed with caution and know that it is okay to put down entirely, or to read in small increments. The author wishes to never take someone backward in the healing process.

For help with healing from abuse, or faith-based support while in abuse, please visit www.abuserecovery.org

INNOCENT VOICES

WHAT THEY SAID...

Congratulations on wrapping up a second amazing book. I'm usually good at figuring out mysteries...I doubt anyone could see this one coming. Your stories continue to grab me. Can't wait to see what happens in each of these situations and how you bring them all together. -Louise M. Gouge, Editor and Award-Winning Author

ABOUT "INNOCENT LIVES"

I knew after reading *Innocent Journeys: Rose* and *Penny* this book would be good. **I never imagined how good though!** ...I read *Go Ask Alice* at a way younger age than I probably should have, **but it stayed with me and shaped my life as well as many others lives. I think this book will too.** -dagaz98

Julie tackles a difficult subject. Hard but necessary to face. She draws you in fully to the lives of two different victims, crosscut stories, but also manages to show you where angels show up. She gives hope in the midst of the trials, and the encouragement to press through." - Cheryl McKay (Screenwriter *The Ultimate Gift* and Co-Author, *Never the Bride*)

Author did a marvelous job of showing the psychological conditioning by abductors towards their abductee. The step-by-step conditioning displayed in the abductor's behavior and actions, without ever having to explain it to the reader their action, is fantastic. I love the way she introduced and displayed her characters. She makes the reader identify and care for these girls, to the point of tears. A deeply moving book." -Richard B.

Prologue
Jem, Age 10

Jem glanced at Mom on the ratty couch. Mom trembled. Thank goodness she could help – Mom sweated, her face red. Jem pulled her earbuds out and set down her book. The song became a tiny sound. "Maybe you should lay down."

"I-I can't." Mom pulled herself up off the couch with difficulty and headed to the bathroom.

Jem sighed and followed. "Out...in a minute." Mom wiped sweat out of her eyes with a trembling hand. She shut the bathroom door in Jem's face.

Jem sighed and rested her forehead against it. Inside, her mom heaved. "Can I bring you something? Ginger ale?" She'd hidden some under her bed a few weeks back.

Mom wretched. Blew her nose loudly. "Ugh! My stomach is killing me! Ain't nothing you can do."

Jem disagreed. She ran to her bedroom and lowered herself to the floor, peering into the darkness. She shuddered, thinking about monsters under the bed, but bravely felt under along the floor until her hand connected with the plastic bottle. She pulled it out, gasping but smiling. Mission accomplished.

"Mom!" She ran back to the bathroom door. "Mom! I got some! I saved it for you!" She tried the doorknob. Locked. She pounded on the door. "Mom?"

"Jem, please. I've such a headache."

"Okay." Jem slid down the door to sit on the floor. The almost empty ginger ale bottle rested beside her. "I'm here if you need anything." She should have brought her iPod with her.

"Jem, get me some of those green pills."

Jem jumped up quickly. Ran to the kitchen cupboard.

On the table, her mom's cell phone beeped. She grabbed it. Clicked a button. Brandon. His message said "K" and that he was on the way. Maybe he could help again. She popped the phone closed. Tossed it on the table. She grabbed the packet of pills and pushed two small ones through the foil. They did seem to help her mom somewhat, just never fast enough. What else? Water. She darted to the kitchen sink and filled a glass. Balanced it carefully on her way back to bathroom. What if this wasn't enough this time? Her heart beat crazily. She tried to forget the bad dream she'd recently woke up from. One where she couldn't rouse her mom. Jem had screamed. Awoke to sweat and tears.

"Mom," she called through the door. "Mom. I have them. And water. Open up."

Mom groaned.

Jem sighed. She had a secret. Time to use it. She set the water down. Tucked the pills in her jeans pocket and turned, rushing to the fireplace. On the rock shelf, a key lay near at the back. A few months ago, after Mom wouldn't get out of the bathtub for hours, Jem finally ran next door for help. When she returned, Mom lay on the couch. Moaning about Jem abandoning her. The next time Mom took a long nap, the neighbor visited and installed a new doorknob. He gave Jem the key.

Jem inserted the key, and the newer doorknob turned easily. She tossed the key on the counter. Mom lay on the bathmat. "Mom." She rushed forward.

Mom moaned. She held her stomach – her hair slicked back with sweat.

The smell of vomit turned Jem's stomach. She pulled at Mom's arm. Tried to heave her up. "Come on, let's get you out of here."

"C-can't." Mom tried to sit up, and Jem was rewarded with a new spray of vomit all over her t-shirt.

She grimaced. Gross. Hopefully Brandon would arrive soon. She grabbed a bath towel to try and wipe up the mess. She sat down, and Mom placed her head on Jem's lap.

"I'm sorry, baby."

"Shhh, can't be sorry for being sick." Jem smoothed Mom's hair back from her pale face. Loud thumps. Heavy boots sounded on the porch stairs. "See, it's okay. Brandon's here now."

Mom groaned louder. Her eyes watered. "For-forgive me," she whispered.

"Mom, stop." Jem frowned. "Just rest. Oh, I have those green pills."

Mom tried to sit up. Failed.

Jem looked up to see Brandon leering. She pulled her mom's head in a bit closer to her heart. "She's sick."

"I see." He straightened his shirt collar and paused to check his hair in the bathroom mirror. "Reeks in here."

"Can-can you help her? Please?"

Brandon refocused his attention on Mom. Put his hands in his pants pockets and grinned at Jem. "Sure." He laughed.

Jem frowned. She wasn't sure what was so funny about Mom being sick.

Brandon knelt. "El, you know what we agreed on, now. You remember?" He pulled a wad of cash from his pocket. Waved it in her face.

She turned away and groaned.

"Three months' rent, plus expenses. And I got the goods for you too. Plus, the other things we agreed on. I must say, it's about time. Need to work on your budget to make ends meet …"

He pulled a rubber tube from his pocket, a bag of white powder and a needle.

Jem breathed a sigh of relief. Mom would feel better now. "N-no…" Mom sputtered. "Jem, go."

"Go sit in my truck, Jem." Brandon glared.

Jem stood. Hesitated. Mom didn't want her to see Brandon making her better.

"W-will she be okay?"

"B-be fine, Jem." Mom's teeth chattered now. Her eyes closed. "Go. Be a good girl. I'm sorry." Tears rolled down her face as she presented her arm to Brandon and eagerly looked at the bag of powder. "Hurry."

Jem turned toward the door. Hesitated again. Why did she have a funny feeling? Mom would be better now, right? She sighed and grabbed the bathroom key. In her bedroom, she changed her vomit-covered shirt. In the living room, she picked up her iPod, earbuds and book. Shutting the front door carefully behind her, she walked down the stairs to wait in Brandon's truck.

Chapter 1
Elenore-15 years before
Seattle

Elenore slammed the bedroom door behind her and bounced down the stairs. Chad was late. Again. She exited the front door and it slammed behind her too.

"Elenore!"

She ignored her mother and instead sat on the steps with her chin in her hands.

"Elenore!" The voice was closer now.

Darn. "I'm here, Mom. On the steps!"

Joy Stevens pushed open the front door and stood with her hands on her hips. "Now, I know you aren't happy with me or your young man."

Elenore ignored her.

"But you aren't to go around slamming doors unless you want to replace them. I don't care how much of an 'adult' you are."

Elenore sighed. "He's late."

Joy's eyes narrowed. "Maybe you should stay home."

Elenore pulled in a quick breath. "No, Mom. He's almost here. I'm sorry I slammed the doors." She jumped off the steps and hugged her quickly. "Sorry." She apologized again as Chad's Beamer roared around the corner and then up the driveway. "See, he's here. Gotta go. Talk later, okay?"

She hurried down the steps, swinging her small denim pocket purse up on her shoulder. Her blond hair, freshly washed, swung around her shoulders in a fragrant cloud. She opened the door. "Hey Chad."

He waved at Joy, still on the porch. "Your mom? Should I say hi?"

Elenore rolled her eyes. "Please. No. We're already gonna be late. Where have you been?"

Chad backed out of the drive. His dark hair blew back in the breeze. She liked it on the longish side. His hazel eyes sparkled. He was the cutest guy in school, and Elenore snagged him, after some cajoling.

"Late to what?"

Elenore bopped him on the arm. "I don't know. Your surprise, remember?"

"Well then, I guess you don't know if we're really late or not."

True. She watched Chad as he steered around the corner. He wore stone-washed blue jeans and a leather jacket. He winked at her – she blushed. She'd wondered how to view those muscles underneath. He probably knew what she was thinking.

"Just get ready for some fun, babe. You know I love you."

Elenore's heart soared. Chad turned her life upside down and topsy-turvy, in a good way. Butterflies fluttered in her stomach, up to her chest, in her heart. If he never said it again, that was enough. "I love you too." She smiled as he swung around another corner and pulled into a parking lot.

"Alki Beach." She breathed in the fresh air. "Let's go walk, Chad. I want to see the water."

"Yeah, sure." They closed their car doors, and she ran around to his side.

He draped his leather-covered arm around her shoulder. "Don't I get a kiss after that?"

She giggled. "After telling me you loved me? Yeah, sure." She swept her hair back behind her shoulders and reached up, wrapping her arms around his neck. "You're the best," she murmured. "I really do love you." She pressed her lips to his as he squeezed her tightly, his hands wandering around on her back…and lower.

"You are *so* sexy." He squeezed her backside.

She squirmed but shivered as she reveled in his praise. They spent several minutes kissing and feeling until they heard whoops and hollers from the beach.

He chuckled and took her hand. "They want to meet you."

"Who?" Elenore laughed as he pulled her along to a beach fire where several people lounged.

"Hey, everyone. This is Elenore."

They smiled and cheered.

"It's about time." One girl smiled. "We've heard about you for only … uh, six months now?"

"Not quite." Chad laughed. "Well, okay, maybe."

Chad had liked her for six months? Elenore sucked in her breath. Maybe she hadn't been the only one pursuing a relationship. He walked to a blue cooler and took out two beers. He tossed one to her. She caught it, then paused. "We're, uh, underage." She spoke quietly, but no one seemed to hear. She looked around. No cops. She would sip it and try to fit in.

"Are you graduated now?" A girl with black hair waved at Elenore. "I'm Kelly, by the way." She shook her hair from her eyes and removed a ponytail holder from her pocket.

"Hi, Kelly. Yeah. Barely."

"What's your plan?"

"Shut up, Kelly-mama. The plan is called *fun*." Chad gathered with a couple of the other guys.

She briefly stuck her tongue out at him. "Really. My parents are bugging the heck out of me because I don't have a *plan*. They won't let me go to art school. Say it won't pay the bills. Whatever."

Elenore nodded. "Yeah, my mom's on me, too. No plans yet really. Working at Charlie's downtown for the summer. Maybe community college. I don't know. I'm kinda burned out on school."

"Burn out!" A blond guy scuffed his feet in the sand. "Cool. Me, too."

"Shut up." Kelly shook her head. "You can't burn out on surfing, Danny. Idiot."

Elenore laughed.

Kelly grinned. "Let's lose the losers. Got your beer?"

"I-I don't really like beer." Elenore turned the can around and pretended to read the ingredients.

"No? Hold on." Kelly went to the cooler and tossed Elenore a berry wine cooler instead. "These are good." She pulled out a bottle cap opener and popped the top.

Elenore shrugged. She set the beer down and sipped the wine cooler instead. It tasted like juice, with a tang. She walked with Kelly farther down the beach, picking up some rocks along the way. "What about the cops? I'm not 21."

"No one is. Well, maybe Chad? Hide it if anyone comes by."

"Chad's twenty. So he says."

"He says, huh? Maybe he's thirty and fooling us all." They both laughed, and Kelly finished her beer. She tossed the can. "Get rid of the evidence." She grinned. "You wait tables at Charlie's?"

"Yeah. Play sweetie-pie until they get obnoxious. What about you?"

Kelly stopped and dreamily gazed at the Puget Sound. "I want to be free. Travel. Write. Grandpa says I should be a travel writer. Then I get paid to travel. Or a food reviewer. Free meals."

Elenore felt impressed. "Are you any good? I mean, can you write?"

"Sure." Kelly scoffed, then giggled. "Can't most anyone?"

"You working now?"

"Unfortunately, yes. In a daycare."

"That's not so bad."

"Some days it *sucks*." Kelly kicked a rock. "If I hear 'Miss Kelly, Miss Kelly' one more time I think I might jump off the ferry."

Elenore laughed and drained her wine cooler. She didn't toss her bottle but found a trash can instead. "So, I guess you wouldn't want to be a teacher."

Kelly's eyes widened. "Heck, no!"

They giggled their way back to the fire, where Kelly replenished their drinks and pulled out hotdogs. Elenore stood by Chad, who laid his arm across her shoulders. He turned back to his friend, continuing the discussion about Duran Duran coming to town. They chatted about buying tickets and maybe even extras to scalp. Elenore wiggled out of his arm grip and returned to the fire. Kelly was more fun. She felt confident now as the alcohol spread warmth throughout her body. She sipped a new wine cooler as Kelly introduced her to Melinda and Lani. This was turning out to be fun. Since their recent move here, she'd been morose and anti-people. Mom would be proud of her for finding friends.

Lani slipped two hotdogs onto a stick. "Who's calling these ones?"

The guys immediately claimed the dogs and Lani sniffed. "I meant the girls. You dogs can make your own dogs."

Everyone laughed, and both Chad and Mike reached for the hotdogs when they were done.

At one point, a police cruiser rolled by up on the boardwalk. They hid the alcohol, and Danny headed out to the waves. No one seemed nervous or scared. The cruiser soon moved on. Chad grabbed another beer.

Elenore wondered how many he had drunk. He was driving, after all. He seemed jovial and raised his eyebrows at her to ask how she was doing. She nodded and smiled.

"I ditched him fast." Melinda was explaining about a blind date who ended up a complete loser.

The air chilled and the girls huddled a bit closer to the fire as the guys walked out to the water.

"How'd you ditch him?" Lani put her socks and shoes on.

Melinda giggled. "We met on the corner, Later, I asked him to wait there while I grabbed my phone I forgot at home. I didn't come back. Since he didn't know where I lived, he finally left an hour later."

Kelly pulled out a cigarette and lit it. Laughed. "Poor soul. Elenore, if you want to do that to Chad, may I suggest a better strategy? Too obvious. He'd knock on all the doors till he found you."

Elenore nodded. Her head followed along with the nod slowly. "No problem there. I don't ever want to get rid of him."

Kelly elbowed Melinda. "She's got it bad. Uh-huh." They teased Elenore until she blushed.

Soon the guys rejoined them at the fire. Chad sat down next to her and hugged her shoulders with his t-shirted arm. His large muscles flexed. His leather jacket lay over a nearby log. "How's it going?" Elenore glanced up as he smiled. "I see you met everyone."

"Pretty much. Except not all the guys." She felt his arm stiffen.

"Why do you want to meet them?"

Elenore raised her eyebrows. "Hmm? Because it seems like the polite thing to do."

Chad glared, and she shrank back. But then he grudgingly introduced her to Sean and Winston. Danny returned from the waves, and Chad nodded at him.

Kelly approached and sat close to Chad on his other side. He squeezed her arm. She laid her head on his shoulder.

Elenore frowned, a bad feeling in her stomach. When Chad shoved another drink into her hand later, she put it back into the cooler while he remained distracted. She gave him another half hour and then asked to leave. She didn't want her mom to worry – the sun now dipped below the water.

"Sure, babe. Give me a min." Chad returned to his guys and drink.

Maybe she should walk home.

A few minutes later, Kelly, Danny, Melinda and Sean all announced needing a ride home, so they put out the fire out with water from the Sound. Other fires flickered around them.

The guys heaved up the cooler and blankets, and they all trooped toward Chad's car. Elenore waved goodbye to everyone else and hugged Lani as she squeezed into the front passenger seat.

Kelly occupied the gear box between the driver and passenger seat. There weren't enough seatbelts for all six of them. Chad patted Kelly's knee.

Elenore's heart squeezed a little.

They turned onto SW Admiral Way and Elenore looked up. Headlights blinded her. Brakes screeched. She covered her face with her hands and screamed as the impact came, shattering the windshield and spinning the car around and around until it came to a rest against a brick building.

Chapter 2
Cienna

Cienna hung up the phone in her office at the Portland Freedom Center and sighed. The calls rang nonstop all day. Claire finally waved at her frantically through the window that separated their areas.

A distress signal. She put aside the grant application she'd quickly typed to meet the Monday deadline and started picking up the phones too. Then followed stories – victims of domestic abuse, someone's sister missing and living on the streets, a mom crying about her drug-addicted son. Trauma was never ending in Portland…and beyond. Her head pounded. Before she knew it, it was past four, but when she saw the time, her heart soared. Tonight, she and her husband, Adrian, planned to meet her friend Jazz for dinner. Her mom agreed to keep Cienna's daughter, Grace, with her for longer than usual, for just that evening.

Although the office closed at five, Cienna finally hung up the phone at 5:30. Her cell buzzed yet again. She flipped it over. Adrian.

Sorry, hon. Phones nonstop. On the way. Jazz there?

When leaving at five, Claire had waved through the window.

How was she supposed to get more grant money to help these victims when her time got sucked up in answering their calls? It was a never-ending battle.

She started her older blue Honda, Queenie, and backed carefully out of her spot. No answer from Adrian. She pushed down the ball of dread in her throat, grateful that she'd even had a parking spot for the day. They'd been hard to come by lately, and when one got a spot, the car was often vandalized anyway. Frustrating. Today, Queenie seemed intact and unharmed, which was great news. She had plans to get to and people to see.

She pressed on the gas pedal and realized she needed the other lane. Her GPS reminded her as she shook her head. Traffic was heavy. Finally, someone let her in, and she waved a thank-you. She sighed, gripping the steering wheel hard as she passed several homeless camps and tents at the side of the road. People sat in old lawn chairs in a circle socializing. Community came in all sorts of forms, she knew. Since the recent rioting, graffiti littered the walls.

Tonight, she should be happy. But seeing Jazz didn't stop the ball of nerves in her stomach. Of course, her husband's silence didn't help.

Hey. She voice-texted, her eyes still on the road.

Here soon? All fine here. Want shrimp cocktail? I'm starving. Already ordered your drink.

Yes. Thanks. She flipped on her turning signal again. Stepped quickly on the brakes as a young skateboarder darted across the street to the tents.

All fine. What did that mean? Did that mean what she hoped it meant? She smiled as she pressed on the gas pedal. Yes! Jazz awaited her too! She wiped a little tear from the corner of her eye as she whipped around a corner. She smiled, waved a gentleman in a red truck to go ahead of her and paused for a pedestrian to cross the busy street. The streetlights started to blink on one by one as dusk descended. Gosh darn it, someday she needed to get out of work before 5:30 during the season of early darkness.

A year before, Cienna required a sabbatical from her nonprofit. She pushed a dark curl behind her ear as she remembered. Started with such passion and excitement, her nonprofit headed downhill after only a year. Two employees quit within a short time, the funding dried up a bit and, at one point, a client spat in her face. To make it worse, the people in her monthly community domestic violence meeting started looking at her like she was an alien. She grew self-conscious, patted her curls constantly and finally asked someone straight out what the problem was. Someone mentioned burn out. Compassion Fatigue. Common when working with people in trauma. Once a powerful advocate of the homeless and survivors of trauma, Cienna's talent dimmed. She no longer felt powerful. Her colleagues admired her as a survivor now helping other survivors. But maybe she should take care of herself for a while?

Cienna dragged herself to the office that next day and picked up the phone. She asked both former employees to chat and encouraged complete honesty with no repercussions. One she had to beg, but finally received the firm opinions of both. She'd harbored control, become overly emotional and neglected to consult her employees when making decisions. In her extreme compassion for victims and in still trying to heal herself, she ran right over her most important team.

Realization crashed hard.

She scrambled to apologize. They both seemed understanding, but there was no relationship left to salvage. Who wanted a Team Lead who didn't truly care what they thought and automatically said "no" every time they brought up a new idea?

Time for a break.

Adrian patted her back that night in bed. "I know you're doing your best." He moved up to rub her shoulders. "But I love you, honey, and I think it's time for a break. You're doing amazing work. Tiring work. But if the world loses you because you're burned out, what good does that do the victims who are out there still?"

Nothing! She yelled it into her pillow, and then realized she hadn't said it all. Instead, she rose, stumbled to the bathroom, and yelled, "I hate Mike!" as she slammed the door.

Mike was in prison now for trafficking Cienna and others and killing little Penny with neglect. But sometimes it felt like he was in the same room with her again. She clenched her fists.

Sinking into a hot bath, she assured herself of her safety over and over again. "Adrian loves you, Ci. Treats you well. You're safe. Jazz is safe. Grace is being raised in a safe and loving home. She will *not* take after her mother or father, she will never be a perpetrator or a victim. Love makes all the difference in the world..." As an advocate now, she knew the stats, but she also knew it didn't have to turn out that way.

She turned into the parking lot of the restaurant and parked as her phone rang. Detective Miller. She needed to answer. Adrian would understand. She turned off the engine. "Working late tonight, Detective?"

"Cienna." She heard the smile in his voice. He was like a proud papa. He and Mollie saved her life – and Jazz's life too. She winced briefly, thinking of the other great losses, specifically of Penny under Mike's house and even Rose, who lived in the farmhouse brothel with Jazz.

"How are you both? And the kids?"

Miller chuckled. "Driving us crazy, of course. But in a great way. Four-year-old twins aren't for the faint of heart. Ha. Mollie keeps threatening to get a full-time job and hire a nanny. How's Grace?"

Cienna texted a quick update to Adrian and leaned back into her seat. "The most beautiful little girl ever. Growing big. And stubborn as heck."

"Yes, um, not sure where that came from!"

She smiled. "Uh-huh. Thanks, Miller. Yeah, Mom always says the kids pay you back double. So far, she's right. You got an update for me?"

He grew serious. "About your request. Just some questions."

She sighed. "I know it's unusual for a survivor to request to visit their perp in prison."

Miller cleared his throat. "You could say that. And you know it's not in my jurisdiction anymore. But if I know more, I might be able to clear something with my Fed friends. So, what are you thinking here? Are you, I mean, are you wanting to find out Grace's parentage? If so, they can easily get a court order for a DNA sample."

Cienna grimaced. Gripped one hand on the steering wheel. Was that part of it? And could she live with whatever the answer was? "I'm...I'm still not sure on that. But I do know one thing." Her jaw tightened. "I need to look that man in the eye."

Seconds ticked by. She imagined Miller was trying to be careful. Very careful. "Why look him in the eyes?"

"As his equal, not his slave." Cienna paused. Wondered if Miller might hang up now. "Not for revenge," she hurried to say. But at the same time, wondered if that truly was what she wanted, given the chance. "For closure. I think."

"You've always been confident, Cienna. I understand. But it might not go as you expect." Miller's voice gentled but remained matter of fact. "He's unlikely to admit to anything. He might pretend not to recognize you. Or he might try to turn the charm on like he was so good at. He might verbally threaten you or get angry, although of course he would be restrained, and they would have guards watching very closely to ensure your safety."

"I know." But she also knew Mike. "I doubt we'll see anger."

"Prison can change a man. Have you chatted with your therapist about this, Cienna? We don't want to see you go backward in your healing."

She rolled her eyes. "No."

"Do me a favor. See what she thinks."

"Fine." Cienna disconnected the call and blew raspberries out through her lips, moving her bangs. How annoying. Why would it be such a problem for her to confront Mike in a safe spot so she could finally move on? She shouldn't have to battle this. It was her right. For her and her daughter's sake, she wanted to look him in the eye, knowing who the victor finally was and who was behind bars forever.

Cienna opened her car door as she readied her mace. She held it in front of her as she approached the restaurant doors. Ah, there he was. Adrian knew. As soon as she saw him, her pulse slowed. Her husband grounded her like no one else could. She tucked the mace and keys into her purse. He reached out, and she quickly grabbed his hand. He pulled her into the shelter of the doorway overhang.

"Darling." He brought her hand to his lips. His blond hair glistened in the porch light of the restaurant.

Weight lifted from her shoulders, and she raised her face to smile at the handsome, amazing man who loved her despite her wretched past. "Adrian. I kept thinking…oh, never mind. I take it the news is good? I can't wait to see her."

His chin dropped, and the message resonated clearly. She gritted her teeth, feeling the black cloud descend. After all the time helping Jazz find her true personality once again and moving her back on track, it didn't matter.

Jazz was still MIA.

Chapter 3
Jem-Seattle

Jem pushed herself against the wall under the overpass, seven-year-old Jade held tightly against her side. Her heart tried to beat out of her chest. She waited, prepared to run out of the other side of the cement structure as fast as she could go. Sweat dripped into her eyes. The sun beat down endlessly. At least the overpass provided some cooling.

"Where'd she go?" Footsteps grew louder. Heavy boots like Brandon's.

"Darned if I know." The man's voice slurred. "But I done saw her. Ran like lickety-split and had a little kid too. Fast runners, those gals."

"A kid?" A loud laugh. "You sure you ain't hitting the sauce too much today? Don't see a lot of kids on the street."

"They aren't from the street, you moron. She's fresh ..." The voices softened, then faded completely.

Jem breathed a sigh of relief. Slid down to the ground. Pulled Jade down with her, but her sister immediately squirmed. Now what? She rubbed Jade's head and tucked her red curls behind her ear. "Sorry, Jade. But I had to take you away. Please understand."

Jade tucked herself in closer to Jem's side as her eyes filled. "Where...where are we going?" Her hand inside Jem's trembled.

Her heart still pounding fast, Jem breathed deeply. Right. Now what? "We need to find Grandma."

Maybe those men would have helped her, but she couldn't risk it. Having a kid made blending in more difficult.

Hadn't the dude just said he didn't see many kids on the streets?

She turned in a complete circle, looking for any potential complications. Quiet enough for now. She let go of Jade's hand.

Jade sniffled and wiped her sad-looking eyes. Dark circles rimmed them. Traffic roared overhead. How long until they needed more food? Their backpacks sported some clothes, two bottles of water, crackers in a baggie, carrots and forty dollars, meant to buy a birthday present for her sister. Now her gift was survival. Away from home and on the streets. And clearing out of Seattle before Elenore awoke from her drug-induced haze.

"Where's Elenore?" Jade sat again – her small body hunched against the little breeze. Her backpack almost tipped her over. She huffed and shrugged it off her shoulders.

Jem considered. Gone for good, she hoped. She shuddered, remembering the conversation between her mother and Brandon. "We have to get to Grandma's. It'll be okay, I promise."

"Will Elenore come see us there?"

Golly, she hoped not! She hadn't thought of that. But if Mom was okay, and sober, she just might. "I don't know yet, Jade. Please trust me, okay?"

Jade placed her hand in her sister's once again and stood. "I trust you, Jem. I love you." She sniffled and wiped her nose on her sleeve.

"I love you too." Her little sister had no idea how much. Jade grabbed the zipper on her backpack, but it stuck fast. Jem reached down and jiggled it, pulling the fabric of the backpack out of the way. She snagged a bottle of water, and they both drank, but Jem only a sip.

Jem kissed her forehead. "We'll figure it out." A tear dropped on Jade's forehead. A large truck rumbled overhead. Two long honks sounded in succession. Sirens wailed in the distance. Jem hugged her sister tightly. They headed toward the bushes at the side of the overpass. Jade rubbed her eyes, complaining as she followed along behind, leaving her backpack. Jem circled around to retrieve it and hefted it onto her other shoulder. For now, she needed to carry both.

Jem worked through some brush and out from under the overpass. She stood near the upper street, looking around. She thought they might cross, but a blaring horn stunned her, sending her three steps backward.

Okay, further down then. She found a crosswalk finally and after crossing, a lady sitting on the sidewalk against a building. Jem paused. She hovered near the homeless lady, who stared at her with beady eyes. "What'cha want? Got money?"

Jem shook her head. "No money. Sorry. We need…we need a bus. Do you know where it is?"

"The boats?" She screeched. She had no teeth.

Jem focused on the wall right above her head instead of the woman's gums.

"The boats are down that-a-way. Down the hill." The woman inclined her head toward the Seattle waterfront.

"No." Jem started sweating. "The bus. The bus station."

The woman smiled.

Jem groaned. "I need a *bus…to…Portland*."

"Oh, there. Yup, there's a station. It's back up the hill, that-a-way." She inclined her head again, this time pointing upwards.

"Oh." In dismay, Jem looked up the long hill. "Thanks." She readjusted the bags and her grip on her sister's hand. One strap kept sliding down her arm. She saw Jade staring at the lady and squeezed her hand, hoping to give her a hint. "How far?"

"Few blocks. And over to the right."

Jem nodded. "Let's go, sis." She whispered. "Grandma's in Portland. She'll help us."

Halfway up the hill, Jem stopped to catch her breath and leaned against the building. Heat radiated from her face. Jade finally smiled at Jem. Jem smiled back.

"Almost there." She found her bottle of water and drank.

"Miss, you gonna share that?"

Jem jumped. An old man sat in the alley behind her. His pants were torn from ankle to knee and he wore no shoes. His long, dirty hair was pulled into a ponytail.

"Um, I..." Jem wasn't sure what to say. She felt sorry for the man, but two water bottles were all they had. She thrust the one over with the least amount of water.

Pulling Jade closer, she hurried further up the hill.

Inside the station, she let go of the Jade's hand while at the ticket counter. "Two to Portland. Myself and ... my daughter." Best to pretend. She wiped sweat off her brow.

"Luggage?" The man in a blue shirt asked.

"Two backpacks."

He eyed the one most crammed full. "One might have to go under the bus. Next one leaves at five. That's $32.50 for two tickets."

She shook her head. A huge chunk, but they needed to get to Portland. She swallowed hard and plastered on her best grown-up face. "The two tickets, please." Her money slid across the counter.

He counted her change out, pushing it back. He ripped two tickets from a hole in the counter. "Boards 4:45."

She nodded and stuffed the tickets and change into her jeans pocket. Her stomach rumbled. "Come on." She turned to find Jade several feet away staring out the window.

"Jade!" She ran to the windows, grabbed her sister's hand again and headed toward the vending machines. Maybe a package of potato chips would be enough for an early dinner. She grabbed the bag out of the machine and crammed it into her backpack.

Jem found the ladies room and hustled Jade into the disabled stall. She set the backpacks down. They both used the facilities. "Time to wash." The door banged against the wall as they opened it, and a woman at the sink jumped.

"Sorry." Jem said. She shouldered both bags again and urged Jade forward toward the sink with one of the bags.

"It's okay." The lady moved over to dry her hands. "Looks like you have a handful."

"We ran away from home." Jade giggled.

"We're traveling." Jem frowned. "Wash your hands now." She smiled at the woman. "Never know what they'll say."

The woman tore a paper towel off. "That's for sure. I have three. My son completely embarrassed me in the grocery store about that age …"

No time to be nice. "Gotta go!" Jem grinned and waved at the woman.

They exited the restroom with wet hands. Jade complained as they headed toward the benches. Bless the bus people. There was a play area with a slide and climbing areas. A boy and two other girls happily played. Jade ran to join them. Jem plopped on a bench with the backpacks, sighing with some relief. She looked nervously around. What if someone they knew saw them?

She took a deep breath, pulled out the chips and tried not to fall asleep as they waited. One mother looked at her sympathetically. She dozed, jolting awake when her sister came back and shook her arm. "I'm thirsty."

Jem, too. She'd better grab another water with her meager funds. She'd keep both bottles this time. Refill them at drinking stations. At the vending machine she struggled with Jade and the backpacks again while scrounging for change.

A man from the playground stepped in front of her. "Let me get that for you." He inserted money and pulled a water out of the dispensing hole. "On me." He walked away. and Jem stared with her mouth open.

"Thanks so much …"

People did the weirdest things.

They soon boarded. The man outside the bus door let them take both backpacks into the bus. She crammed one backpack under her seat and the other in the bin overhead. She settled Jade into the window seat and clipped her into the seatbelt. Settled back in the aisle seat, she breathed a sigh of relief. She shivered. She reached for her sweatshirt in her backpack and as she pulled it out, her cell phone tumbled out with it. Jem swore. Panic welled in her throat. She'd forgotten to get rid of her phone! Could they trace her with it?

"What's ta matta?" A dark-skinned young man across the aisle leaned toward her. "Something I can help ya wit?"

Jem sighed. "I need to get back off the bus now. This needs to go in a garbage somewhere. It's important."

Eyebrows raised, he settled back and nodded. "I get that. Want me ta take care of it?"

Jem paused. "You'd get off the bus and dump it for me? What if the bus leaves?"

"I'll be quick. And I ain't got no kid with me. Actually, I have a better idea." Jem noted Jade blinking up at the guy curiously. He held out his hand. Jem hesitated, then plopped her older iPhone into his hand. He might know what he was doing.

After glancing around, the young man tossed it in the aisle and stomped on it with a heavy heel. People stared. The phone splintered and fell apart as he rubbed his heel back and forth against the floor. "That oughtta do it. We'll sweep it up an' toss it next stop." Wide-eyed, Jem turned to Jade, to see tears rolling down her cheeks. She unclicked Jade's seatbelt and pulled her not-so-little-sister securely onto her lap.

With a shudder, the bus pulled away from the curb.

Chapter 4
Elenore – 15 years before
Seattle

Elenore heard a clock ticking in her dreams and when she awoke, the room blurred. A blob sat near her bed, and the blob touched Elenore, smoothing back her hair. Elenore jerked her head away.

"Elenore, love. It's me, Mom."

"M-mom."

Mom sniffled and grabbed a tissue from the box near the bed. Elenore's vision cleared.

Mom wiped her nose and eyes. "I wasn't sure you were going to wake up. I'm-I'm so grateful…"

Elenore struggled to sit. But wires and tubes held her back. She needed to yank them out and go home. Mom gently pushed her shoulder back to the mattress. "We can sit you up slowly but with support." She tossed her tissue in the nearby trash can and punched a button on Elenore's bed. The bed whirred.

Elenore found herself rising to a sitting position. The room spun.

"Puke!"

Mom grabbed a bedside container and placed it at Elenore's chest level. Elenore heaved, but nothing came up except yellow liquid.

"Sorry, love. Too fast on the bed moving!" Mom said. The TV blared "Friends," and she grabbed for the button on the side of Elenore's bed. "Too loud, too!"

Mom somehow managed to pull the bedpan away from Elenore and turn off the TV at the same time. "Oh, dear." She grabbed another tissue. Wiped vigorously at the tears now streaming down her face.

Elenore closed her eyes. "Mom, you're making me dizzy. Stop."

"What am I doing?" Mom tapped her fingers on the bedrail. "Never mind. Okay, no problem. You want ... quiet? Maybe some music? What can I do?"

"Where am I?" Elenore took Mom's offer of a tissue and wiped the sides of her mouth. A horrible taste rose. A disgusting something coated her tongue. She noted three blankets on her lap, and she wore a hospital gown. Her hair felt plastered to her head.

"Swedish hospital. There-there was an accident." Suddenly, Mom not only hit the call light on the bed but stood and rushed to the door. "She's awake!"

Elenore cringed. She closed her eyes, wishing the bed would go back to flat.

She heard a flurry of activity at the door.

"Hi, Elenore."

"Who are you?" Elenore opened one eye.

"My name is Tabitha. I'm currently your nurse. We're going to check some vitals." She popped a clip onto Elenore's finger and instructed her to open her mouth as she placed a thermometer under Elenore's tongue.

Elenore felt a band around her arm, tightening so hard that her fingers grew numb. "I can't feel my hand!"

"There now." Tabitha patted her shoulder. "You're fine. We're taking good care of you. Dr. Wheeler will be here shortly."

"Can I go back to sleep now?"

"Sure, sure." Mom answered instead of the nurse. "She can, right?"

The nurse mumbled something, her voice growing smaller as she apparently moved out the door. Then all was quiet.

"That boy!" Mom exclaimed loudly. "I'm so mad at that Chad. This is all his fault!"

Elenore felt a buzz around her head. Her arms felt light and floaty. "Where is Chad?" She drifted off to sleep.

Chapter 5
Jem

Jem awoke, startled, and glanced furtively around at the unfamiliar surroundings. A bus. The engine droned. She groaned as the memories crashed back into her head. She immediately turned to the seat beside the window. No Jade.

Across the aisle, her sister laughed. Jem jumped up. Jade sat on the lap of the phone-smasher! The debris seemed to be cleaned up now.

He looked at her apologetically. "She came ta me."

Jem cried out and snatched Jade's hand, yanking her back to her proper seat and pushing her in toward the window. She turned back to the aisle. "You should've woke me up. Who are you, anyway?"

His skin reddened under his darker complexion, and he held out his hand. "Jet."

"Jem." She settled Jade on her lap. Ignored his outstretched hand.

"Girl, I don't mean no harm. She jest came over. Ya was asleep."

"I can vouch for that" A woman behind Jade shuffled in her seat.

Jet settled back and crossed his arms in front of him. Jem saw several tattoos on his arms. As she calmed down, she wondered what they meant. "You going to Portland, too?"

He smiled. "What's in Portland?"

"My grandma." Jem dug in one of the backpacks for the fish crackers. It took her a bit to find the empty baggie under her seat. She groaned. "That was your dinner."

"I was *hungry*." Jade crossed her arms and turned to look out the window, her tears dried on her cheeks. "Where's Elenore and Brandon, anyway?"

Jem shook her head quickly, trying to clear it. "Not here, Jade."

Jade rubbed her eyes with a dirty fist and frowned

"It's okay." Jem patted her sister's arm, wondering what awaited them. She shuddered as she remembered huddling in the bedroom, dreading the heavy footsteps. Getting her sister away was no longer a choice.

When the bus rolled to a stop, Jem noticed Jet sleeping. Quickly she gathered Jade and the backpacks, grateful for no conversation.

The woman behind her stood and smiled. She was heavyset with short, squirrely black hair. "Good luck, honey. I hope you and your daughter are settled in soon. Portland's a nice city."

Jem nodded at her and noticed out of the corner of her eye as Jet stretched his long arms far above his head. Darn it. "Hey, wait!" He stood.

She turned to her side to maneuver out the narrow aisle with people rising on all sides of her, pulling Jade by the hand behind her. She pushed forward.

Jade loudly called "Bye, Jet!"

Jem shushed her. "Don't say goodbye." She wondered briefly if she should change their names like they had just changed cities. Grandma would know what to do.

She stopped suddenly. A vision of her now-smashed cell phone clearly in her head. The phone housed Grandma's phone number. Now what? Did she remember her address? She shrugged one backpack higher on her shoulder and turned right when she stepped off the bus.

"Elenore!" Jade shouted.

Jem startled, realizing a lady a few feet away did look like Mom. She shushed her again. "No Jade! Stop!"

Jade stopped and stomped her foot. "Where's Elenore? Why are we leaving her when she always needs our help?"

Jem ignored her, instead staring into the terminal before her. The entire outside of the building was made of dark red brick. Inside, beige and grey marble shone. It practically hurt her eyes. Jem patted Jade's head and spied several benches. She needed a minute to figure out what to do.

After she sat and gave Jade a bottle of water, Jem pulled out her change. A bit over five dollars left. She must have lost some. She crammed it back deeply in her pocket. They were officially poor.

The terminal bustled. Nearby, a man jumped off the bench and tightly hugged a woman who entered. A mother nearby pushed her bangs off her flushed face as she called to her son who was darting around people's bags. "Simon, knock that off!" A man smiled at Jade.

Jem glared back. She wondered if Elenore was awake enough yet to even realize their absence. Probably not. She usually didn't awaken until at least eight p.m., and a glance at the large round terminal clock told her they still had about an hour to go. Jem sighed.

But now onto more serious issues. She didn't have Grandma's phone number. She remembered an address on 82nd Street. Or was that 182nd? But that was all. Her phone number started with 503. She hadn't seen Grandma in a long time. Surely, the woman would remember them. Take them in.

A uniformed police officer wandered by, and Jem felt sweat roll down her back. He ignored them. Good. Police officers weren't safe, either.

"Hey, girl!"

Jet swept into her vision and plopped down next to her on the bench. "What's uuuup? No need ta go runnin' off on me without a 'bye' or 'see ya.' Geez." He crossed his tattooed arms, pouting. Jade, the traitor, immediately smiled and reached over to give him a hug. "Hey, there." He patted her head.

Jem practically growled. "What now?"

"I'm jest checking on ya. Left awful fast."

"It was time to get off the bus." She ran her hand through her limp hair and tucked the strands behind her ear. "No use dilly-dallying."

Jet laughed. It was a nice laugh, but she still didn't like him. Not one bit. "Go away. Or I'll yell for the cop."

He raised his hands in front of him, palms outward. "Gol, Jem. Jest wanted ta make sure you are a-okay. I'll be outta here." He stood up, crammed his hands into his jacket pockets and sauntered away.

Jem almost called after him. Almost. Instead, she gave Jade the last snack in the backpack as her own stomach growled. The cop wandered by again. How long could they sit here? Maybe she should move to the other side of the terminal. Her back ached. Cushions would be nice.

"Where are we going now?" Jade finished the carrot sticks and held the empty bag out.

Jem snatched it from her hand. "I'm trying to figure that out." She grabbed a book from her backpack and handed it to Jade. "Here, work on your reading."

Jade sighed, then opened it up.

Finally, a woman sat down near Jem and pulled out her phone. After sitting there for two hours feeling pretty much hopeless, Jem figured it was risk time. "Excuse me."

The woman looked up with wide eyes. "Yes?"

"Sorry. I'm sorry to bother you, but I lost an address. Could I borrow your phone real quick?"

The woman seemed to consider, tilted her head and then passed her phone over. She moved a bit closer to Jem. "There's the internet." She pointed to an icon.

"Thank you." Jem pulled up the browser and quickly typed in her grandmother's name: *Joy Stevens, Portland OR*. A ton of sites appeared as Jem sighed. An author, an attorney, a doctor, a therapist. She was pretty sure Grandma was none of those. She was too old.

"Is there a way to find an unlisted number?"

The woman tilted her head again. "Well ..."

Jade disappeared around a large statue. Jem flew to her feet. "Sorry!" She practically tossed the phone on the woman's lap. Grabbed their bags and Jade's discarded book. Hurried to retrieve her sister. Now far away, the woman stood, and waved. "Gotta go! Good luck!" She scooted off.

Apparently, Jade needed exercise. But no play area appeared as they explored the terminal. After visiting the ladies' room, they returned to the benches. Now there were children playing games on the bench.

When Jade approached them, they offered her a colored pencil. She took it. Grinned at Jem.

"Yeah, yeah. I'm keeping an eye on you." Jem crossed her arms and sat.

Jade smiled and started coloring.

The man with the kids nodded at Jem and she immediately grimaced. Moved a little closer to the group. After a while, he removed snacks from a bag. He offered Jade canned oranges and cheese.

"Thank you," Jem whispered. She wondered if there might be extra for her, but the man didn't offer.

"Where're you headed?" He tucked the snack containers back into a bag.

"My grandma's. You?"

"My wife is in a hospital in California. We haven't seen her in several weeks." He nodded at the children. "Forgive the mayhem. They're pretty excited."

Jem smiled. "I understand. She suddenly felt much older than fourteen. "Thanks for the snacks." She hustled Jade into finishing her coloring page. Tried to pull her back to her bench.

Jade yelled and yanked her arm away.

The man laughed. "She can keep the picture."

Jem tore it out of the book and grabbed Jade's hand. "It's just been a long day. We're tired." She stuffed the picture into one backpack. Hefted the strap onto her shoulder and helped Jade put the second one on her back. "Good luck." She'd learned from the other woman traveler. "I-I hope it goes well for you all."

"Thank you." He wiped his son's face with a baby wipe.

Jem hustled Jade away and found a place to sit closer to the bus platform. Her stomach growled again, and her eyes grew wet. But she had no time for tears, not when Jade was so dependent on her. She angrily brushed them away.

Night fell and the activity in the terminal decreased. Despite Jem moving around, the cop wandered by again. She didn't see him after that, but instead saw a lady in uniform with a firearm attached to her side and a scowl on her face.

Jem shuddered and moved to another spot, yet again.

When her eyes grew too heavy to keep open, she finally moved returned to her original bench, Jade alongside. She lay down on the hard surface, using one backpack as a pillow, and tucked Jade in carefully against her stomach in a spoon-type formation. Closing her eyes, she drifted into a warm and colorful world where nothing could hurt them.

Chapter 6
Jazz

Jazz popped her gum and smiled at her supervisor. Pulled back her shoulders. "You know I'm the best there is."

Phil shook his head. "We like you, Jazz. We really do. But there are issues."

She slammed her fist on his desk and leaned forward. "Darn it, Phil. I *care*. You know that. Whether it's a runaway kid who could be in trouble or someone prowling about that apartment community. Last week, it was the teenager crying by the dumpster."

He nodded. He'd already heard it all.

"Did you see my log? A woman on the fourth floor called the cops cuz her boyfriend hit her. And not just once, I hear…"

Phil shook his head. His long beard brushed his chest. "What did you do?"

"I went up there of course! That's why I have a scanner!"

He sighed. "Obviously. And then, what did you do?"

She sat back. Flushed. Shrugged. Closed her mouth. "What did you do, Jasmine?"

She flushed again. Her boss never called her *that* name – he knew better.

"Did you wait for the police? We're basically civilians, you know. Your job would be only to make sure she's safe and wait for the police."

"Oh, I made sure she was safe, alright!"

Phil titled his head. Then he stood up, all six feet, four inches of him. He leaned forward. "Tell me."

Jazz backed her chair up. Her heart fluttered briefly. But she pulled her shoulders forward, stood tall and looked up at him. Her lips pursed. "I backed him into a corner. He's a wimp."

"Did you use your hands?"

She laughed. "No, I used the gun we're not allowed to carry. Ha! I used my baton, of course!"

Phil gritted his teeth. Ground them. "What did you do with the baton?" He spoke evenly, although his posture remained tense.

She shrugged. Tilted her head. "He wasn't a big guy. I backed him into the corner with the baton…"

"The baton *where*?"

She laughed, remembering the look on the perp's face. "I might have threatened…threatened his privates a bit. But it landed in the end right up against his windpipe."

Phil slammed his fist on the desk.

She clapped her hand over her mouth and stepped back. "He deserved it!"

She smiled, remembering how once she'd pinned him against the apartment wall, his partner stood taller. She'd told him to cooperate, or she and kids would leave for good this time. She ran to the bedroom with the kids and slammed the door. As the cops pounded up the stairs, Jazz stepped back and sheathed her baton.

The perp slumped against a wall.

"Good evening officers." She smiled as they entered. "Jazz. Security duty tonight. All is secure on the scene and the vic stepped into the bedroom. Thought it was best to separate them."

As one officer questioned the man and the other knocked on the bedroom door to check on the others, Jazz slipped away.

The satisfaction inside of her rose to the top of her head.

"You need a break." Phil sat and cleared his throat. "I'm processing paperwork now for you to take leave. You can't keep doing this, Jazz. Take a break. Either come back and do it right, or you'll have to find another job. I know you've been through a ton of stuff…"

Jazz's brain started buzzing. *Blah, blah, blah.* Why couldn't people get over her past? She certainly had. She was a different person now. She was strong. No one would ever hurt her again.

She tried a smile. "I got bills to pay, man. Come on. I'll-I'll be more careful."

Phil rifled through a file on his desk. Turned to his computer. "What you're being is a bully. I can't support this behavior. I believe you have two weeks of paid time off coming. You can use that to start, and then we'll talk."

Jazz plopped back onto the chair. Her face flushed, and she clenched her fists. "This is all I've ever wanted to do! Well…"

"Well, not really." Phil raised his eyebrows. "You've made it clear what you're working towards. But, Jazz, at this point, you're not ready. You're a great security guard until something like this comes up…usually with a male perp and a female vic, and all hell breaks loose inside of you. They could slap charges on you for this one, you know. And my reputation and the reputation of this company are also at stake."

Jazz stared at Phil. She couldn't believe it. A required break. She'd pretty much been suspended. Maybe even expelled. Her face flamed. She bit her lip.

Phil held out his hand. Wordlessly, she handed him her ID Badge and set her baton on his desk. He was lucky she didn't put a dent in his precious marble desktop.

Later, as she banged her head on her dining room table, she thought about what Phil hadn't said aloud. She'd never be a cop. She just wasn't good enough.

The story of her life.

Chapter 7
Jem

Jem blinked at the sudden presence near her side. Jade stretched her arms, knocking her in the chin.

"Ouch!" Jem rubbed her eyes, observing marble around her, and the hard, wooden bench. Her shoulder ached. In front of her sat … Jet.

"Hey." He draped his arm across the back of the bench across from her. "Where's yer grandma? Why didn't she come ta pick you up?"

Jem struggled to sit and finally pulled upright. Jade wiggled out of her arms and scooted a few feet away, arms crossed and swinging her feet. Jem wiped her eyes. Her mouth felt like a garbage dump. She looked at the big, round clock. Two a.m. She felt around for the backpack under the bench and groped until she found a water bottle, half full. She took a long drink. Offered a drink to Jade. Jade drank and made a funny face.

"Not sure." Her stomach growled. She wrapped her arms around her middle and rocked as she watched Jade wander along the bench. "I can't find her."

"Got an address?" Jet grinned.

She smirked. "I wouldn't be here if I had an address." What a dork.

He nodded. "So, what now?"

"Don't know. Gotta pee." She grabbed the two backpacks, made her way down the bench to put a firm hand against her sister's back, and headed to the restroom. One boasted a cleaning sign outside. She sighed and walked to the other end of the terminal.

Jem hoped Jet would leave. She noted a rank smell coming from her own underarms and used the brown paper towels and soap to clean up the best she could, leaving red streak marks under her arms.

Unfortunately, Jet still waited for them when they exited the ladies room.

"What? Why can't you leave us alone?"

"A terminal ain't the worst place ta live. But having company might help."

"What are you talking about?" She sputtered. "I'm going to find my grandma, not live here the rest of my life."

"Alright. I'll leave ya alone." He shrugged and turned to walk away.

"Wait!" She shouted, and although the terminal was largely empty, the few around them looked on warily.

Jet turned around, his hands tucked into his pockets. Jade ran to him.

"Traitor," Jem grumbled. She looked up at Jet. She was out of options. Her head swam as she tried to sort her thoughts. Jade deserved decent care. "Can-can you help us? Find my grandma?" She blubbered. Snot and tears ran down her face. "I don't know her address or her phone number. It was in the phone."

Jet straightened up. Hiked up his jeans. "Well, yeah. What else did ya think I was after?" He snagged one of her backpacks and slung it on his back.

Jem walked over to Jade, grabbed her hand and followed Jet out the terminal doors.

The sounds and smells of the street assaulted her as they exited the Station. At Jem's right, a homeless man sat with an upside-down baseball hat in his hand. "Change, miss?" He rattled the hat.

She glared at him and turned to Jet, noting tents lining the street. She shuddered. "Where now?" But to her surprise, Jet darted around her and bent over the man.

"Hey, Gordy. Pretty late now. Probably time ta get some sleep, bro."

Gordy nodded. He picked up his hat and put it on. Struggled to his feet and shuffled to the entryway of the business next to the station. He sat with difficulty, leaned against the wall and pulled his cap over his face. He crossed his arms.

"Alright, then." Jet nodded. "C'mon, Jem."

Jem stumbled behind him down the street. Despite the hour, cars cruised along the roads, and the neon signs from businesses glared out into the darkened street. She heard people partying through the open windows. "Where we going, Jet?"

"Somewhere ta sleep. Can't find your nan at two a.m. Scare the death outta her."

Jade planted her feet firmly and started crying.

"I-I have to get Jade some food." Jem stopped walking and grabbed a nearby wall. "She's hungry. I have five bucks." She dug in her jeans pocket. Held it out.

Jet grabbed it. "That'll do."

She sagged against the wall. Dumped her backpack on the sidewalk. Watched him enter the nearby bar. She squeezed her sister's hand. "It'll be okay, Jade."

Jem guided her sister into the shadows. Jade continued to cry, so she gave up hiding and started walking, pulling Jade with her. Back and forth. Sweat formed on her forehead, and she wiped it away angrily, feeling her eyes wetting yet again. Eventually Jade grew quiet as her steps lagged.

What was taking Jet so long? Did he take the money and backpack and leave out the back door? Anger rose. Jade continued to pace. Buildings loomed around her. On a better day, the lights above her would have seemed pretty. Now they tore at her brain. She wanted to run to the nearest open door and call for help. She wiped a tear off her cheek. "I'm sorry, J. I had to get us out of there. I didn't know where else to go."

"I'm hungry! I want to go home!" Jade wailed and pointed to the neon "open" sign in the bar window.

"Yeah. Food soon. Let's go check on him."

Jem yanked on her sister's hand again and almost stumbled herself. She pushed open the door of the bar and loud music pushed out. She stepped carefully in, pulling Jade behind her and wished for the quiet of the bus station. Maybe they should return there until the sun came up. It seemed safer. She froze as several people turned and looked.

"Hey." The bartender waved toward the door. "Twenty-one and older only."

"I got this." Jet pushed his way around a small group of people and hustled over. "Kitchen's closed." He grabbed her arm. Steered her around back to the door.

Jem stumbled but stayed upright. Jet pushed them both toward the door. "Out, out."

"Out, out." Jade repeated. "You guys are crazy."

"Okay," Jem collapsed against the wall outside and slid to the sidewalk, pulling the backpack onto her lap. "That didn't work. What now? My back is killing me."

Jade laid her head against Jet's shoulder. He patted her head awkwardly. He inclined his head to the right. "Food mart up there. Twenty-four hours."

"'K." Jem took a deep breath and forced herself off the ground.

Jet set out, Jade now clinging to his hand.

Weariness washed over Jem. Before long, the faded 7-Eleven sign appeared. They pushed open the doors, and bright fluorescent light washed over them. Jade saw the snack cakes and strained to pull her hand out of Jet's hand.

"No ya don't." He gripped her hand firmly.

"Where's the money?" Jem held out her hand.

He grinned. "Uh…"

"Uh?" Her face flushed. Jem wiggled her open hand. "Money. Mine. Where?"

At the counter, the cashier stood from his stool and looked at them. "Is there a problem?"

"All good, man." Jet pushed Jade over to Jem and dug in his pocket.

Jem rolled her eyes and decided to let her sister wander a bit.

"I took it out at the bar. But I swear I ... yeah, it's here." He pulled it from his pocket and they both sighed with relief.

Jem headed down the aisle, following Jade. She gaped at price on the potato chips and quickly turned the other direction. Protein. They needed protein after nothing but fish crackers, potato chips and carrots all day. She made her way to the front. Bingo. Snack packs with cheese cubes, meat sticks and crackers, two for four fifty. She grabbed two and headed for the cashier. Behind her she heard Jade identifying candy to Jet.

"Want one more?" The clerk sounded bored. "There's one more at this price. New stock coming in a few hours."

Jem shook her head. "No. Thanks." She passed over her last bill. All she owned. The register popped open, and he inserted her bill and pulled out two quarters, pushing them across the table. "Bag?"

"Huh?"

He grabbed a bag from under the counter.

Jem tore into the snack pack. She snatched the empty bag from the clerk and headed to the doors, with Jet and Jade in close pursuit.

"We should keep movin'." Jet walked quickly.

Jade stopped and stomped her foot, her mouth crammed full.

He sighed.

They settled in an entryway a few doors from the food mart. She groaned. She'd forgotten to check for a restroom sink or water fountain. She sent Jet back into the store to fill both empty water bottles.

They shared the snack packs, Jem cramming more food into her mouth quickly. She chased it down with the water Jet brought back. Jade fell asleep, her head tucked securely into

Jem's shoulder. Jem felt a weariness steal over her, and the traffic and city noises faded away as she closed her eyes.

Chapter 8
Elenore-15 years before

The breeze ruffled the yellow curtains. Elenore clasped her hands in front of her and blinked rapidly. Her gaze fell on a pile of mail at the other end of the table, unopened. She startled as Mom swayed into the kitchen.

"Aren't you ever going to open those?" Mom's voice was light. Sing-songy. She wore yellow too. Canary.

"Why should I?" Elenore's greasy hair hung in strands across her forehead. She glanced at her sweatshirt. Two obvious stains – the ones in her heart much more hidden. "Well, I'm not gonna wear yellow." She muttered.

"Something clean would be nice." Mom sailed out of the room.

Mom might as well whistle a tune on Elenore's worst day ever. Check that. Worst second day ever.

"Make sure you take a shower!" Mom's voice faded.

Elenore snorted. "Why? What's the point?"

She forced herself from the table. Pulled up her sagging sweats. Knocked the pile of mail off the table. The card envelopes flew all over. Some hit the stove. She snickered. Dragged herself upstairs. She turned on the shower and stepped in, barely noticing the cold water. Her body ached. Her muscles cried. As water ran freely down her face, her tears intermingled. Snot poured. She grabbed a washcloth and whisked the gross stuff away. Decided to wash her hair after all. She wished she could step out of the shower and go to bed but no, she had to go to hell first.

Kelly's house was a large brown one on a corner lot. Bikes lined the side of the garage and a camper rested along the curb.

"Mom, why?" She got out of the car and shoved the door closed with her hip.

"Honey, you know why." The worry lines between her mom's eyes increased. "Don't slam the car door again. It's all we have."

"It's all we have," Elenore echoed snidely, but quietly.

Mom frowned and reached into backseat to grab the plate of cookies. She hadn't slaved over them. Elenore had emptied them out of the store container on a plate and stretched the plastic wrap over them. "It's the least we can do since…"

"Since we hardly know them." Elenore glanced at her own black sweater and black jeans. Still, there wasn't enough black. She squinted as she turned her face to the sun. "Stupid sun."

"Come along, Elenore." Mom grabbed a white envelope. Strode along the sidewalk to the front door. Elenore shuffled behind.

The door opened a bit, and a boy peered out. His brown hair was slicked back, and he held a stuffed dog in his arm.

"Mama! Papa!" He called and opened the door wider.

"Hello, young man." Mom shifted the cookie plate. "I'm Joy Stevens, and this is Elenore."

He stared at Elenore. She stared back. The door opened wider, and a man stood there. A hunched, sad-looking man with the same brown hair as the little boy. "Sorry. This is Geoff. Geoff, go push Dog in the swing, will you?"

Geoff shrugged and slipped past them, running to the side of the house.

"Hi. I'm Joy Stevens." Mom shook his hand.

He looked past Mom. "Paul. You are? Oh. You must Elenore. Elenore from the car accident?"

Elenore from the car accident. She wondered if she needed a t-shirt that said that. No, most everyone in town already knew. She nodded her head. "Y-yeah."

"We-We wanted to say how very sorry we are." Joy sighed. "It's been such a hard time…" She blushed.

Elenore wanted to run back to the car. She scuffed her shoes back and forth on a few bits of gravel clinging to the top of the steps.

Mom sighed again. "We couldn't attend Kelly's service. But we're so very sorry for your loss. We brought some cookies."

"Thank you." Paul looked like he didn't want cookies. Elenore agreed. What a stupid idea. His daughter died. We bought some cookies to help. She turned away to look at the camper. Her throat housed a big lump and her stomach ached. Maybe she needed to throw up. Which one of those bikes belonged to Kelly? She turned back to the door, hoping this would soon be over. She crossed both arms over her chest and glared at Kelly's dad.

Paul took the plate and card. Silence stretched. Awkward. "So, you, uh, you were hurt?" Paul cleared his throat. "I hope you're feeling better now."

Was the accident her fault?

"Yes. Yes it was." Elenore stammered. Almost shouted. "I mean, yes, I was hurt. I'm getting better." She turned back to the doorway, despising the man who seemed to hunch even lower now. She fled to the car. As she opened the door, she heard both Mom's muttered apologies and Geoff counting aloud as he pushed his stuffed dog in the swing, higher and higher.

Mom smiled widely as she started the engine. "Well, that wasn't easy. But you did a good job, honey."

Sometimes Mom reminded her of the Joker with that smile. Elenore stared out the window. Her throat burned. "Can we go home now?" She thought it might feel better if she could curl up on her bed...and never wake up.

"No." Mom clicked the blinker. Slowed the car. "I know this is hard. But we need to stop at Chad's, too."

Elenore's heart beat double time. She was going to pass out. She grabbed the door handle. "No, Mom. *Please*."

"This is our duty."

Their duty. *Her* duty. No, she'd failed her only duty – keeping everyone alive. Option one – she could have insisted on driving. Option two – taking Chad's keys if necessary. Option three – calling Mom or walking home and at least saving herself her own injuries. But no, instead she'd pretty much killed the boyfriend who had turned her insides to mush and truly cared about her.

Dang it. All her fault. Now they ran cookies all over town. Avoided the store. Ignored the phone ringing off the hook. Prisoners in their own blackness. Of her own making.

"Let me out. Pull over." Elenore popped her seatbelt open.

"Elenore! Put that back on!" Mom took her eyes from the road to settle briefly on her. "Maybe you should stay in the car for the next one."

Elenore re-buckled her seatbelt. Sighed. "I can't..."

"Oh dear." Mom sighed. "Maybe it's not the right time yet. But it seems like the nice thing…"

Elenore tuned her out. Looked out the window and counted road signs instead.

When they found Chad's driveway down a long windy driveway, she laid her head back and breathed deeply, pretending to sleep. Mom did the next one on her own. It didn't take long. No one even came to the door.

At home, Elenore dug through her bedside drawer. She had pills left over from the accident. As a pill took effect, she felt relief and warmth. Drowsy, she closed her eyes and slept the best since being released from the hospital. And best of all, there were no more tears.

Chapter 9
Cienna

The Portland Freedom Center's lights blinked as the rain and wind howled. Great. Cienna's clock said 6:45. Way past time to head home. Hopefully, Adrian and Grace were safely home already.

She saved and closed the grant application, satisfied with the fifteen pages she'd written, and stretched her arms. It included details of her own experience, budget details and the goals of the Center. One last thing. Incoming emails. One from Detective Miller. She clicked on it. "Wondered how you are. Have you had a chance to talk to your therapist about visiting Mike? And maybe about the parenting issue too? Mollie and I would love an update. Thinking of you."

Cienna sighed. For eight years, she'd tried to ignore the fact that whether Mike or Roger biologically created her daughter, her little girl remained the daughter of a monster. She instead focused on giving Grace the best life possible. Her beautiful little second grader only knew Adrian as dad – with no inkling of the horror before her birth. Cienna needed to think more. And what she wanted to know, or rather, what she really might *not* want to know. Although Mike dwelled in prison since the night of Cienna's rescue, Roger remained at large.

Cienna pushed the lid on her laptop down and reached over to pull the power cord out from the wall. She'd finish it up at home once Grace was asleep. Miller, Claire and the clients who walked through the door had no idea that The Freedom Center absolutely needed this grant to stay running for the next year of services. Without it, the Center would die.

Cienna would rather go to her grave.

Her phone flashed. Adrian. She grabbed it. "Sorry, hon. Still working on the big one. How was your day?"

"Good." He paused. "As much as it can be in this world. Still working on the big one, myself." He laughed.

Cienna smiled, thinking about his grin and the small crinkles around his eyes. But he sounded tired. His team, hard at work on a particular convoluted case, were almost ready to make some final moves – and hopefully help justice occur. She silently cheered him on.

She leaned back in her chair and propped her feet up on the desk. "I'm proud of you. You're so close, I can feel it. You've worked so hard. And remained incredibly sexy throughout, I should add."

He laughed. "Not that you're biased."

"Who? Me?" She grinned.

Outside, the wind howled again, and the rain picked up momentum, pounding on the roof. Something slammed against the front door. Cienna jumped. Probably a wayward branch. Still, her heartrate started pounding. Her hand moved to the mace on her keyring. Why did she keep staying here alone in the evening? She knew the answer. At home she claimed the titles of wife and mama first. Work stayed at the office for the sake of all, at least until Grace was asleep.

"Home soon? The roads are slick. Besides, aren't we going to try and work on a sibling for this poor, only child we have?"

Nervous laughter bubbled out. One track mind, the man had sometimes. And yes, maybe. She'd struggled with thoughts of a new baby for several years. But with good counseling, trafficking recovery services, a weekly support group and a loving, patient husband – she maybe felt ready to consider it. Everything she read recommended having the kids closer together, while still young. That way, you retained a life and time to still have fun as a couple when they left home.

She slid off the chair and went to the window, parting the curtain slightly, her phone still pressed to her ear. Another loud sound banged outside. "It's a little stormy, for sure." She glanced toward the front overhang. No one there. And no cars in the parking lot except for her old beat-up Queenie. Just two tents.

Overreacting, as usual. She sighed. Anxiety appeared only after her trafficking. It took a frequent seat in her life. Frustrating. She started a grounding exercise taught by her counselor and took deep breaths. Told herself that the noise was nothing. Just a bad storm.

"What's going on there?" Adrian's voice startled her. For just a bit, fear reigned.

She answered breathlessly. "Just the storm making noise. I'm-I'm gonna wrap it up here. Be home by 7:30, okay? Maybe we can work on that sibling for Grace."

His chuckle was low, but appreciative. "I'll have dinner waiting. Chicken Alfredo? Wine?"

"Sounds delish."

A lucky girl indeed. A husband who cooked sometimes and helped in so many other ways. Her love for Adrian shocked her sometimes. How could one truly love so much that the other person was a part of your very soul? And yet, that's what their love entailed. With the help of a few angels in their lives, he'd patiently wooed her and waited even when she outright shunned him. He remained only a dear friend. Then one day, her heart couldn't hold him as "just a friend" any longer.

They'd been meant for so much more.

Cienna pressed the end button. She rested her forehead against the cool window. The rain lashed her from the outside. A sibling for Grace. Was it right to think about a sibling for Grace when her daughter's natural bloodlines remained undetermined? What if her bio dad *was* evil Roger, who apparently disappeared underground, but she could bet still trafficked young girls?

She remembered her father's reaction to her unwanted pregnancy at the tender age of just turning fifteen. Even after

Grace's birth, he sometimes muttered about "the other half of the DNA she carried."

Cienna shuddered.

Maybe it was best to never know. Whatever medical or genetic issues arose – they could handle them. Right? And "generational curses" could be reversed, right? Grace didn't have to become monster or a victim just because one biological parent was.

If only she knew for sure.

Cienna pulled away from the window. The curtain fell back into place. She cleared her throat. Maybe she and Adrian could chat more tonight. He didn't want to know Grace's natural parentage. And Cienna agreed at the time. But should they revisit it before trying for another child?

Maybe better to continue pretending that neither of those men ever existed.

Cienna grabbed her laptop and slid it into her shoulder bag. Saw a couple of notes with phone calls she needed to return and slid them up toward her large monitor to remind herself to address them first thing in the morning. She grabbed her bag and her keys and marched toward the front door. She threw it open. Wind lashed at her face. A piece of paper landed at her feet.

What was this?

She reached down and grabbed it. Opened it up and held the doorframe for support as she read it.

> I know where you and your little girl live.
> I'm keeping an eye on you. Be good, Cienna.

Chapter 10
Jem

Just off the highway, down an incline, around three trees and near a river, four tents perched, mostly sheltered from the highway. Tarps tied to trees stretched and covered two of the tents. A bicycle rested outside the green tent. Various pots, pans and litter covered the landscape, and a large barrel in the middle rested on its side. The air reeked. Jem shuddered and clutched Jade tighter, asleep on her shoulder. Golly, for such a tiny girl, she weighed a ton when limp.

She stopped. "Jet?"

He smiled. "Good people. Promise." He grabbed her free hand and pulled her into a clearing. She swallowed the fear in her throat.

"Hey! It's Jet," Slowly, tents unzipped, and heads poked out.

"Whatcha got there?" An older lady with a purple scarf screeched. "A wee one!" She pulled herself out of her tent with effort and trudged toward them.

Jem pulled back but the woman insisted on following.

Soon she was gently patting Jade's head. "Where you bin?" She hugged Jet.

He grinned. "Well, ya see I obviously had a mission ta do. This is Jem and her little sister Jade. Did ya watch my stuff, Mrs. K?"

She puffed up. Stood tall. "You betcha, son. All's good. But I borrowed a towel yesterday. Washed it in the river." She pointed to a large, holey turquoise towel draped over a nearby tree.

Jet ginned again. "No prob, Mrs. K. Sounds like ya keepin' a good eye out. We gonna lay Jade down."

"Here?" Jem straightened up and looked at Jet in confusion.

He nodded and led them to a red tent, zipped securely shut. With one hand, he unzipped it.

She peered inside. The odor assaulted her nostrils. A large mat with a blanket and old, torn sleeping bag lay inside. A battery lamp was in the corner, as were books and a photo album. Although smelly, it appeared cozier than a store doorway in town.

Jem sighed. Her back ached. She looked at both Jet and Mrs. K.

Mrs. K nodded encouragingly. "She's safe here. We all keep an eye out."

Jem ducked and moved into the tent. At least when it rained, the tent would help. She carefully laid Jade on the mat and pulled a nearby old flannel shirt with a thick fleece lining on top of her. She eyed the other two warily, as their heads remained in the tent. Scooted to the door and pushed them away as she exited. She stood. Her back spasmed. She winced. "You live here?"

Jet shrugged. "Good people. I got a job lead now, so maybe not here forever." His cheeks darkened.

Jem understood. It was the best he could offer. For now. She sighed. Hopefully they would find Grandma soon. With her sister along – she couldn't move very fast.

A middle-aged man shuffled over as they stood outside of the red tent.

"This is Zeb. He's in the blue dome." Jet high-fived Zeb, who coughed deeply and nodded at Jem.

"Jem." She managed a small smile. The less these weird people knew, the better. She rubbed her eyes. Maybe all this would go away if she cleared her vision?

"Young lady, how many shirts do you have?" He laughed.

"Zeb's a counter." Jet shuffled his feet. "He only can get to know you in numbers."

Jem shrugged. "Two now, I guess."

Zeb threw his head. Roared in laughter at the sky. "Myself...I have five as of today. Let me show you."

Jem bristled – but glanced at Jet and followed.

He led them to the riverbank where, sure enough, five shirts laid out to dry on the rocks. He waved his hand at them. "But none I can wear. They're all wet! Every last one." He chuckled loudly. Then eyed the sky. "Hoping for more sun before dark." Jem noticed his bare chest under his thin coat.

"Zeb, we need yer help. Mrs. K too." Jet announced loudly. "Jem and Jade need ta find their nan, Joy Stevens."

From several feet back, Mrs. K straightened her scarf. Patted her head. "Well, now..." She murmured. And then something under her breath.

Zeb laughed. Again. "We can keep an eye out. How many buildings where she works?"

"I'm not sure," Jem shuffled her feet. "I lost her contact info. But we need to find her."

"Well, did you call the *police*?"

She turned to the new voice.

Jet slapped the newcomer on the back. "Hey Serv. Jem, this is Servio. Our camp preacher, pretty much." He huffed.

Mrs. K cackled. Strangely, Zeb quieted.

Servio rolled his eyes. Waved at Jem. "Welcome. I'm just kidding. I take it you don't want to call the cops or you would've by now."

Jem felt weak and overwhelmed. She headed to a large rock near the water, within hearing distance should Jade awake. "I just want Jade to be warm and safe. And to find Grandma." She mumbled as she sat.

"I'm gonna find breakfast." Jet headed out. "Mrs. K, check our other supplies, ok?"

Jem wanted to call out and make him stay. But a shadow fell across her. "What?"

Servio sat down. Nodded his head. "You got a kid."

"She's asleep. Everyone better leave her alone." Jem glared at him.

"This is a safe place, Jem. We're a little odd, but we're safe, I promise."

Uh-huh.

"Okay, sorry I made that crack about the *po*lice. It really was a joke."

Zeb wandered down to the river. He started piling up rocks, counting them loudly. "One rock, one building, two rocks, maybe she works where there's five buildings? No...that's five shirts." He coughed.

Jem placed her hands over her face. "Where have we landed?" She was in her worst nightmare.

Servio laughed. "Not Mars. I promise. Need a drink?" He pulled out a bottle of water from a coat pocket and offered it to her.

She shook her head.

"It's just water. At least from me."

She took the bottle. Drank some. Her stomach rumbled again. He waved it at her when she offered it back.

"Finish it up. Refills are free." He nodded at the river.

Ugh. No tap water? Weren't there diseases and plankton and stuff? She would need to limit Jade's intake. She set the empty bottle down.

"Do you wanna talk about it?" Servio grabbed a small rock and tossed it in the river.

"That's another one!" Zeb called.

Servio laughed. "How many is that now, Zeb?"

Zeb placed his hands on his hips and shook his head. "At least fourteen!" He cackled.

"Can't tell if he's serious or not." Servio smiled. "Most of the time he is. Well, let me tell you why I'm here, if you don't want to talk yet. An angel sent me here."

Jem rolled her eyes. Great. Now there'd be angels and maybe demons. Curiosity won out.

"Oh yeah?" She pictured the sky opening up and an angel lowering down on ropes. Oh wait, they had wings, didn't they? "What do you mean?"

"I was living in a shelter. For guys, you know. Can be hard there. Stuff gets stolen. Fights sometime. Sometimes people need more time there for themselves, and other people around them is just too hard. Anyway, I met a Leo – super spiritual. I mean *super* spiritual. He'd quote Bible verses and stuff and even tried to get groups of people to pray. Mostly people made fun of him, but I found myself listening. I at least wanted to get to know him a little bit. You know, from a distance.

"I worked with people like him when I was a mental health aid. I knew he must be a little wacky. But one day he started telling me over and over that he wasn't doing any good at the shelter. He needed to go out and find people to make a difference. And I needed to do that, too. I brushed him off. I mean, it was like a daily message. I liked having a bed and food, even though I had to go to counseling, groups and all that crap.

"One day he disappeared. I swear. No one had heard of him when I described him, and it's like he never existed. Even the workers at the shelter say there was no Leo. But I knew he'd been there, and when he disappeared, that same day I found a note under my pillow from him."

"What'd it say?"

"That he was going out to the people and he wanted me to go too. It's the only thing that would help people out here." He inclined his head toward Zeb, still stacking rocks. "Where we at now, Zeb?"

Zeb grinned. "Twenty-seven and one half, good sir. And I see you have a nice young lady with you. You take care of her, hear me?"

Jem shook her head. Mars indeed. "He-uh-met me…"

Servio shrugged. "Yeah. Sorry about that. Memory issues happen out here a lot."

Jem heard Jade's shout from the tent and jumped up. "And so here you are." She frowned and studied him, not sure why.

Servio nodded. "Here I am. Of course, Leo's nowhere to be found. Go take care of your girl. Breakfast shouldn't be long. Hey, Zeb! Later let's try and see if we can snag some fish for you to count!"

She scrambled up the slight incline to the tent and unzipped it quicky. "I'm here, Jade. Jem's here…"

The little girl held out her arms, tears dripping. Her pants soaked through. Oh, great. She'd probably peed on Jet's foam mat, too. Jade backed out of the tent, leaving it unzipped. Where was her backpack? She found it near the tent and fortunately, an extra pair of pants for Jem. Guess she'd be doing laundry in the river too. After she helped Jade change her pants, she helped her into her extra sweater. Being near the river cooled the air.

Jade was giggly and curious when they exited, zipping the tent behind them. She ran toward the river but tripped and fell flat right before she reached it.

Grabbing the urine-soaked pants, Jem followed her quickly and grabbed her hand to pull her sister up. As she did, something popped loudly.

Jade screamed. "Ow! You hurt me!" Jade fell back to the ground, her arm limp at her side.

Horror filled Jem. She dropped the pants, knelt quickly next to her sister and noted her arm at a funny angle.

"Oh no! I'm so sorry! What did I do?" She pulled her onto her lap and tried in vain to comfort her.

How could the day possibly get any worse?

Chapter 11
Jem

Tears streamed as Jem looked up to find her new houseless community gathered around her. Jade howled in pain. "I-I don't know what happened."

Jade screamed and held her arm with her opposite hand. She'd plopped on the ground and wouldn't move. Panic moved around Jem in a dark cloud. She shook Jem's good arm. "Stop! Shhhh!"

But Jade wailed.

"No matter, child." Mrs. K reached out and grabbed Jade by her good arm.

"No!" Jem yelled. She scrambled to her feet. But Mrs. K turned her back, Jade tucked in gently. Jem heard a crack and then…silence. Jade's tears turned to sniffles and Mrs. K turned back to Jem, all smiles. "All fine now, child."

Jem grabbed Jade and pulled her close, her feet slipping in the mud. "W-hat-what did you do?"

Servio grinned. "Mrs. K is a healer!"

Jem shook her head, holding Jade tightly. She backed away from the group. "I don't know what you mean – you guys are weird…" She looked down at Jade, who grinned up at her. "What the heck!?"

"It's okay." Mrs. K smiled. Her eyes sparkled. "I'm trained as nurse. Nothing to be worried about. Was dislocated, is all."

"You – you're a nurse?! Why are you living here?" Jem huffed and realized how rude that sounded. But that was an honest question, right? She was a nurse! Living on the streets!

Mrs. K nodded. "Come join us at the fire, girls." Zeb's fire burned brightly with gathered branches. A sudden pang pricked at Jem's stomach, remembering campfires in the past when there was not only real firewood, but a stack to the side for when the fire burned low. And marshmallows, and s'mores. Her stomach rumbled.

They gathered around the fire. Jem's stomach growled loudly now, no longer happy with the snacks they'd survived on yesterday and the night before. Her face flushed and Mrs. K looked at her kindly. "Kinda a common sound here."

"Well, that may be." Jem put her arm around Jade and pulled her closer. "But she's too young to be hungry. I need to get her food." She looked pointedly at Jet. Dizziness made him wavy.

"Yeah. I got stuff." Jet left the fireside. In a short while, he appeared with a dozen doughnuts, two bruised apples and a half gallon of milk which smelled slightly sour. "The bakery was late tossin' stuff out." Jade reached for the food and whimpered. Jem sighed. She let her sister eat and managed a doughnut for herself, as well.

Is this how these people lived? Waiting for stores to throw out old food? Apparently.

"I'll go out for more later." Zeb winked. "I know some good spots, missy. Don't worry. You're safe here."

That remained to be seen. Several hours passed with Jade playing at the river and Jem getting to know their new friends. In the late afternoon, Servio scrounged up a ball and they tossed it back and forth in a triangle formation.

"When are we going to go find Grandma, Jet?" Jem felt antsy. He promised to begin in the morning.

Jem wondered about the nighttime accommodations as the evening fire burned down – having no idea that a fire wasn't even an everyday occurrence. Mrs. K found a sweater and Jet led Jem and a sleepy Jade back to his tent. Jem panicked, her eyes wide, and backed away from the tent.

But Jet reached out and pulled her in as her heart beat wildly. It calmed as he motioned to his only mat and after they lay down, covered them gently. With one eye open, Jem watched guardedly as he gathered an extra shirt and bedded down – right in front of the tent door.

Her protector.

She sighed. At least her stomach was finally full and happy. She quickly followed Jade into dreamland.

Chapter 12
Elenore-15 years before

Elenore poked her head into the living room of the double wide. She pulled the cigarette from her mouth and blew out a steady stream of smoke. "Len. Dinner."

He grunted. She turned to head back to the stove. He might complain with just noodles and sauce – she'd only received seventy bucks for groceries that week. The rest went towards his alcohol and the lot rent. Actually, scratch that. The lot rent ran a month behind too. A note taped on the front door confirmed that. Where had the extra money gone? For a moment, as she dished up the bowls, she wondered about leaving Len and returning home. Elenore sniffed. She'd eat better, for sure. Mom cooked delicious meals and baked goods.

Mom would likely kick her out yet again. All because of one stupid night. Stupid Mom. Because of her, she stayed with this jerk-head. Well, sometimes a jerk-head.

Len's arms wrapped around her waist and she yiped. "Len! Hot stuff here!" She squashed her cigarette in the nearby sink.

He sniffed the air and glared at the bowls of pasta. Squeezed her a bit tighter. She wiggled. "Where's the meat?" His voice bellowed in her ear.

"For God's sake!" She finally freed herself from his arms. "I'm not deaf! No meat. Look, we can throw cheese on top." She turned to the fridge. Good, a small amount left of the shredded cheese. She dumped it all on top of his bowl.

Len smiled. "That's more like it. Thanks." He grabbed his bowl and a fork and shuffled back to his recliner.

Elenore sat at the table alone and smoked another cigarette, until her grey, short-haired cat wandered by, wielding himself around her ankles. She reached down to pet him. "Hey Oscar. At least *you* love me for real."

Oscar purred and leapt up on the chair next to her. He stared at her with deep eyes, lifting a paw to lick it and wash his face. He closed his eyes. She laughed. "Are you going to eat with me?" He licked his lips. "Well. I guess you knew I'd be eating alone again anyway. Thanks for the company."

He meowed loudly and then landed on the floor.

Thunk.

Goodness, had he gained five pounds? Maybe the neighbors put out snacks. She pressed her cigarette into a nearby ashtray and wound spaghetti noodles onto her fork. Oops, no drink - the only thing that helped this godforsaken life. She'd purchased a small supply of pain pills that afternoon from one of the neighbors, who kept upping his fees. It came from the grocery money too since that's all Len gave her. With one of those and a drink, she hoped to sleep through the night.

Visiting Neighbor Harley included an interesting twist - a visitor with a nice truck. Brandon looked her up and down when she entered the trailer. A looker for sure. She may have flirted - just a little. Brandon even winked and said hoped to see her again. Her stomach fluttered.

Elenore rose from the table with her bowl and accidentally kicked the cat, who blended in with the carpet. Oscar yowled. She hurriedly bent to pet him. "Ah lovey, I'm sorry!" He immediately purred and rubbed up against her hand. So forgiving. Now why couldn't be humans be as loving and forgiving? Stupid Mom. And stupid Chad, and stupid Kelly and stupid…she forced her thoughts elsewhere. On that track, she'd get no sleep for sure, no matter how much she worked to deaden the pain.

As Elenore grabbed her wineglass, she considered the small brown bag she'd shoved into her sock drawer – the pregnancy test from the dollar store. A late period – and her breasts hurt when she lay on her stomach. Some people didn't drink alcohol when they were housing a little one, she'd heard.

Surely, her cycle would show tomorrow. She slumped back at the table.

Len would never forgive her.

"Oscar, he'd kill me. But Mom would know what to do." Oscar tilted his head and patted the one small sunray on the floor. He rolled on it and curled up with a yawn.

Before she lost her nerve, she grabbed the phone handset and headed to the back porch. Her hand shook as she pressed the buttons.

Mom picked it up on the third ring. "Joy Stevens Consultation". That's right, Len insisted on their number showing as confidential. Most of the time, people didn't even pick up.

"Mom. You still working this late?"

"Elenore." Mom's voice grew guarded. "How are you? No, not really but this is the business line, you know. Thought you might be a new client. Where are you?"

"Home. I'm outside." She kicked a rock off the porch. On the other side of the door, Oscar yowled. She let him out and slammed the door behind him. He jumped onto the porch rail and paced back and forth. Oh yeah, he was out of food. She sighed. "The cat's out of food."

Mom sighed too. "You're telling me this why?"

"Because we had noodles with red sauce and no meat for dinner, the cats out of food, the grocery money for the week is gone and still I can't find a job. And today…today I bought a pregnancy test."

The screech from the other end of the phone pierced her ears. She pulled the handset away from her head. Returned it when it was again quiet and sighed.

"I know, Mom. I know. But maybe it'll be negative. Len would be so mad. Maybe even kick me out. Then what am I supposed to do?"

"How about being responsible in the first place? Too late for that, I guess. I swear, Ellie, you just aren't happy without causing some sort of drama…"

"This is not my fault." Elenore's kicked the stair railing. "That is, if it's true. Well…"

"Well, nothing! It is your fault – even low-income ladies have access to services and birth control. And you hook up with the worst men, I swear."

"Some support would be nice!" Elenore leaned on the shaky rail and wiped tears off her cheek. What was wrong with her? This pre-period emotional stuff bordered on ridiculous. And of course, ever since that night, Mom showed little patience for her negative emotions.

Mom groaned. "I'm sorry. I didn't mean to make you cry. Well, mistakes can be remedied, if that is the case. For goodness sakes, don't give your boyfriend any idea that you're testing or might be. Can you imagine?" She muttered something Elenore couldn't hear.

"I won't." Elenore wiped her nose on her sleeve. "He'd kick me out, anyway. And then what?" Would Mom gain sudden sympathy? Offer her help? "Hey, it wouldn't be all bad. You'd have a grandchild."

Mom sniffed. "I'm too young for a grandchild. And besides, you can't support it. What will you do?"

"I don't – I don't know. That's why I called."

"Elenore, you have to figure this out." *On your own.* Elenore heard the unspoken words loud and clear. "But you start with a test, of course. Maybe it's not the case. And if not, you can be more careful after that. Or better yet, leave that jerk…"

Mom's words echoed in her head as she hung up. Didn't sound like she'd help unless Elenore became homeless. She sighed. Oscar jumped down from the rail and rubbed his face on her arm. "I know, Oscar. I'm a bad cat-mom. We'll go see Beth and borrow cat food."

She set the phone on the porch rail. Poked her head in the trailer door. "Going to Beth's!"

"Why?"

"Oscar needs food!" She slammed the door. The wall shook. She smiled.

Oscar followed her to Beth's, but no one was home. Elenore stared at the open window off the porch with no screen. Loudly, Oscar meowed. "Shush. You can't possibly know what I'm thinking." He sat quietly and licked his paw. Okay, so maybe he did. "Nonetheless, you have to be quiet about it." He stopped licking and tilted his head at her. "Yes, you." She hissed and turned back to the window. She knew where Beth kept her cat food. She'd borrowed some before, and Beth always welcomed her into her home. The window was big enough for her to slip in and out before anyone noticed.

Elenore shook her head quickly. She sat on the edge of the porch. Time to get a grip. She pushed herself up and turned to Oscar. "Let's go for a walk and think about this." He obediently followed her as she walked around the neighborhood.

At the back of the lot was a new double-wide, painted a pretty blue with nice landscaping, bark for mulch and a freshly poured driveway. And sitting at the curb was the brand-new truck she'd noted outside Harley's house earlier. "What do you say? Looks like we have a new neighbor." Oscar meowed.

She'd only met Brandon yesterday. But he must have money. She decided to sit on this porch. Within a moment, he opened the door. "What? Oh – it's you." His face softened and he stepped out, shutting the door. "And – you." He nodded at the cat. "Although I haven't had a proper introduction yet."

Elenore smiled at the same time her insides stirred. Surely this incredibly handsome man would understand her plight. "This is Oscar. We're making rounds around the neighborhood looking for cat food to borrow. Did you just move in?"

Brandon shrugged. "Here tonight. I have a few places."

Oh. A few places. Money indeed.

She heard a muffled scream from inside. Someone else yelled. She tilted her head.

He laughed. "Kids. Uh – my cousin's kids."

Elenore nodded. Must be a busy house. "Do you happen to have a cat?"

He smirked. "Yeah. The cousin, not me. Sure, we probably have some extra food."

Relief filled Elenore. She wouldn't have to resort to breaking and entering after all.

"No old man?" He sat on the porch step above her. Her long hair brushed his knee. She shivered.

She looked over her shoulder. "He can't work. And I'm looking. We'll be okay, just need some cat food until his disability check comes in."

"And yet." He shifted and leaned against the stair post. "I saw you pass some cash for pills not too long ago."

She shrugged. Reddened. "Yeah. Can't go without them. I should've bought less and got cat food instead. I forgot Oscar was out." She rubbed him affectionately behind the ears.

"Sounds like you got financial trouble." Brandon leaned forward.

She repositioned herself to face him. She could drown in his eyes. Her stupid face blushed again. He grinned. "Just need a little to get by." She picked Oscar up, placing him on her lap like a shield.

Brandon stood. "I'll get some." He entered the house and came out with a gallon baggie of dry food. Oscar practically stood on his hind legs to whiff the bag.

"Thank you." She stood and took the bag. Their hands touched, his lingering.

"You can pay me back later."

She nodded as he winked.

Oscar yowled.

Chapter 13
Ruler

The day was bright. Too bright. After waking up to the obnoxious noise of children stomping up the stairs outside on the floors below and screaming, Ruler stepped out to the deck of the overly large apartment complex. As far away from the noise as possible. It still poured rain – the skies darkened as Ruler stepped out.

Why this place to live in? What was Frenemy thinking? Oh, that's right, blending in was key. At work now, Frenemy would likely return and sleep soon.

The top of the apartment complex boasted the fourth floor, reserved for the best amongst them. Where they played above the people and with the people. Where they chose their activities, how much to reveal to others and no one interfered.

Harmless games.

Gregory, the only neighbor, stood short but quick on his feet. Ruler laughed. Reminiscent of a bird. He mostly quirked his head at the ground and sky and never greeted them. He acted eternally fearful. Of everything.

Ruler re-entered the apartment through the sliding door. The dining room wall stayed lined with articles printed from the internet, pictures of people. A checklist. Tasks to do and tasks already done. Petty duties, really. And focused mostly on one gal with curly hair and a wide smile. One gal Ruler had yet to meet.

Why that focus? Oh, that's right, she deserved it. A chuckle escaped. A bit of a thrill, still. To hold the power of fear over someone else. Ruler pulled a piece of paper off the wall and stared at it. An instruction from Frenemy. Fun.

Ruler sat on the lone couch in the living room. A brief memory hovered. Ruler brushed it away with a wrist flick.

This harmless assignment seemed easy enough.

Chapter 14
Cienna

Cienna stared at the note in her hand, fingers shaking. *I know where you and your daughter live...be good.* Was this a warning to not visit Mike? Ire rose as she clutched her mace and laptop bag. She shoved the note into her pocket. Raised the mace. The incessant rain blinded her from seeing beyond three feet.

"Where are you?" She shouted into the greyness. It must be Roger. Who else could it be? How dare he! "Come out right now!" She'd not fall captive to the man again. She'd completed year four of self-defense classes, despite her teacher telling her two years ago she retained expert status. Cienna even helped teach some classes – when they didn't trigger her.

That son of a gun. Just when Cienna started feeling safer again.

The voice in her head encouraged returning inside. And calling the police. But determination reigned. Thunder rolled overhead. She jumped slightly. "You better show yourself, Roger!" She moved out to the porch steps. The rain belted her face. Poured down her cheeks. "You bastard!" Her arm shook slightly. She'd show him.

The rain turned salty, no longer just the Northwest cloudburst dribbling down her chin. Cienna chided herself. She turned around. Opened the door to enter the office. Slammed it behind her.

But wait – what if Roger hid in the building?

She whirled around, pressing back against the closed door. Her breathing quickened. She listened. Only her pulse thundered in her ears. She reached up and wiped moisture from her face, remaining alert. She and Jazz were kidnapped because they chose to walk a trail – without a care in the world.

A casual move never made since.

And where was Jazz? Was she safe? Did she get a note, too?

A loud thump sounded overhead. Cienna whimpered. Adrian wanted to teach her to shoot. As much a gun would be a comfort right now, she'd be tempted to shoot a hole in the ceiling if she carried one.

Guns were better off with the first responders.

Or so she had thought.

Maybe Adrian was right. Now she was a sitting duck, as Dad would say. Cienna decided to move. With trembling hands, she threw open the front door again. Closed and locked it quietly behind her. She ran to Queenie, pushing her key fob to unlock the door. Thought about her training so pointed the mace under the car as she kneeled to look. By now she was soaked and as she stood, her long skirt entangled around her legs.

Pain shot through her shoulder. She heard a board clatter to the ground as she fell.

Chapter 15
Jem

"When do we see Elenore?"

Jem sighed, wishing she could erase Mom from Jade's mind. "We're going to find Grandma." Jade hugged her sister. Jem held her close. They'd camped with the others for a couple of weeks now. Weariness filled her heart. Lately the rain poured non-stop, even leaking into the tents. Both awoke more than once to the surprise of a puddle. The dampness also made outside fires near impossible. Jem always felt cold.

During the days, Mrs. K watched Jade as Jem and Jet searched for Grandma. A tough job – Jem didn't even own a picture of her. But yesterday, they visited the library to use the internet with a Pass the staff kept for houseless people. Jet purchased all-day passes for the Max and they visited all the published addresses they found within the area for someone with the name of Joy Stevens. Many never answered their doors, so Jem left notes with scratch paper and a pen provided by the library. She had no way for Grandma to reach her, so she described the camp. She asked the right Joy Stevens to come and get them.

An odor arose from her sister. Jem smelled similar. Later, when she returned from searching again, she planned to bathe them both in the river with the small bottle of leftover shampoo Jet found in a dumpster.

He'd discovered a decent dinner the night before. Her stomach no longer turned thinking about dumpster diving. People threw away still-decent food all the time. Last week turned up a warmer, but worn, coat for Jade. It hung down past her arms, but Jem still breathed a sigh of relief. And they discovered two freshly packed brownbag lunches. The restaurant dumpsters held the best prepared food finds and the ones behind grocery stores remained a close second.

"Ready?" Jet called from outside the tent.

"Coming." Jem smoothed back Jade's hair. How could she help her sister understand – without the details? "Mom – Elenore isn't in a safe place right now. We need to be away from her and Brandon."

"I don't like Brandon." Jem felt Jade shudder as she tucked her head into Jem's shoulder. She nodded. Perhaps the girl knew more than she thought.

"Jade, did Brandon ever…touch you? You know, in private places?"

The girl stilled. "No." Her voice muffled.

"Okay. That's good." Jem breathed a sigh of relief. "No one can touch you without your permission, okay? And not in those spots at all. Alright? Hear me?"

She felt her sister's head pump up and down. "Now I want you to go play with Mrs. K until Jet and I get back. Then we're going to swim in the river."

Jade pulled her head back from her shoulder quickly and met Jem's gaze with wide eyes. "That'll be fun!"

Jem nodded, patting her on the back. Her mind whirled, a bit of fear attached. Jet promised a secluded spot. She supposed they should take clothes off but keep their underwear on? But then those underclothes would be wet. And how cold was the river anyway? She shuddered. Hopefully, if they waited until almost dark, no one could watch.

Not an experience she looked forward to.

With Jet now nowhere to be found now, Jem passed Jade to Mrs. K and watched for a moment as the two searched for junk to build something crafty. She scoured the landscape. She nodded at Servio and waved at Zeb as he counted the trees around the camp.

"Jet!"

There he stood, under the overpass. She balanced herself carefully on the rocks as she picked her way over. Her backpack strap slipped down off her shoulder, and she pushed it back up. Since arriving, it no longer held all their possessions. Instead, their only belongings lay stacked in Jet's tent. But she still carried the backpack to bring needed items back to the camp.

"Plan today?" She reached him and almost stumbled right into him.

Jet held out an arm to steady her. "Whoa, girl."

"Sorry." She laughed. He joined in and for the first time, she realized what a nice smile he had. And that his hand warmed her arm as it steadied her. She pushed it away.

Talk about adding complications. She needed him only until they found Grandma.

"How are we money-wise? Enough for the day pass again on the Max?"

He shook his head. "Gotta get that first."

Her shoulders slumped. Progress dragged without the proper resources. "How?"

Jet grinned. "Got an idea."

She rolled her eyes. Jet mastered the idea-factory. "Isn't there an organization that could help in some way? A nonprofit or a church?"

"We avoid 'em." Jet took her backpack and they started up the small riverbank. He placed his hand behind his back and she grabbed it. She let it go as soon as they crested the hill. "Some go ta the Portland Freedom Center."

"And?" She caught up and walked beside him. "Did they help?"

Jet mused. "S'ppose. Not sure. I think they got transitional housing for my friend Trezon but that didn't work out." He laughed. "It's a little weird having ta live in a house and follow rules when ya've been out here free." He motioned to the trees, the river and the spans of highways. "Not a lot of rules here."

"Not a lot of money, either." Jem grumbled. Wouldn't the tradeoff be worth it? "Where's Trezon now?"

Jet sobered. "Not good. I think he went back on drugs. Then there was shooting and he got involved somehow…"

"That's sad."

"It's risky getting ya guys help from any organization."

"What do you mean?"

"I mean, ya ain't eighteen and Jade ain't your daughter. She has a Ma, who ya took her from."

Jem snorted. "Mom's a druggie. And worst things than that happens in that house…"

"But ya know what I mean, Jem. Opens up a whole can of worms with a kid involved."

"Yeah." She nodded. Mom and Brandon likely searched all over Seattle even now and maybe even contacted the police. Or maybe Mom was too drugged up to even care that they had left.

Both were possibilities.

They'd better do this without help – until they could find Grandma anyway. Surely, she would know what to do.

"Where we going?" She reached up and pushed a greasy bang out of her eye that somehow had grown longer in two weeks' time. "And by the way, we girls need to hit the river tonight. Phew-wee. Didn't you say there's a secluded spot somewhere?'

Jet nodded. "Has more trees 'round it anyway. I'll show ya." He paused by a trashcan and looked through it. "Here's a box. It'll rip. Jest need your pen."

"For what?"

"Sign. We're sittin' over there by those stores and collecting what comes in."

Jem stopped walking. "We're gonna beg?" How embarrassing.

"Got a better idea? There are other ways ta make money, ya know." He stopped scrounging around and raised his eyebrows. "We've all had ta do other things, at times."

She shuddered. "Begging is fine." She clenched her teeth. Yesterday, an old man stumbled through camp and asked her for "favors". Jet stepped in and told him to get lost. She felt safe with Jet - even if they did have to beg.

Nonetheless, she dipped her head as they made a sign and sat near a busy street corner. The sign read "Lost our housing. Will take anything. God bless you." She'd added the last sentence after Jet wrote the first part.

A few dollars trickled in. The sun grew warmer, and Jem started sweating. She should have taken a river bath yesterday but then again – shouldn't she look and smell the part?

What part? They truly were homeless! Jem looked at the ground again, flushed.

A woman crouched nearby and tried to make eye contact. "Hello. I'm Jamie."

Jem looked up, her face afire. "Jem." Then she wondered if she should even use her real name if Brandon and Mom were looking for them. "Jem - Jemaya." She said quickly. "This is Jet." She motioned to him next to her. Her stomach growled. They hadn't found breakfast yet and she'd given Jade the one-half granola bar found at the bottom of her backpack before they left camp.

"Sounds like you could use some food."

"Max fare." Jet grinned charmingly. "Got someone ta help us-jest need ta get there."

Jem's stomach growled again. Her mouth watered. "Yeah."

He shifted to look at the woman. "Food would be good."

"Have you eaten today?"

Both shook their heads. "I'm sure we'll find something later." Jem tried to sound cheerful.

Jamie stood. "Back in a few." She walked away and entered a doorway two buildings down. Jem figured she wouldn't be back but then the women's shoes again appeared on the cement. She looked up, shading her eyes. Jamie placed a brown bag on Jem's lap. She also balanced two drinks and handed them both one. "You know there's a place not too far away. It's the Freedom Center. They can help you. Take care of yourselves."

As she turned and walked away, Jem called "thank you!" Jamie waved over her shoulder as she disappeared into the crowd.

They dove into the bag. The drink was delicious, sweet tea which Jem both gulped and savored. Jet ate all his large turkey sandwich in a few gulps. Jem ate half of hers and although she was still hungry, she re-wrapped the rest and tucked it away. She ate part of the little bag of peanuts the woman had included instead.

Her little sister needed dinner, after all.

Chapter 16
Elenore-14 years before

Elenore tucked the order form into her apron pocket. It barely fit. Someone looking carefully might note the small pouch at her waistline. She signed. Len might start noticing at any time now.

Brandon signaled from the corner booth. She hurried over with a smile. Her new friend obtained this job for her after she'd flunked several company interviews. She felt so grateful to bring home some of her check, after Brandon took his portion. Oscar ate well, Len drank his booze and didn't mind a lot of spaghetti or rice for dinners, if there was meat. She even dreamed of starting to put some tips aside for savings. An apartment sure would be nice.

"Hi ya." She smiled. She'd splurged on a haircut last week and wore makeup and a spray scent. Today was Wednesday – the day Brandon usually visited and ate lunch.

He patted the vinyl next to him. She slid in. Several other waitresses tossed jealous glances and he smiled their way. His warm hand covered her bare knee. The uniform skirt pulled up quite a bit when she sat. "You smell yummy." He grinned and rubbed her leg on the inside.

She reddened and squirmed. Shivered. Len barely paid attention to her anymore, except when mad or drunk. Kind Brandon proved himself over and over. A job. Groceries. Cigarettes. Cat food. He'd even bought her last set of pills. But she'd tucked those away for later. She smiled.

"How's Oscar?"

She beamed. "He's great. Fat and happy. Still walks around the neighborhood with me."

"Saw that."

"What?" She giggled.

"You and Oscar yesterday. You in those tight blue shorts wrapped around your – ah well." He leaned and whispered into her ear. "He was so close to you, I got jealous. I almost came out and followed you home."

His breath in her ear created butterflies in her stomach. She sighed. Heavenly to have Brandon close. She truly owed him. And her insides grew jiggly. "You can't follow me home." She giggled again. "Len would have a cow."

Still near her ear, he reached up and wound a piece of her hair around his finger. "Nice." He breathed. "Like the haircut."

Was he breathing a little faster? She grinned and pulled away a bit. "Better stop that now, Brandon. I'll get in trouble."

He snickered. "Nah, I know the boss a little too well for that." He smiled at her and tilted his head. "By the way, my fees are going up a little bit. Just not bringing in enough to keep the houses going. You understand?"

She paused. More money out of her paycheck? Wow – he already took like forty percent.

Brandon squeezed her shoulder gently. "I'd like to see you more too. Would that be better than a fee increase?"

She giggled. "You mean visit the diner more?"

"No, goofball. Just you and me."

She raised her eyebrows. Patted her stomach. "You remember I have a sidekick…"

"A sexy one. I'd like to feel that one up close."

Elenore shivered. No one melted her this way, not since Chad. She frowned. Her heart skittered and a sudden lump grew in her throat. She pushed Brandon away. "Stop."

"What?" He growled as she hurried away from the table. Looking back, she saw him wink at Ellen, who cleaned up a table nearby. "She'll be back."

Later, as Elenore hung up her apron in the back and grabbed her purse, she overheard Ellen and Marina. "Did you hear that?" Ellen slammed her locker. "Brandon's upping our fees."

"What? No. I cannot even hardly afford the rent now." Marina started crying. Elenore paused. Other women here paid Brandon too? What?

"He does have other places you could probably stay at with some side work, I hear." Elenore popped open a can of soda and Elenore heard her take a long drink. "Maybe you should check into that."

"Maybe I have to." Marina still cried. "I have no papers here. Nowhere else to go. And now reduced pay when my son and I are barely making it in this Great America!" She left and slammed the door.

Ellen rounded the corner and grimaced. "What are you looking at?"

"Nothing." Elenore grabbed her bottle of water and left quickly. While walking home, thoughts whirled. Brandon charged everyone fees, not just her. Did that mean the others lived and worked at the diner on his mercy too? In property management, he must own several buildings. Did he have apartments for rent for cheap? Could she maybe get out of the trailer park with his help? Leave Len behind?

She spaced out during dinner, yawning more than usual. She cleaned up, fed Oscar and decided to go to bed early. After she changed into her nightgown, she remembered her glass of water in the kitchen. As she walked by Len's recliner, the footrest slammed down hard. "Come here, you witch!"

She looked at him, then looked down. Released from a uniform and now in a comfy, loose nightie, her belly hung out.

Fear filled her stomach.

Len knew.

He jumped out of his chair. Who knew he could move so fast? "And what is this?" He poked her firm stomach with his finger as he leered close to her face. "Fat?"

Elenore recoiled. "Been gaining a little." Breathless, she squeezed her eyes shut as his face neared. She never saw the punch coming. She flew backwards and landed near a bar stool, knocking her head on the metal legs. Len lumbered over and leaned close. She opened her eyes, shuddered, and pulled her legs in to protect her stomach as he kicked her in her hips. "Ow, Len! Stop! I'll scream. Someone will call the cops!" Len had a warrant out. Surely that would stop him.

"You sleeping around on me? You witch. I knew it. You're pregnant! I saw the little booties in your dresser that I thought were a gift for someone else. You're a freakin' liar!"

"I'm not! I'm not! I promise!" She covered her head as he started pummeling. Soon the room grew blurry and quiet emerged. Her head buzzed. She felt like she watched Len beat her from afar. She thought about Chad. Was she worthy enough to join him in heaven? At least he'd once again treat her as a queen. Perhaps that horrible night could forever be erased.

Blackness overcame her vision, and she passed out.

When Elenore awoke, slouched against the bar counter on the floor, she heard rain on the trailer roof. She needed to get outside to drink.

Len hopped up as soon as she awoke. "Had enough?" He yelled as he leered over her again.

"Len…please…" She put up her hand in defense. She was dizzy even on the floor and grabbed the barstool for balance. "Water. I just need some water. I'll leave you alone. This is your baby, you know. There's been no one else." In the far-off distance, she heard Oscar yowl. Oh no. "Is Oscar okay?"

His fist slammed her in the head, and she fell flat to the floor. As darkness overcame her again, she heard him laugh.

***

Hours later, Elenore awoke again. Pitch dark. Where was she? Her forehead throbbed – she touched it. Blood dripped onto the floor. She heard Len snoring in his recliner and remembered.

Oscar ran to her and meowed loudly as he rubbed up against her. "Shhh, Oscar. I'm okay. I'm okay." Was she telling the cat that, or herself?

She slowly started to push herself off the floor with Oscar bumping his head up against her arm. Aww – he tried to help. She patted him on the head, standing with great difficulty. She grabbed the barstool to catch her breath. At least the cat looked untouched. Glancing fearfully at Len still snoring, she whispered. "We gotta go, Oscar."

And then she did the only thing she knew to do. She quietly opened the trailer door and with Oscar at her side, made her way to the back of the lot to Brandon's house.

Chapter 17
Cienna

Cienna peered into the rain as the dark figure ran away. So, they wanted to scare her, but not kill her. Wimp. And apparently, she needed another year of self-defense classes.

 She rubbed her shoulder and seethed as she slid into the driver's seat. Queenie started quickly, as if she felt Cienna's anxiety. The rain was blinding and with the ensuing darkness, Cienna knew she wouldn't get very far trying to find the jerk. She stared hard at the road as she drove. What had she done wrong? Checking under the car? But she'd been trained to do that in classes as predators often hung out there. With shaking hands, she fit her phone into its holder on the dash and punched Adrian's contact icon.

 "Hey sweetheart." His voice was warm. "Was just thinking about you…I'm already headed home. It's Friday – Grace is looking forward to dinner and a movie."

 "Adrian…"

 "Ci? What? What happened?"

 She drew a deep breath. The rain lightened up. But full darkness now covered the city. "I - there was a note on the porch tonight during the storm."

 "A note? What kind of note? Did you call the cops?"

 "Not yet. Don't. I want to figure this out."

 "Well, was it a threat?"

 "It – It was an indication that they know about Grace and also…where we live…" Her voice trailed off. Only part of the story. She hated lying to Adrian. But she downplayed it – or the cops would arrive at the house before her.

"Cienna." He cleared his throat. "That doesn't sound like just a prank. You and Grace could be in danger."

"I know. Yeah. I just have this weird feeling. I know this person, Adrian."

"I'm a gosh darn attorney." His voice tensed. "You know this. I work with the departments closely. And you know I can't encourage you to keep quiet about it. Especially when it comes to our daughter."

Our daughter. She still felt a thrill when he said that.

"We need to talk about that too, Adrian."

Silence.

"Hurry home." He hung up.

She pressed harder on the gas pedal. Then eased up. Was he angry? She shook her head. The man only treasured her, never hurt her. But even Mike had oozed niceness sometimes. What if tonight became a turning point in their marriage? She shivered.

She pulled into the driveway of their duplex. They lived on one side and rented the other out. With Adrian working for the public defender's office, and her at the nonprofit, it helped make the bills. They'd been fortunate last year to find a dependable, older lady named Mel. Dear Mel. With her reduced rent, she showed appreciation via baked goods and babysitting. Adrian confirmed their great decision each time delicious smells started next door – they seemed to penetrate the wall between them.

Cienna braked inside the garage. Finally, out of the rain. She pressed the remote to close the garage door and opened her car door. Her clothes dripped water on the cement floor. She grabbed her bag from the passenger seat, also soaked. Shoot, she better remove her laptop quickly. She pictured her important grant application, completely erased.

Adrian opened the door from the house and gave her a gentle hug and kiss as he guided her into the kitchen. Grace's RC racecar roared at the other end of the house. "Go change. Dinner's in the microwave. Grace is happy playing."

"Until she crashes."

"Until she crashes." He smiled. Grace was good at throwing fits, too.

Cienna removed her coat and plopped her bag on the table, pulling her computer out. It seemed dry enough. The bag on the other hand…ugh. She pulled out some wet papers and spread them on the dining room table to hopefully dry. She handed her soaked coat to Adrian.

"Are you okay?" His forehead furrowed.

"Yes." She headed to the shower. While the water cascaded around her, she winced when lifting her shoulder. A bruise would appear tomorrow for sure. She rotated her shoulder to keep it moving, even as she tensed with the pain. She cleaned up quickly, put on some sweats and headed to Grace's room.

"Mom!" Grace yelled, jumped up and ran to her, throwing her arms around her waist. Cienna blinked, moving her arm to better hold her daughter. "Daddy picked me up from Grandma's." She announced. Cienna smiled at the obvious. "And then I zoomed the car until you came home!" She dropped the remote and Cienna noted the car, upside down, the wheels spinning endlessly.

"Looks like you crashed."

"Dang it!" Grace stomped her foot and ran over to set it upright. "Second time!"

"Watch your language, Gracie."

Cienna sighed. Despite knowing her daughter was safe, she couldn't help the shiver that started at the base of her spine and inched up. Was Grace in danger? She herself? Had Roger discovered where they lived and set out to finish what he started?

"It's Friday movie night!" Grace pushed aside her stuffed beanbag to make more room to zoom the car around. "Dad said we could watch 'Mulan'!"

"Mulan?" Cienna studied her daughter's sweet face. Grace was beautiful with her dark curls, and she still had those brilliant blue eyes she'd entered the world with. She prayed every day for her daughter's safety. "How about 'Tangled'? That's a fun one. No combat."

"Mom." Grace rolled her eyes. "Not the old 'Mulan'. The new one! The real movie! I'm older now and daddy said it was okay. I am going to be eight next week, you know."

"Indeed, you are. And that still has war scenes." Cienna muttered. "Okay. Turn off that car remote, honey. It's time to eat."

Grace hopped to the remote and shoved a switch over on the bottom. "Dad made nachos. He forgot to order pizza."

Cienna laughed as her daughter bounced out of the bedroom.

Life was good. Grace was happy. Oh, how she wanted to keep it that way.

They met Adrian in the dining room. In his hand he held the note from Cienna's pocket. He met her eyes over Grace's head. Nodded. She shrugged. Yes, they needed to chat. They should talk about Grace's true paternity too. Until they figured it out, paternal rights couldn't be terminated, and Adrian couldn't truly adopt Grace. A lot to figure out after their girl fell asleep. Adrian crammed the note into his back jean's pocket.

He put his arm around Grace's shoulders. "Everything's in the living room! Movie's ready!"

"Yay!" Grace jumped up and down and almost hit Adrian in the chin.

He smiled at Cienna. "Getting taller…"

She winced. And almost eight. How was that even possible? She thought back to the day of viewing her daughter on the ultrasound for the first time. Up until then, she'd refused to believe that she was pregnant. For good reasons. Her life turned upside down in the timeframe when Roger sold her to Mike. She silently scolded herself as she followed her husband and daughter into the living room. Not tonight. Not tonight. She wouldn't ruin the evening ahead.

Adrian placed the nachos, all the sides, soda and cookies from Mel on the coffee table. She sighed in relief. Time to relax now.

Talking could wait.

Chapter 18
Ruler

Ruler lay on the couch, resting, and trying to ignore the noise of the children outside – calmed a bit since summer. The days quieted. But with the weather still decent outside of the occasional downpour, the annoying children still hit the pool with a vengeance as soon as the noisy, coughing bus dropped them at the apartment complex sign.

Didn't anyone have homework to do anymore? And weren't they supposed to close the pool soon?

"Knock it off, moron!" One boy yelled. "I'm gonna tell!"

"You did it first!" A girl screamed. A loud splash sounded. Someone swore.

Ruler groaned, pushed off the couch and walked to the glass door. "Shut the heck up!" Ruler slammed the door closed. There. That should tell them. Then, a sudden small feeling of remorse. Ruler remembered well the conversation with Frenemy – the last time she appeared. The memory dimmed. Maybe it was even over a year ago.

"We have to keep a quiet life. No one can know we're here. Only one person in my life even knows I live in this building, and she has no idea of which apartment. Plus, she'd never come without asking first. Discretion. Can you do that?"

Ruler agreed. After moving in, per the arrangement, Frenemy pretty much disappeared. Now they passed in the night, sharing the apartment but never really seeing each other. Apparently, Frenemy paid the bills as there was electricity, cable, and no eviction notice taped to the door. Once in awhile, Ruler saw changes Frenemy made, such as more articles or pictures on the dining room wall.

Today, there was a new note.

> Time to step it up. Nothing really happened last time. She needs to remember the goal and seems to have completely forgotten the promise.

Ruler laughed. It amused him that Frenemy expected more reaction. This Cienna seemed independent and stubborn as heck. Ruler felt shocked when she hadn't run after her attacker. Of course, it was pouring down rain and Ruler easily slipped into an even darker alleyway.

What could be done? It was fun to think of the possibilities. And to be fair, Ruler owed Frenemy much. Due to her generosity, Ruler lived in the apartment rent-free.

Ruler woke up the next morning, knowing exactly what should be next.

Chapter 19
Elenore-14 years before

Elenore stumbled in the dark to Brandon's trailer, Oscar close by her side. If she called the cops, Len might get arrested. And when he got out, the consequences for her fared far worse. She clutched her belly. She didn't want to fail at the one big thing the universe asked of her – to carry this little one into the world safely. She worked hard to avoid pills and alcohol these days. But this baby was no longer safe even in her own home.

She raised her hand to knock, and no one answered. "Brandon! Brandon! Help me!" She pounded on the door and then slid down to sit with her back against the door, her head in her hands. Oscar climbed onto her lap.

When the door opened, she fell backward into the house. "What the heck?"

She recognized the voice and squinted upwards. "Ellen?" Oscar leapt off her lap and trotted into the house like he owned it. From the couch, a back ball of fur arched and hissed. "Ellen. What are you doing here? I – I need Brandon." Darkness clouded her vision, and she reached out to grab onto something, anything – and found herself clinging to Ellen's leg as she passed out.

***

The room spun when she woke up. Was it hours later? Days? Where was she? She heard voices.

"Well, she can't stay here." Someone hissed. That sounded like Ellen.

"She can't leave in this condition." Brandon. Elenore tried to push herself to a sitting position and failed. Oscar, curled at her feet, perked up, stretched, and marched up to her face, stepping carefully around her wounds. Her pillow was wet, and red. "And she needs stitches. Go get Nance."

"Oh, for gosh sakes, Brandon. For once, you go and get a heart somewhere. What the heck? We need to just get her in the truck and drop her back home."

"She ain't going in my truck bleeding all over like she is and she's not going back there." Brandon roared. Elenore heard a slap. "And you'll do what I say!"

Silence from Ellen. Keys jangled. "Fine." Elenore heard tears in her Ellen's voice. What happened to Brandon's heart? What was he so stressed out about? And why was Ellen here anyway? Ellen's voice came from farther away. "Kick her darn cat outside, at least. Oreo's about to kill him over that couch." A door slammed.

"No." Elenore managed in a small voice. She lifted her head further. She tried to talk louder but everything turned grey again. She slumped her head back onto the pillow. Brandon quickly turned to her and before she passed out again, she saw him pet Oscar not-so-gently on his head.

***

Pain awoke her next. "I'm sorry, dear." An older lady poked a needle through her face as someone else held her head from behind her. "But when you're bleeding this much and it's not stopping on its own…" She poked Elenore's temple again.

"Ouch!"

Brandon moved into her view. Grinned. "It speaks. Check on the baby too, Nance. Hold still, El." She squirmed more. "Elenore!" He spoke sternly this time and the hold on her head tightened.

"I-I'll try."

When the dastardly deed of stiches was finally done, Nance asked Brandon to bring a bowl of warm water and paper towels. She gently cleaned the blood from the wounds, then produced a stethoscope. "How far along are you, dear?"

Elenore shifted on the couch, her hand moving to her belly. "Almost five months, I think."

"Good." Nance pulled up Elenore's shirt. "We may be able to hear it with this then." She smiled. "Brandon didn't tell me to bring the doppler."

"Doppler crap." He growled at Nance. She seemed unaffected and just shook her head at Elenore like he was a naughty little boy. "Either you can hear it, or you can't. Let's get on with it."

"Hearing it or not depends on the age. And health, of course. Now hush."

He did.

Who was this older woman who Brandon growled at, and yet seemed to respect at the same time?

Nance moved the stethoscope around Elenore's stomach and finally rested it in one spot. She paused, listening carefully. She smiled. Took the earpieces out of her ears. "Do you want to hear it?" Elenore nodded.

Brandon frowned. "Kid still in there?"

"Yes." She wound up her stethoscope and put it in a small, zippered bag. "Now, Elenore, where else are you hurting?" She turned to Brandon. "If you could leave we ladies alone now, please."

He left the room along with whomever had held Elenore's head.

"My hip. He kicked it."

Nance held a glass of water to her lips, supporting her head as she drank. After that, Nance helped her readjust clothing to expose her hip. Nance felt around as Elenore bit her lip. A tear trickled down her cheek.

"I'm sorry this happened." Nance said. "Doesn't feel broken, which is good, especially since it needs to support your wee one. Where else?"

She continued to examine Elenore and cleaned up blood. Elenore felt badly. With blood on the pillow and the couch, she owed Brandon a cleaning. When Nance finished, she petted the ever-vigilant Oscar while Oreo yowled in the other corner of the room. Oscar arched his back and hissed back. Nance laughed. "Oreo is saying 'I own this place' and your cat is saying 'this is my lady. Leave us alone.'" Elenore laughed too, as pain spiked through her ribs. She grabbed them.

"Ugh."

Nance nodded. "Uh huh. They'll be sore for quite awhile. Now I do have a shot for the pain that Brandon expects you to have…"

Elenore shook her head. "No. Not with the baby."

From the door, Brandon cleared his throat. "Give her the shot." He walked over to the couch and smoothed Elenore's bangs back from her head. He avoided the wound. "You need sleep, El. You won't be able to sleep with this pain, but you need sleep to get better. Don't worry, you're safe here."

"Is it safe for the baby?" Her ribs hurt so badly, it was hard to breathe, and areas of her body started to ache that she hadn't felt before.

Brandon nodded. Nance shrugged.

"One shot. Just for some sleep. Just one."

The poke in her hip hardly hurt. Sleep quickly came.

Chapter 20
Jem

The day ended as discouraging as it started. They'd visited two Joy Stevens' homes. One Joy answered the door. She looked oriental and seemed scared. Jem didn't blame her – she'd caught a glimpse of herself on the way over in a storefront window. She opened her mouth to explain and ended up apologizing instead while Jet shook his head.

After the door slammed, Jem sat on the steps. "My grandma's white. I think."

"Yeah."

They sat until the woman opened a window above them. "Please leave my porch. I hope you get the help you need."

As they rose, a laugh bubbled from Jem's lips. "Did she think we wanted money?" She giggled on way back to the camp.

Her other option included tears, and she grew tired of those.

Now she gathered items in the darkness of the tent, so she and Jade could bathe in the river. She shivered again at the thought, but she no longer saw a choice. The City didn't have public showers, unless you received a referral to live in one of the new little village safe houses.

Pod homes for people like them.

This whole situation edged on ridiculousness. Where the heck was Grandma anyway? But Jem put on her strong face and reached out to Jade.

"I don't want to go in the river." Jade frowned.

"Come on. We'll swim. It'll be fun."

"But it's dark."

Could her little sister get any whinier?

They picked their way over some rocks, with Jet in the lead. He'd promised to show them the right spot, and act as a lookout. Jem felt nervous, but what choice did they have? She plotted various scenarios to not keep their exposure to a minimum.

When they arrived, Jet turned his back.

"Okay." Jem breathed. "Jade, we're going to use our underwear like a swimsuit. We're going to wash our skin and hair. And then – we'll figure out the rest."

Jade pouted but allowed Jem to remove her sweater, shirt, shoes, socks and jeans. "Ouch. Rocks!"

"Be careful. Wait for me." Jem quickly stripped down, glanced over at Jet who still had his back turned and grabbed the small bottle of shampoo. She found Jade's hand again and they waded in.

What about water animals? She felt a something slimy swim past her leg and hoped that Jade wouldn't feel it and freak out. Hopefully, fish cooperated around here and stayed afar from now on.

The river remained still and quiet. Peaceful even. But both girls shivered, and Jade refused to wade in past her knees. "It's cold! I don't want to swim!"

"Look!" Jem stilled herself, took a deep breath and dove in. The cold took her breath away. Her head popped up about six feet from shore. "See?" She tried to keep her teeth from chattering. "Me first." She opened the shampoo bottle as Jade watched and she scrubbed her hair. Dirt poured from her fingers. Yikes. And it was taking more shampoo than she thought. She needed to save some for her sister. Jem bent backwards to try and rinse it all out. She shivered vigorously but when done, her hair felt so much better. *She* felt so much better. She swam in closer to the shore and stood to wash the rest of her body and scrub the underwear and bra she wore as well. She tucked the small bottle in her waistband and waded back out to rinse. The water warmed a bit.

She looked back at the shore. "Ready? I feel better. You will too."

Jade crossed her arms and shivered. Jem didn't want her standing in her underwear on the shore too long. "Come on, J." She begged.

Her tiny "Okay" was enough. Yes! Jem waded forward and reached out for her hand. "You can do this, Jade. Let's swim!"

It was a nightmare with Jade crying the whole time. Even Jet paused to look over his shoulder until Jem yelled that she was fine.

Great. She'd probably fear rivers the rest of her life.

When they finished, Jem held up a towel, instructed Jade to remove her underwear and dried her off as much as possible. She helped her put her jeans and shirt back on. Their underwear needed a place to hang at the camp until dried. Jade tried to hold the towel for Jem to do the same but couldn't hold it as high and still trembled from the cold. Her lips turned bluish. Heck with it. Jem gave up and moved quickly to dry a little with the now-soaked towel and pulled her shirt on first, which hung down over her hips. She quickly finished and called out to Jet. He led them back to the camp, whistling. "Betcha feel better, though."

Jem managed a nod. Jade stumbled along beside her – tears finally dried. Once back at camp and in Jet's tent, Jem tucked her into another sleeping bag they'd just acquired from a dumpster. Gratefulness for finding it just in time overwhelmed her. It was almost October if her calculations were correct. Zeb would probably know for sure since numbers were involved.

Jade coughed loudly. It sounded like a bark from her lungs. Jem patted her back until her sister slept.

Once Jade slept, Jem left the tent and found Servio on the talking log. It seemed to be the place for deeper conversations. "She's gonna have nightmares about that one."

Jem sighed. Her now-dryer hair swung around her face like it was supposed to. It felt light.

"She'll be okay." Servio broke a stick in half. "You though, I'm not sure. Your nose is awfully shiny."

She cracked up. Servio smiled. "Want to tell me why you're here, Jem?"

She sobered. "I told you. I'm looking for my grandma."

"I've noticed something." He nodded firmly. "It's always 'my grandma' not 'our grandma' when you say it. Is she not Jade's grandma too? She's your sister, right?"

Jem sighed and scuffed her feet in the dirt. She'd walked right into that one. Should she spill it? She doubted Servio would tell the others.

"She's not, actually."

Other than the slight quirk of his eyebrows, he gave no indication of hearing her. She knew better, though.

"Brandon brought her to us. She was two or three. Brightest red hair and biggest green eyes you've ever seen." She laughed. "Well like now. Her hair's not quite as red though. Elenore, she's my mom, was pissed. She asked Brandon where she came from. Brandon said she needed a home and that mom had agreed. He spent some time helping adjust things – and then left again."

"Where'd he go?"

"Who knows? He didn't live with us – just popped in once in awhile and especially when mom was sick. He brought her drugs."

Servio nodded. "So, voila! A sister."

"She wouldn't talk. I named her Jade because of her eyes. I was only a kid myself." She smiled sadly. "But mom wanted nothing to do with her."

"And you did." He learned forward slightly.

"She needed me. So I'm the one who made her meals, gave her some schooling, played with her, gave her baths." She laughed. "And again tonight. But I love her. Can't imagine life without my Jade in it."

He reached over and patted her knee. "You did good, Jem. Except now its more complicated, huh? You aren't really even a relative. She has a bio family somewhere."

Jem nodded and sighed. "Yeah. There's that."

Chapter 21
Cienna

Cienna checked her phone and tapped her nails. Jazz promised to show, and the least her friend could do was be on time once in awhile. She sent a quick text to Adrian and answered an email from Claire at the office.

"Sorry, Ci." Jazz stood by the table. Cienna jumped up to hug her friend. "Traffic." Jazz slid into the other side of the booth as Cienna sat down. "Coffee?"

"Ordered your fave."

"Good." Jazz yawned then stretched her arms above her head. "Haven't been sleeping well, I guess. Sorry about missing dinner with you and Ad. Something came up at work."

Cienna frowned. "Yeah. That the day you got put on leave?"

Jazz leaned forward. "The jerk. Can you believe that?"

Cienna's lips twitched. "Well, blunt force and all that..."

"I didn't hit him. Just pressed the baton a bit."

"Still, Jazz. You were mad."

"Heck yeah, I was mad. Bastard hit her and I bet it's not the first time. Poor kids." Jazz looked across at the waitress. "Coffee might help!"

"Jazz, geez. I'm sure she'll be here as soon as she can." Cienna sighed. Sometimes Jazz seemed like a completely different person than her childhood friend. Then again, who wouldn't be after all they'd been through? "I need your opinion."

Jazz turned her eyes on her friend. Intense. "Everything okay?"

"No! I mean yes!" Cienna shook her head. "I don't know. I'm confused. I gotta make some decisions. When I left work last week, there was a note on the porch."

"From?"

"No idea." She leaned forward to whisper. "Seemed like a threat. Said they knew about Grace and about where we live…"

Jazz's eyes snapped. Eyebrows raised. "What?" She whispered back. Then louder, "Oh my gosh. What did you do?"

Cienna pulled down her loose sweater down from her shoulder, revealing a big bruise. Her heart rate increased quickly, remembering the incident. "Adrian doesn't know it all. Just about the note." She'd avoided his touches and advances as well as dressing in front of him for a week now. "It's better. Yellowing at least. It was a board."

Jazz shook her head as the waitress plunked their espressos down in front of them. "Ready to order?" She snapped her gum and looked pointedly at Cienna, who'd quickly pulled her shirt back over her injury.

"That's assault!" Jazz exclaimed. Cienna glared. Jazz had lost some filters after their rescue. With her outburst, people in the diner stared.

"Sorry." The waitress droned. "No assaults on the menu today." She grinned, then she sobered. "Oh wait, aren't you-"

"Jasmine and Cienna, yeah." Jazz raised her eyebrows at the waitress. "It's been nine years, uh…Amanda."

Amanda looked down at her nametag. "Yeah, um. Sorry. So, you want to order lunch or…?"

Jazz rolled her eyes. "Branded for life." Then to Amanda. "But we're different people now and you know, don't really like to be reminded of the past."

Amanda scurried away. Cienna buried her nose in her menu. "Jazz."

"What? I'm sick of it."

"Then move to Argentina." Cienna mumbled, still behind the menu. She pursed her lips. She didn't really want to lose Jazz again. But getting some of the old Jazz back would be nice at some point. "I'm having a Club." She set the menu down and reached for her coffee. "She didn't bring water."

"I scared her." Jazz grinned. "How much you wanna bet we get a new waitress?"

"Or they'll ignore us completely."

A man came over. "Ah. Reinforcement." Jazz leaned her chin on the palm of her hand. "Who are you?" Cienna kicked her under the table. Jazz barely winced.

"Theo at your service, ladies!" He smiled. His white teeth gleamed. "Shouldn't be too long for your food. You came before the lunch crowd. Glad you both are doing well. I heard who you are, even though I was a kid when it happened." He jotted their orders on a small notebook.

Both sighed as he left.

"On the other hand, let's both go to Argentina." Cienna raised her espresso to Jazz and they toasted, and laughed. "Stupid Oregon will never forget us."

"They better not." Jazz sipped her coffee. Cienna wondered at her comment. Well, there was a bit of fame in it after all. Occasionally reporters still pursued them, a couple of TV stations wanted to run a "special" about "how they are doing now" and she'd met with a writer and publisher about a potential book. But the fact remained: with Roger still loose, safety remained elusive. Media attention stayed at a low rumble, at their request and finally with a few threatening letters from their parent's attorneys. And a book needed to wait – if she could even bring herself to do it. And what about Grace? She remained innocent regarding all her mom had experienced but it probably couldn't stay that way forever. Jazz, on the other hand, seemed weird about the attention. Sometimes she acted like she loved it and then other days – she looked like she wanted to hide in a hole forever.

Jazz frowned as if she knew what Cienna was thinking. "So, the note? And the bang on the shoulder? What happened?" Her frown deepened as Cienna explained about the storm, heading out to go home, reading the note and hearing someone upstairs. "No one was there the next day. I had Claire with me, and we thoroughly checked out the second floor before starting work. Then I had the locks changed, just in case."

"And he hit you with a board?"

"Uh huh. I was looking under the car to make sure no one was under there."

Jazz framed her face with her hand, elbows on the table. "You called the cops."

Cienna flushed. "Not yet."

"Ci!" Jazz's screech came just as their sandwiches arrived and she cleared her throat, removing her elbows from the table.

"Here you are, ladies! Enjoy! Can I get you anything else?"

They shook their heads, adamantly, and Theo swept away.

"Wait! Water, please!" Cienna called. He waved at them over his shoulder and headed to the water dispenser. "No cops, yet. There's something about this…this person knows too much."

"Roger?"

"That's my thought. Well maybe not him but someone he lords over." Cienna bit into her sandwich. Some mayo dribbled down her chin, which brought a giggle and Jazz threw a napkin at her which landed in the middle of the table.

Smiles. It was so good to smile with her best friend.

But this was serious, and they both knew it.

Jazz sighed. "Okay. What did Ad think? I'm quite sure he'd insist you call the cops if he knew you were assaulted."

"Hence the secret. Don't tell him, Jazz. I gotta figure this out."

They ate the rest of sandwiches in silence.

"How are you handling two weeks of leave?" Cienna pushed her plate away.

"Bored to tears. Visited mom last night. Dinner was alright."

"Well how is she? And your brother?"

Jazz frowned. "Seth's at the community college. Wants to be a cop. The County just took him on as a Reserve."

Cienna titled her head. "Sorry, Jazz. Painful for you, I bet."

"I don't wanna talk about it."

"Well, your mom okay?"

"Yes, she's very proud of him. Dad too, I guess. Although we don't see him very often."

Cienna knew they were proud of Jazz too – if only she could convince her friend of that. Time for a subject change. She placed her napkin on the table and took a drink of water. Sighed. "Heavy topic ahead."

Jazz snorted. "Getting assaulted isn't a heavy topic?" She laughed.

"Fine. You got me there. Okay, second heavy topic, closer to home. I need to decide if I want to know who Grace's biological unit is. And I put in a request to visit Mike in prison."

Jazz coughed as she almost choked on her last bite. "You have to see him to find that out?"

"No, no. Miller said they can do a court order to get DNA without me visiting. I just need to decide if that's what I really want. And what will that mean, if so? I mean obviously she's either Mike's or Roger's and both have wretched DNA, as my dad would say. They're traffickers and killers. Adrian has really stepped in and is the only dad she knows. So, what good does it do us to know for sure? Except for the fact that we need to know whose parental rights to remove for Adrian to adopt Grace. And, I'll be honest….there's always a question in my mind."

"Cuz Roger was worse than Mike?"

Cienna considered. Her thoughts exactly, until she'd found Penny chained under the house. But certainly, Roger still seemed the worst monster most of the time. And ugly. Mike was handsome and charming – and in that way, dangerous too. "Because what about that DNA? What about potential health issues, medical problems that run in her other person's family? You know. And what about that other side of her family? Maybe there are good people in that family who should be in Grace's life." She shuddered.

Jazz cleared her throat, slammed thirty bucks on the table and stood up. "Aren't you headed to your therapist appointment after this?"

Cienna stared at her. "Yeah. You know that's the only weekday I take off from the Freedom Center. Why?"

"Because I'm coming with you. And hopefully between the two of us, we can talk some sense into you. Come on."

Chapter 22
Elenore-14 years before

Elenore healed slowly. Nance came by often at first to check on her. Ellen glared when she passed the den they finally settled Elenore in. Other gals lived there too, and Brandon helped all of them. And then – the men. Men came in and out for short time periods, and Elenore heard noises she didn't want to hear. Most of the time, she plugged her ears or turned the television up loudly. Once Nadine screamed like she was in pain. Elenore jumped up, only to find that Nadine's door locked. She knocked, and Nadine assured her everything was fine. Elenore slunk back to her den – it was where they all told her to stay, anyway, until it was time to join in for a meal.

In the meantime, her belly expanded. She knew her time for the baby's birth grew closer.

Brandon confiscated her phone. Len would track her, he said. Terrifying. She didn't leave Brandon's double-wide. Len would surely see her and follow her – she lived less than half a mile away.

Next time, she could die. And this baby too.

Brandon provided her pills for free. She took them sparingly, sometimes, saving the rest. Nance and Ellen convinced her that a home birth provided the perfect answer – any other type, the agencies would stick their noses in, do a DNA test and inform the father.

Elenore shuddered. That could never happen. If Len even hit the baby once – it might die.

The den housed a computer and file cabinet. More than once, Elenore tried to sneak a peek into them. The computer was password-protected and little information lived in the paper files. So, what did Brandon really do? He came and went. Occasionally spent the night but mostly stayed at the other properties he managed, she assumed. The women here appeared to maintain clients. Did he understand what happened under his own roof? Should she tell him? He visited occasionally, and then disappeared into one of the other girl's rooms as Elenore pouted in the den.

Tonight, gossip circulated of a visit from him, and butterflies fluttered in Elenore's stomach. Anytime he passed her room, came in to say hello or she saw him in the kitchen without a shirt, she blushed. It didn't help that he paused to kiss her gently or fondle her behind. A little like Chad used to do.

He must like her a little bit, right?

But who would like a whale? She understood. He didn't choose her now because of her large-hanging sidekick, despite what he'd said in the diner. She sighed.

She heard the door slam and perked up. Sat up and waddled to the door of the den – careful not to cross the line.

"El." He crossed to the kitchen and grabbed a beer from the fridge. Nodded at her stomach. "Stay in your room. Unless you gotta pee." He grinned. "I can come watch you then. Or maybe I'll visit you. Have some paperwork to do anyway."

She blushed and at the same time felt a warmth spread through her belly. The baby kicked. She winced.

He laughed. "Keeping you up at night, yet?"

"Oh yes." She flushed. "And – uh, visiting the bathroom more often. Nance says not too long now."

"I hear Nance brough her ultrasound in. It's a girl?"

She beamed.

So did he. Like a proud papa.

A weird, nigging feeling started in her stomach. Well, he could be a father figure anyway. Perhaps. But she might have to insist that he start staying with her instead of having time with all the girls in the house except her.

Yes. Those expectations made sense.

"I want to feel." He set his beer down. "She'll need a dad you know, anyway. Guess I should start getting to know her."

Elenore smiled. Did he mean it? Time with Brandon. Her heart beat double time. She owed him so much. She felt shy each time he neared. Nothing like it was with fat, alcoholic Len who spilled over in the recliner most of his waking hours.

"Okay." She said coyly. "What do you want to feel?"

"The baby, of course. She's moving around now, right?"

Elenore laughed. "Yes. She does most all the time. Doesn't sleep on the same schedule as me, for sure."

"Take your shirt off so I can see her kick." He picked up his beer bottle and tossed it into the recycling bin. He advanced toward her.

Elenore giggled and turned around to re-enter the den. She pulled her shirt off, just as he requested. And sat on the couch, the butterflies in her stomach increasing.

She tapped her fingers on the couch arm. Stretch marks and purple marks decorated her belly. What if he hated how she looked once he came closer? She shifted – trying to look poised and sexy.

Brandon entered and kicked the door closed. Sat next to her on the couch and reached over to rub her stomach, awe in his eyes. "It's like an alien in there."

She laughed as a print of a perfect hand pressed up against the wall of her stomach. "She's pretty active right now."

"Wow." He leaned closer and started stroking her belly, then his hands moved up and slid under her bra. He looked her in the eyes. Her breath hitched and she took a deep breath as his lips met hers. "You're beautiful."

That sealed it. When he led her to her narrow bed, she willingly followed. Allowed him to take her clothes off and make beautiful love to her.

She awoke in the morning to pain. She was on her side. He was behind her, and this time it hurt. "Ow! Brandon!" She tried to push him but couldn't reach him. When she tried to move away, he grunted and grabbed her arms tightly. "Ouch!"

"Stay put. You owe me."

He finished and left the room, while her tears dripped onto her pillow.

***

When Ellen finally left to meet a client elsewhere and all seemed quiet, Elenore quickly searched the house. She finally found a house phone at the end of the hallway in a cupboard. Funny, it never rang. She saw the ringer button turned to "off". She dialed Mom quickly.

"Mom. I'm getting ready to have the baby, and Brandon's not being very nice."

"He's gotta be better than that fat slob." Mom sighed. "What do you want me to say, Ellie? You get what you ask for."

Elenore hung up, tears rolling down her cheeks. And then, to her utter horror, water rushed down her legs and puddled on the carpet.

Chapter 23
Jem

Cold weather seeped into Portland. Jade's cough grew worse. As she hacked at night, Jem held her close, trying to comfort her and help her sleep. Mrs. K found some cough syrup, which helped. And tonight, Jem gave her a second dose.

"Drink, sis." She held it to Jade's lips, praying she wasn't giving her too much.

Jade sputtered as she swallowed. "Ick."

"Sorry. But uou should be able to sleep after you take this. Guess what's in two days?"

"What?"

"Thanksgiving. Do you want some turkey? I can't wait. We're all going to the community center where a big church is giving us all turkey dinner."

"Sounds yummy." Jade coughed, quieter this time. "Jem, when do we get to go home? It's cold here."

"It *is* cold." Jem looked at her little sister. Their previous well-fitting clothes hung loose now. What kind of life had she led her sister to? She held Jade close and cried quietly into her hair as her sister finally went to sleep, still shivering.

"I'll get another blanket." Jet shifted by the tent door. Jem startled. But then again, who wouldn't be awake with the incessant hacking? She hiccupped and dried her eyes on her already damp sleeve. He grinned – his teeth gleamed in the dark. "It's okay, Jem. Maybe we should hitch ta California. Much warmer there."

Jem almost laughed. "Who would pick up three bedraggled people who are obviously homeless?"

"Others get there somehow," Jet mumbled. "Here's my blanket." He tossed it at her.

She caught it. Threw it back. "Don't be ridiculous. You can't give that up. You'll freeze to death."

He tossed it back. "I'll get something else."

He left the tent, and Jem shrugged. Resourceful Jet. She lay down with the extra blanket, holding her sister tightly, hoping her body heat sufficed.

The next morning found all three at the Portland Freedom Center. The receptionist brought them paperwork and turned away. Jet seemed nervous and bounced from one foot to another. "I'll wait outside."

"You will not!" Jem hissed. She felt clueless, with no idea what to ask for. She only knew that Jade needed help. And she'd rather give her own life before taking her back to Mom's apartment. She tapped her fingers on the chair arm.

"Please, Jet. I don't know what to do."

"Yeah." He sat, but still tapped his foot up and down. Jade hacked loudly, and the receptionist looked up.

Jem patted Jade on the back quickly. Sometimes that seemed to help. But now, nothing helped. Jem's face flushed at her inability to care for her sister. "Oh, my word. Jade, I'm sorry." She looked at the lady behind the counter. "Would there be some water for her?"

"Oh, yes." The receptionist stood quickly. "I'll get that." She left the room as Jade continued to cough.

They looked up when a blonde woman burst out of an office. "Ci." The woman called back over her shoulder. "I'll work on it, k? But you gotta make a move on this one. And I don't mean seeing Mike!"

Slamming the door behind her, she stilled suddenly when seeing the three in the lobby chairs. Her eyes riveted on Jade, widening. She covered her mouth. "Oh, my gosh!" She turned back to the office door, opening it again and practically falling inside.

Jem looked at Jet. "What the—?"

He shrugged. "Crazy client."

What were they getting themselves into?

Jade coughed deeply again and buried her face in her sister's shoulder.

"I'm so sorry, Jade. We're going to get you help. Antibiotics or whatever we need to get you better. I promise. I'm so sorry …"

She felt her shoulder grow wet as large, silent tears rolled down her sister's cheeks. She coughed again. "I-I want to go home, Jem."

"I know, baby. I know." Part of her longed for home too. As in, a roof, a mattress and a refrigerator that sometimes held enough food. But never what occurred at home. The trade-off wasn't worth it.

The receptionist came back with a bottle of water for Jade. Her nametag said "Claire". Jade opened it gratefully and drank deeply. She coughed again, and Jem grabbed the bottle before it fell on the floor. "Can someone help us?"

"Yes." Claire nodded firmly. "Cienna will be available shortly to meet with you. Did you finish the form?"

Jem nodded and handed the clipboard over. Fake names only. She checked off "medical care" for requested services. She hoped these people could get Jade the care she obviously needed.

***

Cienna

Jazz slammed Cienna's office door and leaned against it, breathing heavily. Cienna stood quickly and ran to her friend. "What, Jazz? What is it?"

Jazz slid down until she sat on the floor. "Ci, you gotta hear me out."

"What do you mean? I always listen to you." She sat next to her friend.

"No, I mean *really* hear me. You know I'm not nuts."

"I do know that. You aren't nuts. What the heck just happened?"

"That little girl in the waiting room ... red curls. Ci, she looks exactly like Rose!"

"What?" Cienna rose to her feet. "Seriously?" She peeked out her office window. What on earth? She'd never seen Rose for real. Guilt filled her gut. She sat next to Jazz on the floor again. "Look, I know you promised Rose you'd find her daughter. I get it. I know I discouraged it too after a few years of not finding anything. Jazz, I'm sorry for that. I'll talk to Adrian, and we can pick it up again. But I'm quite sure that little girl out there has nothing to do with Rose. I know you want to find her ..."

"You don't know crap!" Jazz lifted her head. "When did you see Rose? Oh, okay, I guess probably online after we were rescued? But that's it. That girl ... her head tilt, her eyes, her hair, her smile ..." Tears filled her eyes.

"Okay." Cienna patted her friend's arms. "Whoever they are, they need help, and we can probably learn more then. Look ... I promise to help start searching again. Okay? I promise. Now let's get you on to your day so I can help them. Aren't you starting back at work today?"

"Maybe," Jazz mumbled. "I have to meet with stupid Phil first."

"Well, okay! You go do that!" Cienna grabbed Jazz's arm and hauled her up. "Come on. You gotta go tell your boss that you get it and that you won't hurt people again when responding to situations. You can do it."

Jazz grimaced but allowed herself to be pulled up. "And *you* can go to the police with the note crap!"

Cienna nodded. Recognized the deal. "I can. I will. Now go." Deciding she should walk Jazz out the door, she guided her out of the office and to the lobby.

But Jazz stopped. And stared again at the three strangers.

Well, now they'd probably leave.

"Jazz." Cienna urged her friend toward the door by pulling her arm. But Jazz stood firm.

"I will. I know who you are." Jazz put her hands on her hips as she addressed them.

Panic filled the older girl's face. She lifted her chin and stood. The boy and younger girl stood with her.

"Jazz!" Cienna yanked on her arm. Practically pushed her out the door. Out of the corner of her eye, she saw Claire staring with wide eyes.

Jazz finally left, grumbling.

Cienna turned back to apologize. Their guests swung their backpacks onto their backs.

The older girl glared. "We better leave now."

The boy nodded. "Sorry ta waste yer time, ma'am." He inclined his head at her, then nodded at Claire.

Polite then. At least the boy. The girl, not so much. There was something else going on here.

"Please stay." Cienna rested one hand on her hip and smiled gently. "I hear your girl's cough. She needs a doctor. We can help. You're safe here. I promise. No one else will bother you."

She winced, thinking of her best friend's reaction. But she couldn't force them to stay – only they could make that decision. The younger girl obviously needed medical care. That was her card to play. As if on cue, the littlest one started hacking and lifted her arm to her mouth. She bent over at the waist, holding her stomach and chest.

"Look. This cough she has. It's hurting her. I bet she's even struggling to breathe. Please let me help." Cienna touched the small girl's shoulder. "Let me help you. What's your name?"

"J-Jade."

"Jade. What a beautiful name. I bet you were named for those beautiful green eyes."

The older girl grunted. They were still on their feet, ready to run.

"Are about ten, sweetie? You look a couple years older than my daughter."

"Seven." The older girl almost growled.

Your names and ages don't matter." Cienna straightened up, looking the older girl straight in the eye. "In fact, we can make up new names right now. No one will have to know but me, and maybe the doctor. Will you let me help Jade?"

The older girl sighed and glanced at the young man. After a very slight nod of his head, she turned back to Cienna. "What do we need to do? My sister needs help."

***

It was much later that evening when Cienna arrived home. They checked the smallest girl into the hospital for treatment of pneumonia. Cienna's legal team filed paperwork for temporary guardianship so Cienna could give permission for treatment, and the judge had approved it only hours ago on an emergency basis. Turned out the older girl had no ID and admitted that she was only fourteen.

Well, so much for Jazz's theory. Rose's little girl didn't have a big sister, at least that they knew of. And if she was indeed seven years of age, the timeline failed for that hypothesis. But long after Cienna arrived home, she tossed and turned.

Something wasn't adding up.

After Adrian was asleep, she grabbed her phone. With a lump in her throat and heart, she scoured the headlines, going back nine years to when she and Jazz had been rescued. Nine years ago when Rose had passed. Her body, still unclaimed, was unburied at the farm only after the arrest of Sam and Kella.

Staring from the screen was a picture of Rose. And Jazz was right. Add eight or so years to Jade's face, and she could have been Rose's twin.

Chapter 24
Ruler

Not enough has happened! You're not doing a good job!
 Ears plugged, Ruler tried to escape the voice.
 It was obvious. Ruler sucked.
 "You have no idea how stubborn she is," Ruler muttered to Frenemy, who wasn't even in the room. She would be by later. Maybe to leave more instructions. More likely to leave a scathing note. "And what is the point of this anyway?"
 She broke a promise. That's inexcusable.
 Ruler moaned. Truth was, this living arrangement wore thin at times. Sure, Frenemy took care of the bills and left food in the fridge. Mostly. Ruler found a yellow note on the front door from the power company the week before. But the power was still on, so obviously someone paid.
 But what kind of life was this? Ruler running around following instructions. Sometimes hurting people. Sometimes just threatening. Still, noisy kids around the apartment complex. A headachy complication for sure. Ruler read books and sometimes watched TV or played video games, but mostly zoned out when not focused on the next assignment.
 Maybe Ruler should look for a real job.
 But no, the head pain intensified even thinking about it. Worthless Ruler. Disability just out of range. No choice in this case.
 Ruler needed to keep placating Frenemy. For now.
 In fact, Ruler required improvement. The fridge's shelves lay almost empty, a noticeable consequence when Ruler struggled to follow the exact instructions. Better performance was needed. Eating was a pain, and something

Ruler wished to do without, but the body had its way of being in control.

Ruler slammed a fist on the dining room table.

Control! Ruler knew it was time. Ruler needed the control here, not Frenemy.

But how could this be accomplished?

Chapter 25
Cienna

Cienna tapped her foot impatiently while waiting for the receptionist to take her debit card. She rolled her eyes at Jazz, who stood nearby. The phone rang again, and the receptionist raised one finger.

"Look, I need to go." Cienna frowned.

Sorry, the receptionist mouthed it to her. "Springhaven Counseling. How can I help today? Oh wait – can I put you on hold? No? Okay then …"

Cienna ached to leave. Screw them. They could bill her. Instead, she turned to Jazz. "Well, are you satisfied? Meena didn't really agree with you."

Jazz frowned. Cienna expected to hear a growl come from her lips. "Not sure what *you* heard," she muttered as she wandered across the lobby and sat in a chair by a large fish tank.

"What does that mean?" Cienna marched over and plopped herself next to her friend. "She said it was up to me."

"That's what therapists are supposed to say, dingbat."

"Dork." Cienna rolled her eyes. "She said it might bring some closure."

"She also said it might be triggering, painful and bring back your nightmares."

"Oh." Cienna shrugged. "Sure. She also said that."

They sat for a moment in silence. Sudden memories rushed over Cienna of sitting with their moms in another waiting room, waiting for a doctor to insist on Cienna's pregnancy. Confirmed to them all with a picture of Grace on the screen and a "wa-woosh" on the Doppler. A knot settled in her stomach. Why did she want to bring all of this up? Was it that important to know Grace's heritage? Why couldn't she just wipe it out of her head?

"What happened with the little red head?"

Cienna sighed. "We got her help. Pneumonia. She's in the hospital but hopefully released soon. You're right. She does look like Rose. I looked up her picture."

"Uh-huh. Told you." Jazz nudged her in the ribs.

What? Cienna looked up to see the receptionist waving her over. She rose and went to the counter.

"I'm sorry for the delay." The receptionist eyed her carefully. Cienna recognized *that* look. She sighed. She and Jazz needed wigs and sunglasses, apparently. Whoever thought they could have a normal life after trafficking was seriously demented.

"It's fine."

Jazz appeared at her side and glared at the woman. "You don't have to look at us like that."

"Jazz!"

The receptionist blushed as she took Cienna's card. "I know nothing."

"*BS*, she knows nothing." Jazz frowned as they exited. "This is ridiculous, you know. Why can't we be forgettable?"

"I don't know." Cienna's stride slowed on the way to Queenie. "It's a pain in the rear, for sure. Changing counties didn't even help."

"Well, Mike was apprehended here." Jazz yanked open the passenger door. "It was pretty heavily covered on the news, I suspect. There's still an online board, and it's all they talk about. Sick fans or something."

Cienna gritted her teeth as she settled in behind the wheel. It would be nice to just blend in. But of course, they were more recognizable together, and she wasn't going to give up their friendship for something as stupid as that. If anything, she should use it. Yeah, how could she use it a bit more to help the Freedom Center? Maybe raise more funds? There had to be a way. If Jazz agreed, of course.

"But Roger wasn't." Jazz clipped her seatbelt in.

Huh?

"Oh. You mean caught?" Cienna nodded and started the car. "Yeah, we thought Roger was maybe dead. But-"

"But, heck no, he got away with almost murder and is still out there doing it." Jazz stared out the window.

"We don't know that for sure."

Jazz laughed.

Cienna noted her friend's laugh was no longer one of sweet innocence – but rough and raspy sounding. "Oh, you think he retired?" She smiled grimly.

"Shoot no. Probably just still lying low."

"Yeah." Jazz cracked her window open and pushed down her visor. "Hey, maybe he's writing you those notes, though."

"One note." Cienna yawned. "And, okay, there was a board involved." She suspected Roger as well. But why would he come out of hiding after all these years? Just to show them up? To try and abduct them again?

Sick bastard.

Didn't matter. He'd find himself flat on the floor if he tried anything. And he certainly couldn't scare her anymore. "So, time to involve the cops, you think? I guess I promised you I would. And Adrian wants me to."

"Course he does." Jazz grinned. "You do have a daughter, you know. And you can bet Ad doesn't want you abducted again."

"Nor you." Cienna turned her head briefly to her friend as she steered onto Second Avenue.

Jazz shrugged.

"I'm tired of all this. I'm going to do something. And it starts with me telling Mike he can go you-know-where." Cienna gripped the steering wheel. "I'm gonna visit him. And petition the courts for a paternity test."

"Are you sure?" Jazz frowned deeply. "What if it's Roger? He's still loose. Is there a chance he could fight for custody or something weird like that? Geez."

"I doubt that. It's more like, how could I live with it if she's *his* daughter? Ugh!"

"'Cuz he's so much better than Mike?" Jazz shook her head. "Either way, you're screwed, my friend. Why not just forget this wonky idea? Grace is yours and Ad's. That's it. Be happy. You have a new life. A good one."

Cienna poked her friend's knee. Jazz had a point. "You have a good life too. You're off drugs. You don't have this alternative personality thing going on. You're working again. Time for you to be happy too."

Jazz grunted and stared out the window.

Cienna knew what she was thinking. "Maybe you could still be a cop, somehow. Maybe your brother could put in a good word. And look at all the healing you've worked so hard on."

Jazz sniffed. Her voice cracked as she said, "I know my record was expunged for the drug charges, but still, I bet they know. And antidepressants galore? Clonidine? They won't take me now. They know me. They know us."

That they did. Maybe they should move to Canada or something.

No matter. Their rescue and their friend's deaths landed on the national news several times over. Someone once told Cienna's mom they'd heard about it while on a trip to Japan.

Sheesh. Maybe there was no real way to start over after all.

Cienna pulled into Jazz's apartment complex. "I get it. Adrian wants a baby. I do too ... I think. But I just can't yet. I don't know why. This other thing just isn't done for me, and I'm afraid of the memories, afraid for the baby's safety. I have bad dreams about it occasionally. Hey, how'd you get to the diner?"

Jazz rolled her eyes as she pushed the button on her seatbelt. "I'm getting used to the bus. Don't look at me like that. I'm safe. I'm packing."

"You're what?"

"Packing." Jazz patted her small backpack. "Got a little Ruger right here."

The blood drained from Cienna's face. "You have a *gun*? Dang. I mean, I get it. I carry mace. But a gun, Jazz? You don't take it to work, right? You aren't supposed to have a gun at your job, right?"

Jazz laughed as she slipped out of the car. She leaned in. "Ain't no one messing with me ever again. Or you either."

Cienna drummed her fingers on Queenie's steering wheel. "I don't suppose I could come in? We could chat more about this."

"Gotta go." Jazz slammed the door and waved.

Cienna grimaced. Shook her head. Waved back.

As she pulled out of the complex, Cienna hit the speed dial on her mounted cell phone. One thing at a time. But her next move stared her clearly in the face.

"Adrian? I want to see Mike. Any way you can push that forward? I want the DNA test too."

His loud sigh came across the speaker. "I'll put a colleague on part of that. Better call Detective Miller too. Can we talk about this more?"

"No. I'm done. But I love you." She smiled and hung up the phone. She was ready to face Mike, whatever it took.

She pushed another button for Miller's phone, surprised when Mollie answered.

"Cienna? Everything okay?"

She smiled. "Better than okay. I want to move forward with getting DNA. Can Miller put that into place? And a visit? I contacted my legal team too, just in case there are issues."

Mollie was silent for a moment. "Rob's busy. But I can talk to him. Are you sure, Cienna?"

"One hundred percent." Her voice resonated clear and strong. The only thing she wasn't sure about was how she felt about Jazz carrying a gun.

Chapter 26
Elenore-14 years before

Elenore gritted her teeth as another pain hit. She lay on the narrow bed on a plastic sheet, sweating, as Nance decided without warning to "check her cervix" again.

"Ouch!"

Nance pulled her hand out and took off her glove. "Don't be a baby. Once you have one, you gotta grow up a little, Elenore."

Elenore glared. Brandon was on his way. Nance tended to nicen up in his presence. In the meantime, she'd like to punch her in the face. "How about some of that pain medicine?" She moaned, held her belly and turned on her side.

"Oh no you don't." Nance shoved her roughly back into position on her back.

"But it hurts more that way." Elenore knew she sounded whiny, but for once she didn't care. "Can you call my mom?"

"Sure. I'll call your mom."

Right, she would. Elenore watched her leave the room and head the opposite direction from the phone. The pain lessened, and she took deep breaths, knowing the respite was temporary. She wished she could leave the house and have the baby elsewhere. But where would they go? Len's? She snorted. Brandon kindly supported her with anything she needed. And now, she needed childcare to work. He assured her of his "continued support", but he required her staying in the house for her own safety from Len. And once she was back on her feet, Brandon expected her to work at home and pay back rent, groceries and the medical care.

She didn't mind so much anymore when he spent the night with one of the other girls. He never even apologized for hurting her.

"Geez!" She yelled.

Nance poked her head in. "We'll have to close the door, sweetie. Can't have the workplace distressed." She slammed it loudly.

Elenore almost laughed. Like she hadn't heard worse in the house.

When Brandon arrived and walked in, Nance followed quickly. "How's your day been, handsome?"

He grinned as he headed toward the bed. "About to get much better."

Oh. Okay. He was going to be sweet now, apparently. Well, at least he was looking forward to the baby.

"We gotta keep her quieter. Don't need the neighbors calling the cops."

"Certainly." Nance snapped to attention and hurried to her bag. As she drew the needle out of her bag, Elenore cried happy tears. Finally, some relief. Minutes before, she'd considered rolling out of bed to find the handful of her hidden pills. Now, her stomach rolled. She felt dangerously at the point of puking.

"Thank you." She glanced at Brandon. Why did he have to be so darn cute?

He winked. Squeezed her hand. "I'll always take good care of you and the baby too." He smoothed her bangs back. "Nance, at least get her a cool cloth. Golly. No need to be archaic just cuz it's a home birth!"

"Coming right up!" Nance jabbed the needle into Elenore's hip and capped the syringe, tossing it back into her bag. She hurried from the room.

Elenore snorted. Yeah, so now she hurried. Now, she was nice. Elenore should tell him the truth. Never mind that. As much as she hated Nance, she needed her right now.

Another pain started even as the medication eased into her system. She moaned, and Brandon soothed her, reminding her to breathe deeply. She looked into his eyes as she squeezed his hand. His gorgeous eyes. Something inside her melted just a little. "I forgive you," she whispered through clenched teeth.

His face hardened, just for a moment, then he winked at her again. "Oh that. I forgive you too."

Forgive her for what? She grew drowsy and her eyes closed as the contraction ended. Despite her unanswered questions, she sighed deeply as her body started to rest.

***

Elenore awoke to searing pain. Her nightgown crunched up by her waist as Nance shoved her knees apart. "Time to push. One, two, three, go."

Brandon held her hand as she took a deep breath and pushed.

The pain seared her insides like fire, but she couldn't wait to meet her little girl. After pushing, she fell back onto the bed, out of breath. But seconds later Nance told her to push again.

Again? Wasn't it time to rest now?

Brandon patted her knee. "No rest for the weary." He glanced between her legs. "Wow. That does look painful. Guess it'll be a while before you're healed up."

She glared. Sweat poured down her face, intermixed with tears.

"But I can see her head."

Elenore barely heard him. Thinking she would surely pass out soon, she raised up a little on her elbows and bore down hard.

Little girl better be worth it.

She groaned and yelled as she pushed out her baby.

Finally, after hours of pain, Nance held a little one in her hands. Elenore heard a small cry, and a wail. As Brandon cut the cord, Elenore fell back, out of breath but relieved.

"Not quite done yet. Need to deliver the placenta still. Wait for another contraction."

Still not done?

Nance handed the slippery baby to Brandon, and he grabbed a towel. He rubbed her little body clean. She stopped wailing, and he constrained her wiggles by wrapping her in the towel. "She looks like Len. What's her name?"

Elenore reached out her hands, but he turned his back, still holding the baby. Well, she did have more work to do apparently. "Jem," she whispered as she pushed one last time to finish the job.

Then she promptly passed out.

Chapter 27
Cienna

Cienna clicked her blinker to cross into the right lane. She glanced into her side mirror and turned to the back passenger window to ensure no one drove in her blind spot.

And saw a box with white paper and a bow on the backseat.

Her foot hit the brake. Her mind raced. She'd glanced back there as she unlocked Queenie after lunch. She always did. Nothing graced the seat at that time.

Had Adrian left her a gift?

No, he worked diligently through the day at his office. Rarely even took breaks. Their anniversary loomed. But he knew how surprises still made her nervous.

Her hands sweated as she pulled Queenie over to the side of the road. She hit Adrian's picture on her mounted phone.

"Hon, did you ... did you leave me a gift in the backseat of the car?"

His sharp intake of breath came over the phone. "No." A long pause. "Cienna, get out right now. Call the police! Or I'll call them. Where are you? Get away from Queenie! Please! And do not turn off the engine."

Cienna's hand shook as she fumbled for her seatbelt, released the latch, and gripped the door handle. She grabbed her phone from the holder and laptop bag from the passenger seat. She opened the door and almost fell out on a grassy embankment, leaving the keys, and the attached mace, in the car. "O-Okay," she stammered, but Adrian had hung up. She grimaced, sprang to her feet, and ran about ten feet from

Queenie. There she crouched, feeling naked without her mace. She nervously glanced around as she hit 911 on her phone.

"911. What's your emergency?"

"I-I ..." Cienna felt breathless. Recognized a panic attack as her heart pounded and sweat formed on her forehead. She should run. Run far. No, she needed to stay to keep a visual on Queenie. "This is Cienna Rydal-Hower. I-I was a trafficking victim, and someone's been harassing me. I talked to Detective Peters the other day. But now – now there's a box in the backseat of my car. It's a gift, wrapped like one, but my husband didn't leave it. He told me to get out ..."

"Mrs. Hower, are you a safe distance from the vehicle at this point? And is the vehicle still running?"

Cienna heard the dispatcher typing. "Yeah. Yeah, I am. It is. But my mace is still inside Queenie! Sorry! That's my car, Queenie. I'm about ten or so feet away."

"I want you to move farther away from the car. Is there anyone else near the car?"

Cienna scanned the area. "No, just cars driving by. But I can't go farther. Not ... not without my mace. I can't."

"Ma'am, you need to." The dispatcher was firm. "I'm here with you, and we've notified officers. Please move farther away from your car."

Cienna's hand shook. She took a deep breath. She must follow the instructions. But without her mace, she felt powerless.

She scrambled over the grassy hill and found herself in an almost empty parking lot. Took a deep breath. Crouched there, her phone tight to her ear. "Okay. I'm ... I'm farther away. I'm sorry. How's your day?" She felt guilty suddenly taking up the dispatcher's time when likely there were other calls, too. A tear leaked down her cheek, and she angrily brushed it away. She heard sirens in the distance.

The woman chuckled. "A good day, so far. I want you to stay on the phone with me, okay? How are you doing?"

"Nervous!" Cienna grinned and then sobered. "But safer with you on the phone. Thank you. I'm sure you have other calls?" Sirens sang in the distance.

"No worries. We have plenty of staff today."

"I think I hear them coming."

"I'm glad you called. Don't worry. We've notified them that you need help."

"Thank you." Cienna took a deep breath. The phone trembled in her hand. "They're closer. Let me check."

She scrambled up the hill even as the dispatcher said firmly, "Ma'am."

Yes, she got it. Stay away from Queenie. But how else was she supposed to check to see if help had arrived? She peeked over the hill and saw two patrol cars, lights spinning. Fortunately, the piercing sirens silenced now. She saw Officer Elianna Matthews, who attended Cienna's monthly domestic violence and homelessness task force meetings, speak into her radio and head toward her. Cienna sighed and dropped to the ground as all the strength drained from her legs. "Yes. Elianna's here. Thank you again." Her hands stopped shaking as she disconnected the call and took a deep breath.

Elianna reached her. "Hi, Cienna. How are you doing?"

Cienna almost laughed but controlled it. Instead, a fat tear made its way down her cheek. "I'm okay! But now I'm worried about Queenie!"

"Queenie?" The officer quirked an eyebrow. "Oh, your car?" She threw her head back, laughing at the sky, and Cienna instantly felt better.

She laughed too. "I know she doesn't look like a queen …"

"Well, who am I to judge!" They shared another laugh, and Elianna pulled out a notebook after her radio crackled. She adjusted the earpiece in her left ear. "Sounds like they're sending a bomb squad, just in case. Just a precaution, Cienna. I'm sure all will be fine. In the meantime, let's chat a bit."

***

In the police station, Cienna tucked her knees up and wrapped her arms around them as she waited for Adrian. She'd enjoyed sitting in the front seat of Elianna's cruiser and talking about a Measure from last month's meeting they hoped to help pass. One that would require domestic violence training for all the judges and court officials. Long needed in their county, and in Oregon State too.

Once they passed the lobby and found a place for Cienna to sit near some desks, she felt safe. She knew several officers through her work and a few waved as they walked by. A couple stopped by to ask what was going on. While activity buzzed around her, a friendly lady named Dolores Rae brought her water and asked if she needed anything else. "I have chips." She raised her eyebrows.

Cienna giggled. "I'm good." In truth, her stomach churned.

"Okay. You just let me know." Dolores winked at her, returned to her desk chair, and typed on her computer. She answered calls occasionally and waved a few times at Cienna.

Such a friendly, and busy, lady.

Finally, Adrian burst through the door from the lobby, his face red. "Cienna!"

"I'm fine." She went to him. Buried her face in his shoulder as he held her tightly. "I was scared. Sorry to interrupt your day."

"Okay to be scared," he replied gruffly, which is what his voice sounded like when holding back tears. He squeezed her gently and pushed her away slightly with his arms. But still held onto her. He met her eyes. "I'm glad you're okay. Always best to get things checked out."

She laughed. And felt exhausted suddenly. "I don't know how Queenie is."

He squeezed her shoulder gently and led her back to the chairs. Sat next to her with his arm around her shoulders. "I'm sure she's fine."

She leaned her head on his shoulder.

***

Elianna pushed through the door. "Let's chat."

Cienna rubbed her eyes. Adrian grasped her hand and led her past the desks and into a side room with a small table and two chairs.

They sat and Elianna leaned forward, her elbows on the table. "Detective Peters is on her way. We've got some things to chat about, for sure. But just so you know – that box was not a bomb for real."

"What does that mean?" Adrian raised his eyebrows.

She sighed. "Well, it was made to look like a bomb. Wires and all when we opened it. But no power behind it."

"So …?" Cienna frowned.

"A scare tactic, Cienna. Someone's trying to scare you. Now we still need to address it because it may escalate. Someone broke into your car without you knowing, and I know you already had that … incident with the note and the board. But you and Queenie are safe for now."

Adrian squeezed her hand. He cleared his throat. "Safe for now. Thank God. But I'm worried about Cienna's safety moving forward. How can you and Peters help us, so she stays safe, since that Roger is still out there?"

Chapter 28
Elenore-Present Day

Elenore took a long drink straight from the vodka bottle. She stared at the bald, gross man on the bed. He snored loudly.

She should kill him. She did have a knife in her purse.

But no. There would be aftermath, and she still had to find the girls. Teach them a lesson. How dare they run away? She clenched her fist. The guilt laid with Jem, she knew it. And now, sentenced as Brandon's Bottom Girl until they were found, she seethed. He'd even moved her out of the apartment into a stupid Victorian with eight other women. She clenched her teeth.

Maybe Brandon needed to leave the world. She turned every penny over to him. He at least threw new clothes at her occasionally, gave her a mattress to sleep on with three others in a bedroom, fed her and provided alcohol and drugs.

No way could she make it through without those.

No way could she ever leave.

Elenore glanced in the mirror at the hard woman staring back. Without warning, a memory of Jem's birth surfaced. Soft brown hair, red face and a wrinkled brow. Jem looked like her, not Len, she realized when Brandon finally placed her daughter in her arms. He'd said that just to be mean. Her heart softened thinking about Jem's whimpers and sweet baby smells when she was clean and cuddly.

She'd remained stuck in that trailer for six years with her daughter and not allowed to leave lest Len saw them and realized they lived less than a half mile away.

Prison. Then abruptly released.

Unfortunately, her release came with conditions.

Elenore shook her head to try and erase the memories. No use going back.

She needed to call Mom. Once they'd arrived in the apartment, Mom visited once, meeting her granddaughter for the first time, before Jade arrived on the scene. She sat with her on the couch. Read her a book. Gave her hugs. Said the wonderful words, "she looks just like you." And as she left, "you got a chance now, Ellie. Do it right." She had no idea what was truly happening in Elenore's life and how she'd scrambled in providing a great impression when Mom visited.

She moved away from the mirror. When Mom relocated to Portland, she'd called Elenore. She'd acquired another business and combined it with Joy Stevens Consultations. They chatted occasionally now, but Mom never visited anymore.

Elenore reached up and pushed her long, thin, tousled hair back from her face. She glanced over her shoulder. The man, whatever his name was, was still sleeping soundly.

Well, screw him. She grinned at the words. He'd already paid her, but all of that would go to Brandon, of course. She tiptoed over to his slacks on the floor and felt around the pockets. Found his wallet.

Paydirt.

In a hurry now, she rifled through. Paused at the picture of this man with his arm around a beautiful woman and two boys in front of them.

Happy family? Why, then, was he here?

She shrugged as she pulled two hundred dollars from the wallet and then tossed it onto the hotel table. She gathered her things and the man's vodka bottle and quickly slipped out the door.

Time to report to Brandon.

But she'd be sure to get sloshed first.

Chapter 29
Jem

As Jade finally slept peacefully in a real bed, Jem hovered. Nearby, an IV bag hung on a pole. Her sister struggled with too much pain to even care when the nurse poked her tender skin. But first she'd needed several breathing treatments.

"Hello." Nurse Barb entered the room with a stack of clothes. "Oh good. I'm glad she's finally resting. I bet you didn't get much sleep, either one of you, with a cough like that."

Jem smiled. She'd shook like a leaf as her brave little sister received the treatments. By the time they arrived at the ER, Jade could hardly breathe, and her skin held a bluish tone. What if Cienna hadn't helped them? Jem shuddered.

Relief came as they moved the little girl out of breathing distress and then into a room upstairs when she was stable.

"Would you like a shower?"

"Really?" Jem turned from the bed. "I-I would love a shower. Thank you. I'm sure I smell …"

"Never mind that." Nurse Barb plopped the pile of clothes and a towel into her hands. "Everything you need is in the room." She pointed the bathroom door. "I'll sit with Jade."

Jem hurried into the bathroom, secured the lock on the door, and undressed. She opened the shower curtain. With a surreal feeling, she reminded herself how to turn the knob to get water going and stood shivering until it was warm enough to hop in.

Hot water cascaded over her skin. She stood for several minutes before she noticed dispensers on the wall for liquid body wash, as well as shampoo and conditioner. The nurse left a plastic razor wrapped in plastic.

Was there a time limit? Would the hot water run out?

Curling up to bask with hot water running tempted her. She felt warm for the first time in weeks. She sighed with pleasure and found herself humming a silly song.

Filling her palm with shampoo, she washed her hair three times before it squeaked. She threw on conditioner for good measure and soaped up the rest of her body.

Were her hip bones sticking out more than before? It looked like it.

She blinked the water from her eyes. It was only the thought of little Jade waking up and not having her by her bedside that pushed her to finally finish up and turn the water off.

When she exited the bathroom, she saw the nice lady, Cienna, sitting in a chair by the window chatting quietly with the nurse.

"Well, hello, whole new person." Cienna grinned at her.

Jem wasn't sure what to think of the curly-haired lady who seemed stubborn as heck and insisted on helping Jem and Jade. But she certainly felt grateful. "I-I'm so sorry we gave you a hard time, ma'am. Thank you so much for helping my sister."

Cienna dipped her head. "We all need a hand up now and then." Her voice sounded rough. "Looks like Jade's doing much better."

"She needs sleep for sure. We haven't slept that much." She yawned.

Cienna smiled. "You need some rest too now that she's getting better. What do you think of that? And how about some food? I know you're missing having turkey at the community center."

Jem's heart raced. Were they going to make her return to the homeless camp without Jade? And how could she let Jet know that they were doing okay? "I could eat." She cautiously stepped over to the bed and looked down at Jade. "Her color is better now, don't you think?"

Cienna agreed. "Why don't we go to the cafeteria? We'll get some food. I'm starving. They might even have turkey. We can talk more down there without waking your sister up."

"Where's Jet?"

"He headed back to camp. But he said he'll check in. He waited to hear that Jade was stable before he left. I hear he's been taking care of you?"

Jem nodded vigorously. "We'd be in trouble without him. There's mean people out there and even homeless people who think they own certain areas. You gotta pay them or camp elsewhere to stay safe."

Cienna raised her eyebrows. "Have you been friends with Jet for a long time?"

"We only met when Jade and I came here." Jem knew she shouldn't say too much. By now, Mom most certainly looked for them. Jade needed safety from her and Brandon, no matter what it took.

Fear again snaked down her spine. Would Cienna make them go home?

"How about we go chat and get some food? I promise you they're keeping an eye on her."

"I guess so ... if we're not gone too long."

Cienna grinned and jumped up from the chair. "Come along, then. They do have the best sandwiches here. Unless you prefer salad?"

Jem's mouth watered. She'd be happy with fresh food no matter what it was. Taking some to Jet became her second goal. She followed Cienna out of the room after glancing one more time at the sleeping Jade, and they walked side by side down the hallway to the elevator. The lights seemed bright, and most people they passed smiled at them. Her new stretchy pants and sweatshirt comforted her. The new tennis shoes squeaked against the floor. She'd brushed her hair with the brush the nurse left near the sink. She yawned again, then plucked up some courage. "I don't have any money to pay for the clothes or food." Inside, she told herself three times to shut her mouth.

"This is my treat. You can treat me another time."

A nice thought. Maybe someday. She sure would try. "My sister could have died."

The elevator door closed, and they were alone when Jem burst into tears. Cienna placed her arm around her shoulders and squeezed her gently. Jem cried on her shoulder and then attempted to gather herself together when the door slid open.

"I understand more than you know. But you don't have to do it alone anymore, Jem. I just need you to be willing to accept our help."

"But what does that mean?" They joined the line at the cafeteria counter, and when Cienna pointed at the posted menu above, Jem gasped at all the listed food. "What … what can I have?"

"Anything you want. Your choice. Again, my treat this time, okay?"

As they sat at the table, Jem stared at the tray in front of her. She'd ordered a burger, fries, salad and a cola. Her mouth watered. "Some of this is for Jet. I need to take some food to him and the rest too. They helped us. Mrs. K even put Jade's arm back into place when it came out of the socket."

Cienna winced. "Sounds painful. Hope she did a good job."

Jem nodded, mouth stuffed with fries. "She used to be a nurse." She swallowed.

For the next several minutes, Jem wolfed down her food. Cienna ate too, just slower. Jem stared at her plate in amazement, and then dismay, when it was almost empty.

"Don't worry. I'll make sure your camp family gets a meal too." Cienna smiled and leaned back. "I hope your stomach won't hurt after all of that."

Jem laughed, and then for some reason, could barely keep her eyes open. She laid her head on her arms on the table after pushing her tray away.

"Come on." Cienna urged. "Our talk can wait. You need sleep."

The room looked different when they returned, although Jade continued to sleep. Another bed had arrived – with a fluffy pillow and several blankets. Cienna helped her into it and covered her with a blanket.

Jem smiled as she drifted into a peaceful sleep.

Chapter 30
Cienna

Cienna's hand shook as she signed the clipboard and passed over her ID. This visiting Mike crap quickly became an arduous process. She'd ridden two buses, experienced "patting down" twice, questioned at least once and stared at with raised eyebrows several times.

The message was clear. *Why* would she request a visit with her trafficker?

None of their business. She raised her chin and tried to not think about Adrian waiting. He'd expressed many concerns. She might not be safe, although he knew the guards would try. And what if seeing Mike completely took her backward in her healing? They'd lain awake discussing it until the early hours of the morning, and when he couldn't convince her otherwise, Adrian finally took her to bed and held her tightly like he couldn't let go.

Like she'd see Mike and never return.

She feared that a little bit too.

She called her parents beforehand. That hadn't gone so well. Mom bawled her face off and Dad took the phone from her and tried to talk Cienna out of it. It didn't matter who Grace's bio dad was, and how could she think of putting herself into this situation … facing that monster who had forever damaged her life? All of their lives?

Cienna hung up. She felt bad but understood they wouldn't let it go until she'd changed her mind.

She shouldn't have called.

No one understood.

"Wait over there." The woman guard motioned to the hard plastic chairs.

Another waiting room. Dread settled in her gut. This was the last step before the visit, she suspected.

Cienna hoped the wait would pass quickly. She couldn't deny the desire to flee – about twenty times in the past hour. She might lose her cool in front of Mike. And she needed to get back to the hospital to check personally on Jem and Jade. She took a deep breath and took her mind elsewhere. A green meadow. A beautiful running stream. Putting her feet in the water.

The sounds of the prison resonated around her. Someone yelled outside. She heard a scuffle and guards yelling back. "Winters!" The speaker squawked and a man near Cienna jumped up and headed to the door as they buzzed him in.

What was Mr. Winters story? Surely, he hadn't been trafficked.

Cienna tapped her foot. She still wasn't sure what she was going to say to Mike, only that she needed to face him.

The biggest improv of her life.

Maybe not. Maybe the biggest improv happened as she struggled so hard to survive. Obedient Cienna. Compliant Cienna. Whatever-you-need-from-me Cienna.

Hmmm.

She decided to go back to the world with the river until her name was called. Otherwise, she risked running to the window and asking to be let out ... to go back home to safety and a husband who loved her with all his might.

This didn't feel safe at all.

But the urge pulled at her with strength she didn't understand. She would obey after months, no, *years* of protesting.

When another lady sat next to her, she opened her eyes. The woman smiled. With deep eyes, she gazed at Cienna, and Cienna felt warm from her head to her toes. "I don't suppose you're here on a fun visit."

Cienna smiled and cleared her throat. She loved that the lady's eyes were as blue as the river she'd imagined. "You know who I am?"

"Not from news reports." The woman chuckled. "But yes, I've been told."

"What do you mean?" Cienna smiled again. She couldn't seem to stop smiling at this woman. "Who told you about me?"

"Oh, I have my sources." The woman laughed then, a happy sound that made joy bubble in Cienna's heart. She felt a kinship with this new friend, no matter her "source".

"Well, I have to face him sometime."

Her new friend nodded. "I understand."

"You do?"

"I do. This is a battle you've been victorious in. But it doesn't feel like it's over quite yet."

Cienna scoffed. "That's for sure. Especially since the real bad dude is still out there." She wondered again how this lady knew so much. But for once it felt comforting instead of threatening.

"Ah yes. There's that. He has eyes on him, though. Have no doubt. This won't be how it is forever, my dear. And it's time for closure for you. I have a feeling that today will truly be your release."

Cienna felt a bit drowsy and closed her eyes, her river instantly filling her mind with peace. When she opened her eyes, the woman was gone. "Rydal-Hower!" The speaker squawked. Cienna jumped up. Finally.

It was time to face the man who'd held her physically captive and had also, for a while, retained just a little hold on her heart.

The guards guided her to a table, where she sat with damp hands clasped in her lap. They'd spent some time explaining the safety measures. Restrained and guarded, Mike couldn't touch her, only talk to her.

But Mike maintained a gift for talking. And putting on the charm. They didn't know him like she did.

No matter. She didn't come to have a one-sided conversation.

She heard shuffling and chains. The door opened, and Mike scooted slowly in. Her breath caught as she leaned back in her chair. For a moment, so much fear rose in her throat, she thought she might vomit. But she remembered her calm friend in the waiting room and a strength rose. Strong Cienna. Fighting Cienna. She stood. Raised her head. Faced her demon. Her eyes sparked with confidence, and a whole lot of annoyance too.

Mike looked older and grayer. No red baseball hat. Prison garb didn't compliment his slightly greyish skin color. "Hey ya, baby." He shuffled forward and sat at the table across from her as two guards flanked either side of him. His still brilliant blue eyes met her for the first time in several years.

And, she realized, a DNA test wouldn't be truly necessary, after all.

Chapter 31
Ruler

Ruler shifted positions on the ratty couch to stare out the open glass door. Rain pattered gently on the porch, despite the overhang. Ah yes, sometimes in the Northwest, rain slanted and came in sideways. Perhaps the carpet would suffer.

Ruler didn't really care.

At least the pool was closed finally. Those stupid management people finally got their act together on Thanksgiving Day. No more screaming kids every afternoon and weekend.

Ruler sighed. It echoed off the walls. Liking the sigh, Ruler tried it again. And then laughed.

A knock sounded on the door. Ruler jumped off the couch. Usually, Ruler ignored it, but for some reason, the sound generated curiosity. Scooting along the wall, Ruler made it to the door before peeking out the peephole as a second knock sounded.

It was the tiny neighbor man, Gregory.

Ruler gagged but threw open the door. Gregory stepped back quickly and looked at the ground. The man always looked for a coin perhaps, or maybe for weeds to sprout from the cement. Gregory held a container.

"I ... hi. I was cooking." Gregory shuffled his feet. "And it's just me, so I have extra and I thought, I wondered ... you seem by yourself too. Would you like some cookies?" He thrust the container out.

Ruler's jaw dropped. Their eyes met. Curiosity in Gregory's. Questions in Ruler's. The container hovered close to Ruler's face, so Ruler grabbed it roughly.

INNOCENT VOICES

Gregory glanced to Ruler's left. "I see you have a picture wall."

Darn it! Maybe Frenemy should move the location. Wouldn't the hallway be less obvious? Not that they ever had visitors. "Sure. Family and stuff. Notes from the roommate." Ruler slowly lessened the gap in the door, so the neighbor's view was lessened.

"Oh, so you *do* have a roommate."

"Yes," Ruler mumbled. "We work opposite shifts. Rarely see her. Thanks for the cookies." Ruler wondered if it was breaking a rule to mention Frenemy.

Gregory nodded even as the door slammed in his face.

"Argh!" Ruler tossed the container on the dining room table and then went to work carefully removing the pictures, notes and instructions from the wall. Ruler piled them on the dining room table and then stood in the hallway, thinking. It wasn't too hard to pin them all in the hallway, although Ruler struggled to remember what order Frenemy had placed them in the first place.

Did it really matter what placement they occupied? Ruler felt a stirring of dread. Even if pinned back into the dining area, the system might end up awry.

Why hadn't Ruler just taken a picture of the wall first?

Stupid! Stupid! Ruler smacked the hallway wall. Well, only the best attempt would work. That morning Ruler determined to change things, take back control of the situation. Maybe even pull another person in. Two against Frenemy. They'd be so much stronger.

Gregory just might be the answer. But not if the map was in full view right off the bat.

***

The next time Gregory knocked at the door with a plate of burritos, Ruler smiled. "Why don't you come in, and we can share those?"

Gregory hesitated but entered. His gaze landed on the now-blank wall in the dining area, then moved to the one couch in the living room. "Looks like you could use some furniture. Th-there's always throw-aways at the dumpster. I've pulled out several good pieces. Should I keep an eye out for you?"

Ruler shrugged. "I suppose we could up the décor just a little. You know how people get stuck in their ways."

Gregory nodded. Placed the plate of burritos on the table. "I do get it. But sometimes we can also get stuck. Know what I mean? Not want to improve our lives at all. I have that issue sometimes."

Ruler frowned while removing plates and silverware from the kitchen. What did Gregory mean? Searching the fridge for vegetables, carrots presented themselves, so Ruler carried them to the table, along with the ranch dressing. "I'm afraid I don't have much for drinks. Oh, wait. I might have wine." Re-entering the kitchen, Ruler did find a large bottle of white wine in the refrigerator, Frenemy's usual stash. Ruler returned to the dining room, where Gregory now sat.

"Thank you for the invite." Gregory accepted a glass of wine and then scooped a large, still steaming burrito onto his plate. "I'm afraid I didn't bring any sour cream or salsa."

Ruler smacked the table. "I'm afraid I'm not being the best host."

"No, no. You're fine." Gregory grinned. "I did surprise you, after all."

"You did indeed," Ruler murmured. No, not really. Prepping for Gregory returning occurred the very night the neighbor brought cookies. Cookies! "Oh, I have your container too. The cookies were delicious." Ruler moved back into the kitchen to get the empty container and the salsa. They rarely stocked sour cream.

But when Ruler brought the items back to the dining room, Gregory's chair sat empty. Ruler almost dropped the salsa but managed to place it and the cookie container onto the table before springing into action and hurrying to the hallway.

There Gregory stood, staring at the newly constructed plan-o-gram and notes on the wall.

Rage rose. Ruler's face flushed.

"I'm sorry." Gregory calmly turned to Ruler and smiled. No longer a whiny, stuttering, unassuming man, he seemed to gain more height as he looked Ruler in the eyes. "I needed to borrow your restroom. And of course, I found your art wall along the way. Why don't you tell me what's really going on here?"

Chapter 32
Elenore-6 years before

Elenore hardly contained her excitement. Butterflies danced in her stomach as she opened the door of Brandon's trailer and propped it open with a large rock they kept there.

"Jem, let's go! We got boxes to move!"

Eight-year-old Jem shuffled out of their den bedroom and glanced wearily outdoors.

"Come on. Outside won't bite." She wondered suddenly if Jem presented a problem. Hadn't thought that restricting the girl only to her trailer and backyard, and even "homeschooling" her for years, might create a fear of everything else.

But it wasn't her fault. And it was time to move! Brandon had rented them an apartment. And Len finally died the week before. It was safe to move out and about. Finally. "Woo hoo! Let's go, baby girl!"

Nadine wandered by to the kitchen and frowned at the noise.

"Quit it, Nadine. You're just jealous. You're stuck in this hellhole while Jem and I finally get our own place."

Nadine rolled her eyes. "I'm sure it will be a loads of fun." She wandered into the kitchen.

"What the heck do you mean by that? Are you being sarcastic? Sheesh. Jealous hog." Elenore frowned but shook it off. Stupid Nadine was always jealous. Jealous when Brandon spent the night in Elenore and Jem's room. Jealous when he seemed to favor them. And especially now that he'd rented them their own place. The envy seemed to ooze from her very pores.

She had better things to think about.

"Whatever," she mumbled. "Jem, come on. I need your help!"

Jem grudgingly picked up a box and moved toward the doorway.

"Thanks, love. That's it. Brandon gave us a car to drive for now. That black one right in the driveway there. Trunk is open. We don't have much. But we're gonna fill our new place with lots of stuff. Stuff only ours that we don't have to share! Won't that be fun?"

She didn't miss the worried wrinkle crossing her daughter's brow. "Jem, you have your *own* room. You won't have to share with me anymore, and when people come over, well, you know …"

Jem's frown deepened, then she smiled. "Maybe the new place isn't as noisy?"

"For sure!" Elenore placed her hand on Jem's back and guided her out the door. "Won't that be nice! Quiet. Just you and me."

"But Brandon will still visit." Jem stomped to the car.

Elenore ignored her as she grabbed a couple of garbage bags crammed full and followed Jem. The girl needed to adapt. Nothing could ruin Elenore's mood. But her back was already sore. She grabbed her purse from the passenger seat and rifled through it. Found two pills and popped them both in her mouth. She looked at Jem. "What?"

Jem sighed and handed her a water bottle from the car's drink holder.

"You're my good girl." Elenore almost choked on the chalky pills, so she opened the water bottle quickly and took a big drink. She capped it and handed it back to Jem.

"Hey!" Nadine yelled from the open door. "You're letting all the heat out!" She slammed the door.

Elenore sighed. Nadine was a pain in the butt. Now they'd need to hold the door open for each other with each load coming out. Oh well. There wasn't much left. She glanced at the sky as clouds hovered. "Let's hurry. We gotta make a stop."

Jem pouted. "I'm sick of carrying boxes."

Elenore smacked her on the behind.

"Ouch!"

"Ouch yourself!" She snickered. "I told you to get a move on."

Jem shuffled back into the house, grabbed a garage bag and dragged it to the car.

"Pick it up!" Elenore screeched – her face reddened.

Jem huffed, blowing her bangs up from her face. Then looked down at her wet pants. Elenore looked down at the same time. "Go clean up right now." She hissed. The nerve of that girl to piss in her pants again!

Jem dropped the bag on the porch and ran back into the house, her face bright red, and slammed the door.

Elenore sighed. She ought to slap Jem. Maybe that would wise her up. She muttered as she grabbed Jem's discarded bag and heaved it into the car. That might be the last one. She entered the house one more time to check on things and almost ran right into Mynx, the newest resident. Mynx resided in the real bedroom, the one that by all rights should have been her's and Jem's. Elenore snarled but decided she'd ended up with the best deal, their own apartment. That made the long years stuck there worth it. She'd get settled in the new place, maybe put Jem in a real school and find work.

"Watch it!" Mynx rubbed her forehead. She was scantily clad in a see-through robe. But her makeup and hair screamed perfection.

"Oh, did I hit you? So sorry!"

The ladies looked at each other in the eye, neither backing down.

"Thought you moved out."

Elenore clenched her teeth. "I'm trying. I need to do a last look-through and grab Jem. Let me back in, please."

Mynx grunted and moved aside. Elenore heard a car park by the curb and Mynx smiled. Elenore brushed by her.

Would have been nice to get Jem out before they ran into a client, but the girl peed herself. Of course. She sighed.

"Jem! Hurry up!" She passed the bathroom door. Her daughter peered out with wide eyes. "Golly, Jemmy!" The den seemed empty of their things anyway, but she saw Jem's wet pants on the floor. Mynx could clean up. She kicked them to the corner of the room and walked back out.

Jem shut and locked the bathroom door.

"Jemmy!" Elenore pounded on the door. "Hurry up!"

Silence met her. She sighed and wandered back into the living room. Mynx was already in the arms of Donovan, a regular. They kissed.

Elenore cleared her throat. "Don't mind me. We're outta here soon."

Donovan grinned. Broke away from Mynx and looked Elenore up and down. "Two for the price of one?"

Elenore shook her head. You never could be sure what a client might come up with, but she had no interest. Today was moving day. But Jem still lingered in the bathroom.

Mynx batted her eyelids. "What do you say, Ellie?"

"No. I'm busy."

Mynx raised her eyebrows. "We can get away with a quickie, I suspect." She winked. "You-know-who wouldn't want to know that you turned someone down."

Elenore placed her hands on her hips. "Is that a threat?"

Quickly, Donovan stood in front of her. He shoved her against the wall by the shoulders. She stumbled. Then his gross, fat lips sucked on her neck as Mynx laughed.

Elenore attempted to shove him away. She finally broke away. "I-I said no."

"Then you forget what you're here for." He grabbed the waistband of her jeans.

"Mom!"

They froze. Wearing a pair of gym shorts, her arms crossed in front of her, Jem stood trembling at the edge of the living room.

"Baby girl!" Elenore took advantage of Donovan glancing at her daughter and landed a punch on the side of his nose. As he raised his hands to his nose, she slipped out under his arm.

"Ow! You witch!"

Mynx glowered.

Now she *would* get in trouble. But she didn't care. Nothing could take the dream of this day away, even a gross, disgusting pig of a man who just took what he wanted. She reached Jem, grabbed her hand and pulled her to the front door.

"Not so fast." Mynx stepped in front of the door. "You're turning down a client, Ellie. A decent one. I don't recommend that."

Yeah. Now Mynx's job was at stake too. Donovan might not be satisfied with just her. Elenore understood, but as Jem clung to her with her eyes wide, Elenore took a deep breath. Spoke softly. "Look at her, Mynx. She can't be here. Where's your heart?"

"Put her back in the bathroom. We won't be long. Trust me." She inclined her head at Donovan, who glowered. She laughed.

"I won't." Elenore reached out and shoved Mynx to the side of the door, not caring when the woman almost fell to her knees. "Goodbye."

She opened the door. She and Jem fled to the waiting car.

Jem cried as Elenore buckled her in and hurried to the driver's side. "You're okay, Jem. Everything's going to be okay. We have a new home now. Forget any of that happened."

"Th-that man was gross! He wanted to hurt you!"

"He ... well, not exactly. It would have been okay, Jem. But you and I have things to do today. Want to see your new bedroom? I decorated it especially for you." She started the engine and backed out. "We still have a stop."

Jem cried. "I don't want a stop. I mean, I want all this to stop!"

Elenore paused. She backed out of the driveway, threw the car into drive, and turned the wheel. "This is the start of it all stopping, Jem. We'll be safe at the new place. I promise. Now be a good girl. Stop crying. Remember I told you that there was a man down the street who died last week? I gotta stop there. I have some important stuff to pick up …"

Jem wailed.

"Shut up, Jemmy! Trust me!" Elenore ignored her tears. Getting to their new apartment where johns weren't visiting became almost the highest priority. But first … first, she had to get a journal, clothes, pictures of her and her mom, the Family Bible, a special quilt. Things she'd missed since running from Len years before.

She screeched to a stop in front of Len's house. Wow, it looked different. A fresh paint job, new shutters, new landscaping with some fairly matured shrubs. A red rose bush. And a blueberry bush. The bush looked a few years old at least. Len had never really cared about the landscaping.

She frowned. Eerie. Yet it looked pleasant and safe. Nothing like the way it had looked before.

Maybe her memory was really off?

Elenore shook her head hard. No, she remembered it well. Grey, peeling paint. A front porch sagging where she'd often sat on the steps. Gutters hanging halfway off the roof. A carport that leaned to one side, now removed. And Oscar. Her heart pinched. After Jem turned two, loyal Oscar disappeared. Brandon laughed it off. The other housecat, Oreo, lorded over everything ever since. But Elenore desperately missed her furry friend with such a personality who led her to safety and even followed her around the neighborhood as she walked before she'd moved to Brandon's house.

Weeding the front bed was a woman with white hair and darker skin, who straightened to greet them. Who the heck was this? Len had only passed a week ago. Was this a caretaker for the trailer park? She opened the car door and stepped out. "Stay here, Jemmy."

Jem sniffled. Her tears stopped as she looked out the window. Oh yeah, she kept forgetting the kid had only seen the inside of Brandon's house and the fenced backyard for her entire life. Did she even know there were other trailers and houses out here? She shook her head.

"Hello. What can I do for you?" The older lady stepped forward, removing her garden gloves.

Elenore walked up the sidewalk until they stood about five feet apart. "The house looks really nice."

"Thank you, young lady. It's been a lot of work. And of course, things take a few years to mature." She smiled. It reached her ears. "But I'm proud of it." The woman surveyed the house and the yard. "Strawberries and blueberries even. There might be an apple on the tree if you'd like one."

Elenore felt warmth. A good woman stood here – she could tell. She wanted to sit with her on the new porch and explain her whole life. And receive a hug. "You don't even know who I am."

The woman laughed and stuck out her hand. "Hi. I'm Esmerelda."

"Hi, Esmerelda." Elenore smiled and shook her hand. "I'm Elenore. I-I…you take care of the place?"

Esmerelda lifted her chin. "Well, yes." She giggled. "It is my house, after all."

Elenore felt her knees turn to jelly. She felt breathless. "W-What do you mean? This is Len's house. I have stuff here. He died last week and … and I came to see if I could get some of the stuff I left …" Even as she lifted her chin and looked into Esmerelda's kind eyes, her stomach dropped.

Esmerelda smiled gently and tilted her head. "I'm so sorry. We did buy the house from a Len Thompson's family when he passed. But my dear, that wasn't a week ago. That was over five years ago."

Chapter 33
Cienna

Cienna's brain flooded with memories even as she recognized Grace's "sperm donor." Mike tying her up in the barn. Mike lying to her about Mrs. Mike. Mike leaving her alone for days while Roger tortured her. Tying her to a tree. Using her as a domestic servant. And then, the day she discovered poor little Penny tied up under the house. Sneaking the girl food. Sirens and lights flashing as cops pinned Mike to the ground and Cienna stumbled out of the truck into her guardian angel's arms. Salvation.

The memories chilled. Settled somewhere in the back of her mind instead of the forefront, where they might damage her more if she chose to dwell on them. She lifted her chin. "I'm not your baby." She stared into Mike's eyes, daring him to challenge her. Hopefully, he would never even know about little Grace, who thankfully looked the most like Cienna ... except her eyes. Her mind stilled. Peace flooded her soul.

Time for closure. "Today is your release," the woman in the lobby had claimed. Cienna smiled.

The startled look on Mike's face told her he'd expected her to look intimidated. But intimidation haunted her no longer. And she saw something new.

Before her sat an older man. A broken one.

He no longer had the strong muscles he'd once used to pack her over his shoulder and toss her back into the barn. To restrain her. With the wrinkles on his face and a shrunken body, she felt taller and stronger than he had ever been. Mike the coward. A wimp.

"You will not call me baby. My name is Cienna." She spoke loudly and clearly. One of the guards at Mike's side straightened up. Nodded. "I'm going to talk, and you will hear me out."

Mike leaned back in his chair. He raised his handcuffed hands behind his head. "Gotta stretch." He grinned. "Close quarters in this joint."

Cienna breathed deeply. Gritted her teeth. Mike was in for life. She was in no danger here. Despite that, her heart started pounding at this familiarity, his grin, their closeness. "Let me say that again. I'm not your baby."

He nodded. "True."

"Thanks."

Thanks? Was she returning to his conditioning? His power over her? At one time he required her to thank him regularly. No, but she would remain polite – and firm.

He looked at the table and placed his hands again in front of him. He moved them closer to her. She pushed her chair further back.

The guard slapped his baton on top of Mike's hands. Mike winced. "That's warning one, sir. There won't be another. You're looking at Solitary if you don't behave. This young woman deserves your time, and you will be on good behavior."

Mike grinned directly at her.

Instead of feeling charmed, ire rose. She jutted her chin out. "*My name is Cienna.*"

His grin dimmed a bit. He nodded. "Cienna." It was quiet, but still an admission. A nod to her humanity and perhaps what he had ruined.

Her thoughts whirled. What next? If she only visited this one time with him, what was the most important thing to say? "Why, Mike?"

He leaned back. "Well, ya know I lost Mrs. Mike."

She vividly recalled the night she'd plotted her first escape by trying to accompany him to the clothing store. He'd shared his deepest pain. "I know. But people lose their loved ones every day. Most do not choose to bring in young girls … and … and replace their wives with them. Make them their servants. Prevent them from even calling home. Tie them up. Rape them. Hold them captive. Starve poor Penny under the house. *Why*, Mike? I need to know! Penny died!"

Mike's eyes flickered.

She paused, flushed. One guard remained stoic, but the other's eyes widened as she spoke.

Yeah, they probably had no idea of the whole story. And she was quite sure they'd received the full version of Mike's side.

But never hers.

"Why?" She looked into his eyes and inside her heart, she pleaded. "You even won me over a bit. You *know* this. You were saving me from Roger. Remember? But the reality is, you were a monster too, just like him. You *are* a monster."

Mike shook his head hard. "I dunno whatcha talkin' about, darl–, er, Ci-Celina. Guards, you need to let me outta here now."

But the guards stood still, their eyes riveted on Cienna. Clearly, his refusal to use her correct name not lost on them.

"Yes, you do know what I'm talking about. You locked me in the barn. You were supposed to take me back to the campground. You tied me up for days. When I tried to run, you threw me back into the barn! You let Roger come and torture me. Then you moved me in the house like I was a prized guest, but it was to cook your meals and get locked in the guest room when you ran errands! You raped me, Mike. It was under the guise of your protection and care and all that crap, but I was under the age of consent, and you know it. I didn't consent. I couldn't. You held power over me! And poor Penny!" Her eye twitched – blinked rapidly. She must not cry. Holding it together became a painful priority – no matter how much his presence angered her. "You *bought* us! How wrong is that?"

He sighed. "Fine. But ya wanted everything ya got. And so did Penny. Flaunting about with yer ... bodies." His eyes dropped to her chest. One guard used his baton to move Mike's chin upward. He again met her eyes. "Or maybe not."

There.

She leaned forward. Firmly. Held his gaze. Felt a little gratified when his head moved back as if wanting to avoid her.

Who was in charge now?

But she felt no peace with that, just sadness. "You're a sick, sick man," she whispered. "You hurt a lot of people."

One of the guards sighed. Yeah, they were getting the script of a lifetime right here. But she no longer cared who heard. Mike needed to understand the gut-wrenching truth. And by golly, she'd survived. And she hadn't survived to just wilt in the presence of the man who'd damaged her without thought. Without a conscience. And, obviously, still no regret.

Plus, she thanked God for Grace. She couldn't imagine her life without her beautiful, blue-eyed girl. Grace would grow up to do great things, she was pretty sure. She couldn't thank Mike for the circumstances, but someone, somewhere, was responsible for turning those horrible, nightmarish months into a little blessing that continued to daily bring light to Cienna's life.

She couldn't thank *him* for that. She wouldn't.

But should she tell him about his daughter?

A battle raged inside. Mike – locked up for life. Roger – still out there.

How could they truly be safe until they found and convicted Roger?

Her desire for revenge shrunk like a muscle never used. Like Mike's.

He couldn't know about Grace. Not safe – even with Mike behind bars. And what if he defied the odds and got out someday? Escaped? Jazz would probably hold that little Ruger directly to his head. She shuddered.

She met his eyes once more, surprised to note a tear in his. Perhaps prison could change a man. Who knows what he had been through in the past nine years? She'd heard what could happen to the incarcerated who hurt or killed children. A little pity poked into her heart. Had he suffered some of what he gave, not just to her and Penny, but also to girls before them?

"You deserve anything and everything that's come to you since you were caught, Mike. What you did was horrendous. Do you see this at all? Do you understand the damage you've caused?"

Mike shrugged. Threw her a little grin – a grin formerly charming despite her captivity. Now, with all her heart, she hated that grin. Hated his actions. Hated his charm.

But she realized now more than ever that "survivor" was her identity – no longer "victim". And that others received continual help due to her journey and because of her hard efforts at the Portland Freedom Center. And as awful as the time of torture remained in her brain sometimes, then came Grace.

"I need to tell you something." The purpose and hassle of the trip became clear. Out of the corner of her eye, she saw one guard's eye twitch and the other lean forward. She smiled. "You no longer have power over me, Mike. I renounce the nightmares, the PTSD, the anxiety and the memories. I choose to erase everything you ever did from my heart. You broke me, but I'm no longer broken. I guess that means, in a way, that I forgive you. Because forgiving means to release that hold you've chained me with now for nine years. As a monster, but you created a thriving force. Instead of giving you the rest of my life, I now give it to other people – ones trafficked, and those struggling in other ways. You poured pain into me like I've never experienced. But I choose to pour out some grace now. Not only to the people I work with, but to you. In this, I heal. And you no longer have any say or power in my life. I only feel sorry for you. I hope that someday when you die, God will have some mercy on your soul. But if not …" She shrugged. Pulled her shoulders back and held her head high. A sweet release filled her entire being. A large weight lifted from her shoulders. As her friend in the waiting room so confidently mentioned, the time for her second release depended on this visit.

Cienna stood. Nodded at the guards. The dazed one shook his head as they hauled Mike to his feet.

"Aw, come on." He protested. "It weren't all that bad, Ci-Cilena. We had some good times."

The guards yanked him out of the room, and Cienna released a shaky breath. She grabbed the table with one hand and thanked the guards who led her out back to the lobby. She exited the building, climbed on a waiting bus, and eventually walked off into the arms of her husband. Only then did she let the tears come.

She was finally ... and *truly* finished.

Chapter 34
Jem

Jem sat by her sister's side as Jade opened her eyes. "Hey, sis," she whispered. A roomie lay in the bed next to Jem. According to Cienna, they benefitted from "public" dollars, whatever that meant. But apparently it meant Jade gained a roomie. The new addition meant no room for Jem to stay overnight, so last night Cienna drove her to her own home. She'd even met the nice lady next door, Mel, and enjoyed a fresh doughnut.

Jade smiled and squeezed Jem's hand.

"Am I still in the hospital?" Jade stretched and rubbed her eyes.

"Yeah, for now." Jem's eyes filled as she realized how close she'd come to losing Jade. "But almost done. The doctors say you're doing so much better. You can leave soon!"

She frowned when Jade's eyes darkened.

"But to where?"

Silence filled the room. Jem's heartbeat sped up. "I-I'm not quite sure yet. But we'll figure it out."

"It's warm here. With soft pillows." Jade yawned.

A lump rose in Jem's throat. Yeah. Not a tent. Not sleeping on the ground. Ordering from a menu versus scrounging in a dumpster. No flooding. Best of all, real showers instead of bathing in the river in the middle of winter. "Look, I brought you a doughnut from a nice lady named Mel." She unwrapped the brown wrapper.

As Jade devoured the custard-filled doughnut, Jem mused. Where could she take Jade? Where could she get her what she needed but still be safe from Mom and Brandon? She paused. The hospital might release them back to the camp. But Cienna mentioned their "minorship". Did that change things?

No matter. Taking care of her sister persisted as the priority. "We'll get a place." She reassured Jade as much as herself. "I'll figure something out."

"I know." Jade squeezed her hand. Her green eyes sparkled. Something Jem hadn't seen a long time. "Hey, where's the remote?"

Jem rolled her eyes. Her sister watched television way too much since she felt better.

But what could that hurt? What if their next step was returning to camp and living without all the perks of the last week? She found the remote and placed it in her sister's hand even as her heart squeezed. She missed Jet, and Servio, Mrs. K and even Zeb. They were the kindest Street Family ever. But they'd all lived there a long time – the conditions became normal at some point.

Didn't Jade deserve better? She was too young to stay houseless. Jem noticed that they both gained weight in the past week, and Jade's face no longer paled. They looked … healthy, and even happy.

For the first time in a long time.

Later as Jade slept, Jem sat quietly near the door. A kind volunteer brought a cart of books, and Jem snagged one about a far-off world with dragons and King Pricolai. Absorbed in his fight to keep his Kingdom from the Elite Monsters, she paused as voices raised right outside the door.

"I can't let that happen." Cienna's voice sounded steeled. A bump sounded against the wall. "No, no and *no*. Foster care isn't always beneficial."

A lower, male voice sounded soothing. "It's what the system is built for. They'll be safe. We have good families ready. You want them off the streets, right? You don't really have a choice, Cienna. Without known relatives …"

"There *is* a known relative. A grandma. We've been looking. Can't we hold this off until I can find her?"

"Jade will be released very soon. The doctor says she's doing well."

"Well, what about a temporary place?"

"What do you mean?"

The voices faded and Jem strained to listen. A temporary place. What did that mean? Visions of Mom's apartment filled her head. Adults who treated Jem like garbage. She'd had no choice but to flee with Jade. Her heart quickened. She glanced at Jade, now awake but absorbed in a television show. Jem thumped her book closed.

"There's not a choice, Cienna." The voice strengthened. "Let's get some coffee and talk. But the fact is, they're wards of the State."

"I heard from their mom!"

Jem stood quickly, dropping her book and bottle of water on the floor. Her palms started sweating.

Quiet from the hallway. The conversation grew quieter. Finally, silence came.

Jem ran to the door and peeked out. No one there.

Jade needed released soon. Mom knew their location, And Mom meant Brandon. Jem shook off the swirling memories of the first time Brandon entered the den ... and got into Jem's bed instead of Mom's. He'd felt her all over that night and at the same time, murmured in her ear that he would hurt Mom if Jem told. Then he rubbed against her leg and groaned, leaving a sticky mess. Gross. She wanted to scream. No way on earth could she return her sister to ... *them*. The apartment? Such a ruse. It became only a way to hide the activities as more men visited Elenore, and Jem hid in her bedroom, plugging her ears. When Elenore met with men outside the apartment, Jem sighed in relief.

Her life had changed dramatically when Brandon brought Jade home.

As Jem mothered her new little sister, she became mostly untouchable. Jade became her shield, and she fiercely protected Jade, sometimes daily.

They could never return – not after what she overheard.

Jem shook her head and commanded her legs to move. She scrambled to the closet in the hospital room and found the plastic bag with Jade's clothes. They smelled like flowers – how nice of someone to wash them! She quickly added the few new things. A teddy bear from Cienna, a greeting card from the local church, a business card from the hospital chaplain and a comic book and socks a nurse brought in.

"What are you doing?" Jade, distracted from the TV show, swirled her head to look at Jem.

Jem grabbed the two packages of saltines from her sister's bedside table, crammed them into the bag and smiled. Wiped the sweat from her forehead. "They're releasing you."

Jade tilted her head. "Really?" A tear rolled down her cheek.

"Really. Don't cry. I'll keep you safe, Jade. But we gotta take care of that first." She eyed the needle in Jade's arm, covered with white tape. She glanced at the bag dripping into a tube above her.

Well, how hard could it be to pull out a needle? Her sister couldn't go anywhere with a stupid pole attached. "Okay." She kept her voice low, unconcerned. "I'm going to unwrap your bandage, Jade."

"Okay." Her sister presented her arm.

"Watch your show. See? There's *The Odd Squad*." At home, Jade enjoyed the show often in their bedroom. Jem peeled back some of the tape.

"Ow, Jem!"

"Sorry! Shhh. Let's get this over with." She ripped the bandages off Jade's arm and pulled the needle out. Blood squirted.

Jade screamed.

"Jade! Shush!" Jem grabbed the corner of the sheet from Jade's bed and held it against her sister's arm. Finally, the blood stopped. Still, a band aid would be good. She ended up grabbing some of the same tape she'd ripped off and sticking it over a Kleenex folded several times on her sister's arm. It barely stuck.

Jade shook her head and whined. "What else?"

"Time to get dressed. We gotta go." She helped her sister out of bed and pulled her hospital gown up and over her head. Yanked her clothes out of the plastic bag and helped her into them.

"I stink." Jade frowned.

"I'm sorry. We'll wash soon ... somewhere."

With her sister fully clothed, Jem grabbed her bag and Jem's hand. "We gotta leave now. Quietly, okay?"

She bent down and scooped up her book on their way out the door.

Chapter 35
Elenore-6 years before

Elenore shook Jem's shoulder and, when that didn't work, yanked on her daughter's arm until she almost fell out of the car.

"Ow, Mom!"

"Sorry." Her cell buzzed and Elenore let her go abruptly, scrambling back into the car. Boy, if it was Brandon again, she planned on giving him a piece of her mind.

Mom. **Are you out? Safe to text?**

Yeah, Mom. Just got here. That stupid Brandon. You won't believe what he did. Len died five years ago!

What?!? You've been stuck in his house all this time for NOTHING? Are you dumb or what? OMG.

Elenore hissed. Well, some things never changed.

Jem trudged to the trunk as Elenore popped it open. "Is that Grandma?"

"Yeah. Checking up on us. Hurry up. Get some stuff. We gotta go up some stairs to get to the new place." She dug in her purse to look for a key and found a cigarette.

Jem wrinkled her nose. "You're smoking a lot now."

"Mind your own business. Besides, I'm in a much better mood now with my cigarettes. You're better off."

"Why are we in such a hurry? I'm tired. And hungry." Jem scooped up a backpack and one of the lighter garbage bags. "Do I get my own bedroom?"

I told you that you do, idiot. It's all ready. You even have a TV."

Jem brightened and smiled.

Huh. The girl was even pretty when she smiled. Even though she did look a little like Len with that mousy straight brown hair. Probably good that she was moving her away from Brandon before she grew some boobs.

"You can't watch it all day. You gotta do your schoolwork. And I need to get a bed for you still, but there's a mattress."

"That's okay, Mom. I don't mind a mattress. And I always do my schoolwork."

"True." Elenore propped a box on her hip and slammed the door of the trunk. She drew in deeply on her cigarette and paused against the car door as she blew it out. "Thank God we're away from him. Free." She turned a bright smile toward her daughter. "Free! This is all ours!" She swept her arm toward the grey, two-story structure.

Jem frowned. "All of it?"

"Don't be stupid. A piece of it. Still, it's ours. Now we can go to the store and not be locked in the den all the time. We can go for walks. Go to the lake. Get a cat. Oooo, how about cooking? You should learn to cook for us, Jem. That's fun."

Jem looked fearfully around the parking lot. "I-I liked the den."

"That's because you're dumb. Hurry up." She winked at Jem. "Aw, come on. You know I love you most of the time." She used her free hand to put out her cigarette against the car and let it fall to the cement. Guided her daughter toward some old-looking stairs.

Jem bounded ahead. Elenore thought she heard her singing. She should definitely turn on more music now – not allowed when Brandon was around, except when he turned it on. But she always made Jem listen to it with her earbuds when not working on her schoolwork. It not only kept her quiet, it blocked some of the the noises in the house as the girls worked. Once she'd shoved Jem in a closet when a client arrived for her much sooner than Jem's bedtime. She'd tossed the iPod and earbuds in with her and told her to use them, no matter what.

Elenore inserted the key in the lock with a shaking hand. What if it didn't work? It was an older building. The apartments seemed on the larger side, and the buildings more spread apart. But not very modern. Brandon paid the rent – it likely meant cheap although he could afford better. Not the best part of town. But it didn't matter. Freedom awaited them.

The door sprang open. They stepped into a living room with a few feet of tile placed inside the door.

Blue and tan carpet. A large rock and slate fireplace with some rocks sticking out as shelves. Dirty fireplace. No worries. Jem could scrub that right up. Everything else seemed somewhat clean.

"Wow." Jem stopped and stared. "It's a pretty fireplace, Mom. Can we have fires in it? And roast marshmallows?"

"Sure." Elenore set her box on the floor and tossed her keys on the kitchen bar. "Let's look around. I set up your room earlier." She tried to ignore the smell of the carpet that assaulted her nose. They'd open the windows and air it all out that night. Oh, well. She might ruin it with cigarette smoke anyway.

She led the way to the hallway and opened a door to the left. "Voila! A Jem room." Jem carried her backpack and garbage bag and peeked in. A mattress. Some shelves. Sure enough, the promised TV. Even pretty flower curtains at the windows.

Elenore saw tears in her daughter's eyes and pulled her in for a brief hug. "Do you like it? I still need to get you a comforter and a bed frame … maybe a dresser."

"I love it!" Jem dropped her things and threw herself on the mattress. She rolled around. "It's a mansion." She sighed with delight.

"It's pretty small." Elenore frowned. The master bedroom was a lot bigger, but of course, that was for Elenore.

"It's huge," Jem murmured into the mattress. "I love it, Mom."

"Oh, I get it. It's because it's all yours. Okay then. But you can't live just in here. It's not like the other place. We have a living room and a kitchen. Come on and see."

Jem bounced off the mattress and followed. "Wow! Your room is huge!"

Elenore's room, painted beige like Jem's, held a huge bed in the middle, a matching dresser, a big mirror and smaller dressers by each side of the bed. And a huge fluffy cover on the bed with three large pillows. Jem threw herself on top of it as Elenore tried to show her the master bathroom and big tub.

"Jem, knock it off! You'll spoil the bed!"

Jem slid down the side. Her feet hit the carpet with a soft *whoomp*. "Sorry, Mom." She looked at the floor.

Elenore sighed impatiently. "Stay off my bed. You have your own."

"I will." Jem obediently checked out the master bathroom and followed Mom into the hallway to see the other bathroom and the kitchen too. They peeked out of a sliding door to see a little deck outside, with another door. Jem's stomach growled. "Is there a pool?"

Elenore reached out and shoved Jem's shoulder. Jem fell against the fireplace. "Are you dumb? We can't afford the ones with a pool. Now go get yourself busy and unload the car. I'll look for something to make for dinner."

Jem scrambled to the door, propped it open with a box and disappeared.

Elenore sighed as she saw her keys on the table.

Her kid really was an idiot.

She grabbed her keys and went out to the patio. "Hey!"

Jem's small face looked up in time. Otherwise, Elenore's heavy keyring would have landed on her head. Jem's hand darted out, and she caught them, sending a grin up toward her mother.

Elenore shook her head and wandered back inside. She checked her phone. Three calls from Brandon. Well, he could wait. Especially after keeping them captive for five years after Len passed. Five years she and Jem could have walked the neighborhood, found a school and job, checked in with Beth, maybe met some other neighbors.

But no, imprisonment ruled their lives.

Maybe Brandon hadn't realized until last week that Len had passed.

She shook her head. Brandon drove in and out of the trailer park several times a week. He talked to the neighbors. Certainly, he would have seen the remodeling and added landscaping at Len's house.

By the time Elenore found a box of macaroni and cheese in the packed boxes and made it with water instead of milk and butter, five more calls showed on the screen. She sighed.

Jem wandered to her room after dinner to check out her TV. Elenore's phone rang with an unknown caller. Cable or utility company? Both she waited for. She grabbed it while scrubbing the macaroni pan.

"Hello." Oh golly, it was Brandon. Her face flushed.

"I'm at your door. Check this out – *you never turn down a client, witch*. I'll be making a copy of your door key tonight, And if you don't let me in *now*, you'll be very, very sorry."

She dropped the pan in the sink, tossed the phone on the counter and ran to open the door.

Brandon glowered at her.

Chapter 36
Ruler

Ruler reached out and patted Gregory on the shoulder. The usually nervous Gregory didn't even flinch. Instead, he intently studied the wall of notes, pictures, timelines and articles. "I guess I started in the middle." He moved to the far left. "Ah, the beginning of it all. When they were kidnapped." Ruler stepped slightly away from Gregory.

Ruler sighed. "My, uh, roomie has quite the fascination with the case. She helps with the investigation."

"I see. How so? This note … looks like instructions to someone." Gregory stroked his chin, and Ruler noticed pokey hairs he'd missed while shaving. Gross.

Ruler backed away more. Ruler's hands were shaking. Ruler's hands never shook.

No one except Ruler and Frenemy viewed the wall … the timeline … the potential future plans. Ruler's heart raced. "Right. Well, she's a private investigator, you see. Hey, let's talk more in the living room."

Gregory nodded and followed Ruler to the one ratty couch. He perched on the edge. "I do think you could use some other furniture."

Ruler nodded and patted the arm of the sofa. "Sure. This one's special though. His name is TC."

Gregory laughed nervously. "Never known anyone to name their couch. What's with that?"

Ruler shrugged. "Dunno. Roomie named him. He's ugly."

Gregory laughed again. "Little smelly, too. I mean, no offense." He colored.

"None taken." Ruler opened the glass door for some air. "I guess I'm used to it."

Ruler slid down the wall next to the fireplace and sat on the carpet. "Now, we should talk."

"Uh, sure. I'm an auto mechanic, by the way. Is … is there a way I can help with the case? I'd heard of those girls, of course."

Those girls. For some reason, the bland statement irked Ruler. Ruler itched a knee. "They were rescued."

"I know. But why would your roomie be helping unless there are things still going on? Still must be something. And … and now I know you're, uh, helping, right?"

Ruler shrugged. Okay. Gregory needed more information, or he'd develop wrong assumptions. "My roomie is heavily involved. Helps the cops and all that. Yeah, I guess the main guy is still out there. Plus, one of the girls broke a promise."

Gregory quirked an eyebrow. "What kind of promise?"

"To find someone important."

"I see. Hmmm, I would imagine that might happen with someone who's had a lot of trauma. Or so I've heard."

Ruler scratched the other knee. "Maybe. No excuse though. Anyway, Frenemy knows more."

"Frenemy is your roommate? That's an interesting name."

Ruler nodded. "She's working right now. We do opposite shifts."

"What it is you do?"

Ruler thought quickly. Gregory probably realized Ruler rarely left the apartment. "I'm a writer, and I do customer service here at home on the computer for a shipping company."

Gregory nodded slowly. "I heard a lot more people started working at home after Covid. Guess they don't need all those office buildings after all."

Ruler snorted. "Tell them that. They're still building."

"So, what company? One of the online giants?"

Ruler ignored the question. The too-curious Gregory needed to shut up. Ruler shifted and sat cross-legged.

"I don't need the whole couch. There's room for you." Gregory sat back into the couch, almost sinking in. He crossed his legs. His hanging foot bounced up and down. He folded his hands over his knee.

A studious look. Was he getting ready for more questions?

Ruler realized that Gregory, with his professional knowledge, could be valuable. The question was, how to win him over?

"So, here's what's up. But wait – this is top secret information. Both our lives are at stake if you can't keep quiet."

Gregory's nose twitched. "I understand."

Ruler frowned. Perhaps Gregory helped on other cases. His neighbor seemed calmed. Or maybe he wanted a friend. Ruler breathed deeply. "We ... we've located one of the major guys involved in the kidnapping."

"Wow." Gregory's eyebrows almost disappeared into his bangs. "That's something."

"Yeah." Ruler shifted again and slid up against the wall. Gregory seemed to shrink. Was Gregory afraid of Ruler? Well, that could come in handy, Ruler supposed.

Ruler should chill a bit. Ruler walked over and sat backward-style on the dining room chair. "But we must be careful, you know. The cops don't have enough information to bring him in yet. That's where we come in."

Ruler puffed up as new ideas flowed. Maybe writing as a career fit. Ruler certainly appreciated a good imagination.

Yeah, this could work.

"So, with you being a mechanic and all, we could really use the help. Specifically, to plant a tracking device and some other small things on this guy's car. Heads up, though. It's quite a beater." Ruler laughed.

This would finally give Ruler power over Frenemy. To go outside the plan and to make it more successful. To finally *win*.

Truthfully, Cienna just needed to die.

Gregory cleared his throat – quiet for a moment. Probably wondering what *other small things* included. He shifted as his Adam's Apple bobbed up and down. "Okay. What's in it for me?"

Chapter 37
Cienna

Cienna tapped her fingers on the table. Adrian's feet shuffled back and forth. Detective Miller and Detective Peters both entered the room. Cienna jumped up and Miller gave her a large hug and squeeze.

"Commuting a bit far these days?" Cienna grinned and pushed her curls behind one ear. "And I hope you have pictures!"

Adrian smiled and crossed his arms over his chest. He stood. Shook both the detectives' hands.

"You bet!" She smiled as Miller pulled his phone out. They sat at the table as he scrolled quickly through pictures of the twins, laughing, smiling and sometimes pouting. Adorable. Mollie grinned from the images, too, and there was even a squirrel who photobombed a selfie of the whole family. Cienna sighed happily. "Everyone looks really happy. I'm so happy for you. Mollie hire a nanny yet?"

Miller smiled. Shrugged. "She continues to threaten. But I think she's happy at home except for taking the occasional case."

"Missing kids?"

He nodded.

"I hear she's the best." Peters smiled.

"We're grateful." Adrian leaned forward. "Without her, Ci and Jazz may have never been found. But what's today all about? Did you find Roger?"

Peters sighed. "Roger remains at large. I think you know they pulled in the FBI a couple of years ago. I hate to say it's a cold case, but it's starting to look …"

Miller, Adrian and Cienna frowned in unison.

Cienna's eyebrows wrinkled. "But … but no one is safe as long as Roger is still out there."

"Agreed. That's where you come in." Even as Peters said it, Miller's frown deepened. His foot started tapping quickly on the floor.

"What does that mean?" Cienna pushed her chair back. Her shoulders tensed. Her jaw tightened.

Miller sighed. Put his face in his hands. Looked up again at Cienna. "I don't even want to ask you this. Cienna, you're not required to do this. In fact, if it takes you at all backward, Mollie and I don't even want you to do this."

"Do what?" Adrian stood. He towered – something unreadable in his eyes.

Cienna tugged on his hand, and he sat. "How about we listen?"

Peters tapped the paper file in her hand on the table. "What would you think of visiting Mike again and wearing a wire? We think he's in contact with Roger. You're right. Until we bring him down, girls are not safe. And that may include you and Jazz."

Silence resounded from the walls.

Adrian cleared his throat. "Absolutely not." He coughed. Stood and walked to the window, where he stared outside. "You must be joking. Intentionally put Cienna with her *trafficker*? Make her be friendly? Just to get information? What are you thinking?"

Cienna giggled. Three pairs of eyes stared at her. She continued to laugh. So hard that she grabbed some water and took a drink before catching her breath. "I-I know you didn't hear the last conversation I had with Mike but we sure as heck didn't end with 'let's be pen pals and stay in touch.' I stood up to him. Made sure he knew that he wasn't in control any longer, and … and that I wanted to nothing to do with him." She wiped her mouth with her hand. Bit back another laugh. "I'm sure he hates me."

"Since then, he's asked twice for you to visit again." Miller quirked an eyebrow. "I don't know, Cienna. You know we care about you. I'm not sure it's worth it. But we have truly exhausted all current clues for finding the head honcho."

"I'm supposed to be done with Mike!" Cienna slapped the counter, no longer laughing. "That was a final act for me, and you all know that. I'm not an actress anyway. Don't you think he'd figure it *out?*"

"He's not the smartest block in the cell," Peters murmured.

"We do know you're a good actress, Cienna." Miller glared at Peters.

"This isn't your case anymore, Miller. You're here as a *courtesy*." A knock sounded, and Peters let a burly, bald man. The buttons on his shirt looked ready to pop off.

"Hi, hi." He set his coffee on the table and pulled up another chair. "Gerald. FBI. Sorry to be late."

Cienna put her face in her hands and sighed. Adrian crossed the room and rubbed her back briefly before sitting. "Officer ... Gerald, is it?"

"Well, technically, Officer Clark." He mumbled, his face flushed. Then turned to Cienna. "We feel you might be healthy enough to consider this. You've worked hard on your healing, we hear. And of all people, you might be the one to get in Mike's head and bring us Roger. You've sucked up to him before."

Cienna wanted to slap him. Adrian's face flushed bright red.

Of all the things to say.

Clark shook his head quickly and held up a hand. "I'm sorry. I didn't mean it like that."

"I did suck up." Cienna stood, her hair awry and her eyes wild. "We do those sorts of things to survive, Clark."

He mumbled something about needing to be more trauma informed. Cienna stared at him, then landed in her chair again with a solid thump. "What safety measures would be in place?"

Adrian sighed.

"Same as before." Peters took some papers out of the folder and placed them on top. "Chains. Guards. He can't get to you."

"He tried."

"Better guards this time. We can't take a chance. We don't want you hurt. This is important."

"Her life and healing are more important." Miller flicked a dust bunny off the table.

"No, not really, when thousands of girls could be a stake." Peters matter-of-factly pulled a pen out of her pocket as Miller glared at her.

"You don't have to do this," Adrian said loudly. "And what about Devon James, the other dude who helped with the kidnapping? Isn't he around?"

"Cienna, you can say no," Miller replied at the same time.

Cienna shook her head quickly, her eyes darkening. "Yeah, what about James?"

Clark sighed. "That's the other reason for this meeting. He was harassed in prison. Beat up a few times. Hung himself with a bedsheet yesterday."

Cienna blanched.

Adrian sighed again.

Peters scribbled quickly on the notebook in front of her. Cienna turned and looked into her husband's eyes. "Well, then, I have to. Don't you see? Roger's hurting more of us even as we speak. I can't let any more Pennys die. And what about Grace?"

"Grace is safe, and Penny was not your fault." Adrian pulled her to her feet. She clung to him. "You did everything you could after you discovered her."

"I did." Her voice muffled in his shoulder. "But Grace might not be safe with those notes. Someone put a fake bomb in Queenie. What if it *is* Roger? What if he takes her? And if I hadn't been so focused on the other things and escaped Mike a lot sooner, the department would have found Penny a lot sooner. Not after she was ... dead." She felt her husband's deep sigh this time as his shoulders rose slowly and dropped.

"Still not your fault." Over her shoulder he addressed the rest. "We need time to talk."

"Sure, sure." Cienna heard a chair scrape the floor. "I'm sure the rest of us can find something else to do for a bit."

They left, and Cienna pulled away from Adrian. She found her phone and sat. Dialed Mollie. Punched the speaker phone button. "Hi. What an offer. Did you hear?"

The twins played loudly in the background. "Hold on, Ci! We're at the park. Hayden, it's Herbie's turn on the slide!" Rustling and wind came through the speaker.

Cienna smiled at Adrian. "See what we're in for if we have another one?" His grin reached both ears. She paused for a moment, admiring his handsome features. But most of all, she admired his heart.

"I did hear." Mollie was back on the phone, the background bit quieter now. "Whew! All day kindergarten next year!"

Cienna laughed. It felt good. She sobered. "All day kindergarten helped me too. What do you think I should do? It's gotta be Roger or his thugs making these threats. And if they know about Grace, she's in danger."

"Cienna, we can easily move you and your family away from the area."

"What? With the Protection Program? Ha!"

"Yes. It's a good program." Mollie sounded firm.

"So good I can't talk to my family or Jazz. Adrian would have to leave his job. Probably couldn't work as an attorney, which he loves. And what about my Freedom Center? What about my parents?"

"All considerations. But you know, the program doesn't have to be forever."

"True." Cienna chewed on her lower lip. "But as long as he's still out there …"

Mollie grunted. "Yes. There's that."

"Well then that settles it. I gotta do this wire thing. Jazz is gonna kill me."

"Jazz doesn't have to know. Maybe you should tell your folks, though."

"Jazz would want to know."

Mollie sighed. "Except that she might insist on coming along to protect you."

Cienna giggled. "That's true." Her heart grew heavy, thinking about the gun Jazz now carried. "I felt so much more freedom after I saw him. Ready to move on. Start a family with Adrian. Maybe hire more staff for the center. Help Jade find her family because we suspect Rose was her real mom. We even got her DNA taken at the hospital for testing. Now it feels like everything is on pause again."

"You still have that freedom, Ci. You've already let him know that he has no power over you. And you aren't the same girl anymore."

Wasn't that for sure.

Mollie sighed. "He can't affect you anymore. But on that same note, we want you to be smart if you do this. And if it sets you backward in your healing at all, you'll have to turn up the self-care and maybe even stop meeting with Mike. That's okay. Your healing is the most important thing of all. To all of us."

Cienna nodded. Adrian covered her hand with his own, and she squeezed it. "I don't want to back out. But … but I promise I will if that's a problem, okay? And there's one other thing I feel Jazz and I really need to do."

"What's that?"

"Visit River Falls."

Chapter 38
Jem

"Where're we going?" Jade yanked her hand from her sister's and pulled up her jeans, which still hung a bit low on her small frame.

"Shhhh. Trust me!" Jem pulled her into a stairway and hunched down, meeting her sister's gaze. "We gotta go. Mom … Mom's looking for us. She's not safe, Jade. Please trust me. We gotta leave now."

Jade pouted and crossed her arms. She paled and wavered a bit.

Jem frowned. What if she passed out? They better hurry. "Come *on*."

They followed the stairs down and ended up in a long, white hallway. There. A sign for the lobby. Jem shifted their backpacks on her shoulders and walked quickly, trying to look as normal as possible.

"But I'm hungry, and my show's gonna be on soon," Jade whined as they reached the lobby.

"Time to go for now." When the glass door slid opened, Jem firmly pulled her through, ignoring lady behind the reception desk who looked at them with too much curiosity. Outside, Jem breathed deeply and shivered. Were those snow clouds in the sky? It was about two p.m. Two hours until dark.

She suddenly thought of the Thanksgiving dinner they'd never ate at the community center. It was almost Christmas now. Lights appeared on stores and trees twinkled in the park. Someday, she needed to settle Jade so her sister could enjoy some real holidays.

She stopped at the end of the street, her breath forming little clouds around her. At the same time, sweat beaded her forehead.

Now where?

Jem hoped to recognize the area more once outside of the hospital. She sighed at the confusing streets. She'd only been in and out only a few times to spend nights with Cienna and to eat yummy things the funny old lady next door, Mel, made. She shivered again. At least Jade had a proper-fitting coat Cienna brought a couple of days ago. Hopefully, the borrowed hooded sweatshirt from Cienna would suffice for herself.

They needed to walk. But to where?

The homeless camp, always welcoming, may have moved by now. And if not, where was the site from here, anyway?

As they trudged up the city blocks, the answer flooded her brain. Jet originally found her at the bus terminal. He could find her there again.

Too bad she didn't have money to hop the bus and just get out of town. Could they hitch a ride? That seemed dangerous.

Jem huffed. She couldn't risk her sister's health but going home screamed the most danger of them all. She remembered the street the homeless camp was close to. But how far were they?

Ahead was Gordy, the man she and Jet first greeted when they'd landed in Portland. Jet's friend must be safe. She hurried over.

"Got some cash?" Gordy lifted bleary eyes and held out his hat. A puzzled look briefly crossed his face. "Know ya?"

"Gordy." Jem leaned down. A strong body odor filled her nose, and she almost puked. She swallowed hard. One backpack slid off her shoulder, so she set it on the pavement. "I know it's been a while, but I'm Jem. I'm looking for Jet. Have you seen him?"

"Jet." He grinned. His dark teeth looked about ready to fall out. "Jet's my friend."

"Yes, I know. We ... we met a while ago. I need your help. Do you know where his camp is? Or the bus station where I met you?"

"He lives by the river!" He announced this as if everyone should know.

"Still? Good. But where is that? How do I get there?"

Gordy's eyes narrowed. He shuffled around behind him and pulled out at bottle. "Some for the lady?"

Jem recoiled, her heart pounding. "No. No thank you. I just don't know how to get to the river."

"It's a ways." Gordy took a long gulp. Jade stared at him, and Jem pushed her behind her.

Wow, she wasn't getting very far. She pushed her long hair behind her ear, wishing for a hat. And maybe gloves. "It's cold out here, Gordy. Why don't you go to the mission tonight?"

She remembered Servio and his complaints about staying in the shelter. But still, wasn't it worth it in this weather? She also remembered the nurses mentioning warming places. "You should probably go get warmed up and get some dinner." She grabbed the bottle out of his hand, sloshing it on hers.

What had gotten into her?

Concern flooded her heart for Gordy. That made no sense at all. Was it because he was Jet's friend? Perhaps because she'd slept in those doorways and now ... now was looking to go back. But no other options presented themselves – at least for her and Jade. "Safety. That's the most important thing."

"Hey, gimme that." Gordy whipped his hand out, and she handed the bottle back with a trembling arm. "It's all I got."

Ire rose. "You can't drink all the time, Gordy. And there are shelters when it's so cold. Please think about going there and getting a meal and maybe a cot. Please. Now, can you tell me how to get to the river? I have to go. We have to go. Jade isn't safe where we were anymore. Please."

He mumbled directions. She thanked him and started out.

Three blocks later, Jade started dragging, and Jem looked at her with concern. Her sister paled. Then Jem remembered. Hadn't the doctor and Cienna both said that Jade needed pills for a while even after discharge? She groaned. They'd run off without them.

They'd have to figure it out. At least for now the coughing seemed fixed.

"Let's sit down for a bit." She glanced at the darkening sky. They needed a break. Hopefully the darkness would hold off. She'd no sooner settled Jade against a wall full of colored graffiti when someone grabbed her by the arm. She screamed.

"You can spend the night with me, girlie. Leave your kid here." A stinky man with long grey hair yanked her into an alleyway. One backpack dropped off her shoulder.

"Jem!" Jade screamed and ran after her.

"Jade! Go back! Leave!"

Jade froze.

The man pushed Jem roughly against the wall. Shoved his hand up her shirt. She screamed and tried to push him away. She remembered something she'd learned on TV. "Hey, you over there! Help! This man is hurting me!"

As the man looked over his shoulder, she brought her knee hard up into his groin. He stepped back, leaning over with his hand at his crotch. As soon as he stepped back, she ran to Jade, grabbed her hand and raced out of the alleyway, completely forgetting the dropped backpack with Jem's clothes.

Jade coughed when they finally stopped running. The wind dried the tears streaming down both their faces. Jade's bright red face pinched with worry. Jem bent down and held her close. "I'm so sorry. So sorry. We're okay, sis, I promise."

The reality of what that man could have done to them both hit her hard, and an hour later as she hurried into camp after making several wrong turns, she burst into tears again.

Quickly, Mrs. K appeared as she blurted out the story. Zeb arrived. Servio walked over. Jet hovered by the tent. They were all there. "Oh, he's in big trouble. What'd he look like?" Jet scanned her up and down. "Ya okay?"

"Good. Fine." Jem wiped her eyes with shaking hands. "He had long grey hair. Smelly. A few blocks away from where Gordy is. We can't go back. Mom's looking for us. And they said … they said we might have to go into foster care." She gulped. "I didn't mean to put Jade in even more danger!"

Her knees gave out. She sat hard on the ground. "I'm so scared. I'm glad you all are here." Fresh tears rolled down her cheeks.

The girls felt comforted that night. Zeb built a rare fire and caught a fish. Mrs. K served that plus stale muffins for dinner. It wasn't enough for all. But Jem figured after what they'd been through, a small meal worked better. She glanced worriedly at Jade, who coughed a few times throughout. Mrs. K brought the large teal towel to drape over the girl's shoulder and held her tightly. As the darkness descended fully, Jem shuddered.

What if the man followed them?

No matter, they'd be safer here.

"You can't stay." Servio broke a stick and tossed it into the fire. "You're safer with the housed people, Jem. And foster care can be a good thing. You're too young to be out here."

"No! I heard we could get separated."

He tilted his head. "Separated, warm, fed and having school is still better than out here. You could have been seriously hurt tonight."

She shook her head. "We … we can't. Mom will fight to get us home. I just know it. And someone else controls her every move." She glanced at Jade. She wanted to explain everything. The full story. But she couldn't. Not with Jade listening.

"Well then, there's only one other option." Servio stood. Surveyed the group.

"Time to move?" Jet leaned forward, looking at him pointedly.

"Yeah. First thing tomorrow, we break camp and find another place."

In unison, they nodded.

Chapter 39
Elenore-6 years before

Brandon pushed his way past Elenore into the apartment. "I think you forgot who owns you and who owns this place."

The smell of whiskey slimed past her. She automatically looked at the ground. "It's just been busy. I was gonna call you back."

"Sure you were. Look at me, you witch."

"Brandon, Jem's here."

"*Look at me.*"

She peered up just in time to see his fist coming at her face. The room swam around her. "Brandon, please." He'd never hit her before. He must be really, really drunk.
How could she placate him?

Elenore stumbled to the kitchen with Brandon close behind. "Need dinner? I don't have much but let me look." She started tearing into boxes. Her eyes watered and she could feel an inflamed bump rising on her cheek.

"Mom? Are you okay?" Jem stood at the doorway. Elenore saw her tremble.

Brandon headed toward her daughter. She thought quicky. "Jemmy, honey, I need you to go to your nice bedroom for the night now, okay? It's getting late."

She saw her daughter glance warily at the sunlight pouring in through the kitchen window. "Will be late soon. Brandon, leave her alone!"

He bent over and peered right into Jem's face.

She recoiled. "You stink!"

Brandon shoved her. She landed on her backside on the floor and looked up fearfully.

Elenore stood helplessly by the open box of food on the counter.

He grinned. "You heard your ma. Trust me, you don't want to be around tonight."

As Jem fled, Elenore shuddered. What did Brandon mean?

She shook her head to clear it. "I think I might have wine?" She pushed aside boxes. Found towels in the next box. "Don't worry, she had mac and cheese for lunch. She'll be okay."

Brandon marched back into the kitchen area. He shoved her against the opposite counter. "Don't worry, she had mac and cheese!" He mimicked her in a high voice. "Witch, you better listen to me."

"Okay, okay. I am." Her words pitched in fear. She remembered another night, so long ago, when Len knocked her unconscious. Brandon took most of her paycheck at the diner, forced her to do things she didn't want to do and brought over men she had to satisfy like all the girls in the house did. But he'd never, ever been like Len. She suddenly longed for faithful Oscar. She and Jem could maybe get another cat now.

A slap out of nowhere landed on her ear. Ouch, that hurt. Her hand flew up to cover it.

"What?" She snapped. "What's wrong with you, Brandon? You're scaring me!"

He laughed and slapped her again. She cringed against the sink. He stepped back. "You don't have this place unpacked yet? Lazy."

She wanted to remind him they'd been there only four hours. That she'd spent most of that time unloading the car, putting away things in her bedroom and acclimating Jem. She swallowed those words. "I'm sorry for not calling back yet. I planned on it. We were unloading."

He sat, almost carefully, on one of the barstools that came with the apartment. "I'm your priority." Brandon glared. "I call, you pick up. Period. I thought I could trust you. That's why you got this place. But no, as soon as you're away from me, you *ignore* me." He blinked.

Elenore stared at him. Was he going to *cry*? Oh, for gosh sakes, she'd really screwed it up this time. "No, no." She rushed over – still drawn to this handsome man who'd rescued her from the worst man ever.

But wait, what about *that*?

Before she reached him, she skidded to a stop. "But, Brandon, I gotta know something."

He narrowed his eyes. "You don't need to know anything."

"But I do."

He stood, walked over and picked her up. Carried her to the bedroom. Deposited her on the bed and slammed the door. She pushed herself up, against the pillows. If he wanted her, he would take her. She already knew that. She started preparing herself mentally and reminded herself that only a bathroom separated her room from her daughter's. "Please, Brandon. I do gotta know. I do. Len didn't die last week like you said. He's been gone for years. There's an older lady at the house, older landscaping that wasn't there before. She even painted. She said-"

Her head moved sideways as the punch came. She heard a bone crack up near her eye. Pain filled her head.

"Shut up." He punched her again. "I was only trying to save you from that nasty man. He would have killed you."

Buzzing started in her head. From far away she heard what sounded like a sweet voice singing. Jem, singing in her room. Singing away the pain. Tears gathered. They dripped down her cheeks. She prayed that her little girl was tucked in the closet with the door closed and her earbuds in. "Kill me?" She managed. "Yeah, you want to, don't you?"

"Witch." He pulled her to a sitting position. "You'll forget this day even happened."

He reached toward the nightstand drawer and pulled it opened. Her eyes widened. He'd put supplies in there. When had Brandon entered the apartment? But instead of pulling out the usual pain shot he and Nance sometimes gave her, he grabbed a mirror, flat razor blade and white powder. He clenched her arm, looking for a vein.

Elenore leaned back from him. "Brandon! No! What is that?" She wiggled her arm free. Tried to scramble off the bed. She might be under his control mostly. But she wasn't stupid. He had hard drugs. Those could kill.

But Brandon sat on her hips and as much as she tried to push him away with one arm, she just wasn't strong enough. Despite her efforts, the needle entered her arm. Within seconds, a warmth filled her body like never before. She lay limp, not caring anymore about anything. The room spun gently. She felt like she floated. And didn't care about anything else.

She barely noticed as Brandon undressed her, bit places on her body and then forcefully raped her. She might have moaned in pain. Later she awoke to a fist beating and wild eyes above her. For a moment she thought Len returned to life and found her. But no, it was Brandon. She opened her eyes briefly to see him flicking a lighter and then blowing smoke in her face.

He smiled as he enjoyed his cigarette and then smashed it out on her sheets. She recoiled as the hot cigarette butt glazed her ear.

Elenore closed her eyes. Bit her lip. Tasted blood. She tried to move but felt stuck to the sheets. He gave her more drugs. Then came hours of blow upon blow, pain in areas she'd never felt before. As she drifted off, Brandon awoke her with punches and burns until she looked at him and acknowledged him as boss. No choice. No argument. She'd die under him today, with no way to get help.

***

When Elenore awoke, all was quiet. The apartment silent. No Brandon. She raised her wrist to look at the time, noting the dried blood all over her arm. But wait. She squinted. That couldn't be right. Her watch said it was the sixteenth. She and Jem arrived at the apartment on the fourteenth.

Her watch must be seriously off. But it said 4 a.m., and that matched the darkness outside. She looked down at her naked body and blood-soaked sheets. She barely recognized herself, she was so covered in purple and black bruises. Bruises took time to develop. She'd been out of it for some time.

It really was the sixteenth!

She tried to heave herself out of bed but screamed in pain. She slid down the side instead. Crawled on her hands and her knees toward Jem's room.

Where was her daughter? Had Brandon hurt her too? Tears rolled down her face as she slowly crawled down the hallway, still naked. "Jem? Jem!"

No answer.

She managed to reach the door handle on Jem's door and slid her hand down one side of it until it opened. She fell into the room.

Only darkness met her.

Jem was gone.

Chapter 40
Cienna

Cienna slammed her hand on the steering wheel and cursed. Drove slowly through the darkened streets. Hit the contact button on her phone. "Adrian? I need you. Jem ran away from the hospital and took Jade. I'm looking for her now, but it's so dark. Can Mel watch Grace?"

"What? Yeah. She's here already. Brought stew over. Hold on."

Cienna heard muffled conversation in the background. Then Adrian picked up the phone again. "Where are you? I'll meet you."

"Good idea. Queenie's kind of sputtering weird. I need to use the restroom and get some water anyway." She spied a convenience store up ahead. "Meet me at Wallaby's on 141st. I'll find something to do until you get here."

They hung up. She pulled into Wallaby's, parking in the small lot by the air pump and water dispenser. Cienna grabbed her purse and held her mace as she exited the car. Took a deep breath as she entered. A friendly jingle bell on the door announced her entrance.

"Evening." A woman with short blond hair chomped on gum at the register. Tats covered both her arms. She eyed Cienna's mace.

"Hi." Cienna moved her mace down by her side. The bright overhead lights comforted her. "Sorry. Restroom, please."

The clerk snapped her gum. "Customers only."

"I'm buying." Cienna reassured her. "Long night ahead, probably."

The woman looked her up and down. "Traveling?"

"Not really. Hey, have you seen a couple of girls?" She pulled out her cell phone and found a picture of the girls, a selfie Jem took after borrowing Cienna's phone. Jade grinned from the hospital bed, her bright red hair and green eyes standing out against the white sheets. "They ran away."

"You don't look old enough to be their mom." The woman raised her eyebrows.

Cienna noted her nametag. "I'm their guardian, Lou. I'm afraid they might be in danger. Have you seen them?"

"Nope." Lou snapped her gum again. "Bathroom in the back." She inclined her head as Cienna pocketed her phone.

"Thank you."

In the restroom, she paused to read the poster on the stall door. *Are you being trafficked? Held against your will because you owe someone money and must work to pay that off? Forced to do things you don't want to do? Missing your ID or passport? Call the National Trafficking Hotline.*

She shuddered.

Yet gratitude filled her. It took the media announcing the cause and others educating the public to provide thousands of victims with help.

About time.

She flushed and exited the stall. This store seriously needed an upgrade. Cracked and dirty tiled peeled in several areas. The walls didn't look much better. The stalls boasted phone numbers and names and claims of a good time. But this store at least had walls and warmth.

Better than what Jem and Jade likely experienced tonight.

Why, oh, why had she not given them money? She knew why – a fear they'd flee. But at least a hundred plus a few bucks might have provided a cheap but safe hotel room. Now the girls carried nothing but the clothes Cienna and a local church had purchased.

She washed her hands, taking her time. She preferred to wait inside the store for Adrian. Lou looked like she wanted Cienna to just finish her purchases and leave. Well, she couldn't hurry her along if she stayed behind a closed door.

Had Jem returned to the camp? Or hitchhiked out of town?

She picked up her ringing phone. "What's up, Jazz?"

"Getting off work. You?"

"Glad to hear Phil's letting you work again. I'm in the restroom at Wallaby's."

Jazz paused. "Uh, I can call you back. You didn't have to pick up."

Cienna smiled. "Done with the necessities. Killing time. Jem took Jade and ran from the hospital. I'm waiting for Adrian so we can drive to the camp where she stayed before. I'm scared for her." Her voice dropped.

"I'm sorry, Ci." Jazz sighed. "Why would she do that? Run when they were being taken care of?"

"Not sure. But that's her history. I mean, running away when things get bad."

"So, what happened?"

Cienna heard a screech on the other side. Bus brakes. "You bussin' tonight?"

"Best for me. I shouldn't be on the road with my anti-you-know-what meds. And got my sidekick. So, think back, what happened? Did she maybe overhear something?"

"Overhear?" Cienna's brain scrambled, then clicked. "You're a genius, Jazz. Yes! We talked just outside her room. Her mom's looking for her. I'm gathering all the evidence I can that she shouldn't have custody – we didn't say that part. But we talked about them being wards of the State and needing foster care since Jade was close to release. Gosh darn it!"

"I should be a detective."

"You should be, Jazz. What the heck was I thinking? Well, I thought she was asleep. Or at least that the walls were thicker. It was the social worker. And when he walked up to talk to me about it, I didn't even think about that. Ooooo, I'm so mad at myself!"

"Don't be. I'm sure she's at the camp. Aren't you their guardian?"

"I am, but not certified for the foster system. Guess we should be."

"Well, that's a big decision. Hold on. Seatbelt."

Cienna heard her friend click herself in. "It is a big decision. I wonder what Adrian would think? I mean, of course I have their best interests at heart."

"Maybe you should ask him. You waiting for him before searching?"

"Yeah." Cienna exited the restroom, ignored Lou's glare, and browsed the aisles. She grabbed a water, and some chips. On the other hand, if she found the girls, they'd likely be hungry and thirsty. She propped her phone between her shoulder and ear and went back for more water and more chips.

Her text messages pinged. Adrian. "Oh, good. He's close. Jazz, gotta go. I miss you. Let's get together."

"Sure. Hope you find 'em. Time to go for me too. Stupid bus people already glaring at me."

Cienna smiled as she hung up.

Ever faithful Jazz. And smart too.

She was finally at the counter when a large boom sounded outside the store. Both she and Lou dropped to the ground.

"Oh, my heavens!" Lou yelled as Cienna covered her ears.

After a moment of nothing but a "whoosh" and then quiet, Cienna slowly rose to look outside. What she saw made her drop her phone.

Fire consumed Queenie.

Chapter 41
Elenore-present day

Elenore slammed the door after she entered the old Victorian where she and several other girls lived. Hmmm – quiet house for once. She kicked off her heels and didn't bother to glance in the entryway mirror. She knew how bedraggled she looked after servicing a john. Plus, she'd be sick soon without her drugs. Brandon should be more understanding. Lately, he'd been sending her out without some of her usual needed prep.

She walked to the entry table, lit a cigarette and breathed in deeply. Why had she taken up smoking again?

Oh yeah. It helped her deal.

She missed her girls. It wasn't fair they ran away. Elenore missed unloading about her day to Jem. And Jade? Yeah, she was a strange kid when Brandon brought her home, but she always looked at Elenore with love in her deep green eyes. Like she had years of knowledge, knew what Elenore really was and yet loved her anyway. Elenore grew lonely when most of the other ladies worked and because Brandon mostly hung out at the other houses. He trophied a new, young sidekick. Yeah, the blonde he brought over last time. New recruit, apparently.

Never truly a loner, Elenore befriended a guy named Hendrick, via text. But it wasn't *that* kind of texting. They'd met online and now conversed frequently. He helped with some of the loneliness. Of course, he had no idea of her real occupation. She'd mentioned past bad relationships and abuse – so he understood her hesitation to get together in person. But at least he helped pass the time. Maybe he even cared about her a little bit. Unlike Brandon, who "cared" about all his gals equally.

She snickered as she slid open the glass door and stepped out onto the porch with her cigarette. She leaned on the rail. The woman next door on her own deck stared at her. Only a chain link fence separated the yards.

"What?!" Then she looked down and realized she still had on her hooker-wear. Oh well. She sure as heck couldn't please everyone. She went back inside and grabbed her phone. She texted Brandon.

Hey, done for the day. Need stuff. Where you? She got some food, practically gagged on it, and took a picture of her face trying to look sweet and vulnerable to Hendrick. **Missing you. When can we text again?**

Probably best to gag on her food. She'd put on a few pounds, and Brandon wasn't happy about it.

Elenore opened her laptop and clicked around. She entered Jem's name, then Jade's, to no avail. A few friends kept an eye out – someone claimed they were in Oregon. But they appeared houseless and quite bedraggled.

"Not my girls." Elenore shut that down fast. But later, she heard "Portland" from more than one person and Elenore considered someone she hadn't heard from in a long time.

Mom.

Mom moved to Portland a couple of years before. Was that where Jem had taken Jade? If so, pity on the girl. Elenore cracked up. If Jem showed up at Mom's door, the door might slam in her face. After all, Mom had screeched at her for getting pregnant via Len in the first place. And even though Mom visited the apartment once before leaving for Portland, she'd acted disdainful the entire time.

But still …

Elenore picked up her phone before she lost her nerve and clicked Mom's last known number.

"Hi. You've reached Joy Stevens Consultation Services. I'm mostly retired now but take clients on a part-time basis.

Please leave a message after the tone, and I'll call you back as soon as I'm available. Have a great day!"

Elenore practically growled into the phone. "Mom. Call me. It's important."

Her phone dinged with a text, and she eagerly switched over. It was Hendrick, not Brandon. Darn it. Her stomach churned and head ached. Where was Brandon?

Hey beautiful. How was your day?

Good. How's the wife? She giggled. She didn't really care, but she knew it irked him, and tonight, she needed attention from someone other than a john.

Oh baby, come on. You know you're the only one for me. She moved out anyway. For the best. Now I can see you for real.

Oh yeah? I think they all say that. Her vision blurred a bit and a drop of sweat dripped on the phone. Where the heck was Brandon? She sighed.

For real. Let me see you. Video? Meet? I'll prove it to you.

She grinned. **How?**

Now, her mind wandered.

Baby, meet me for real. I'll fly out. Stay in a hotel. Just please ... I want to see you for real. I know you're the one for me.

Elenore laughed. She imagined opening the front door to an actual decent man. What would that be like? She sighed. What *would* that be like? She didn't deserve such a man. He'd drop her like a hot potato after realizing what she really was.

She set the phone next to her on the couch. When it rang, she snatched it up without looking. Brandon, she hoped. "Yeah?"

"Elenore Melodie Stevens, do not greet me that way." Shoot!

"Uh, hi Mom." Seldom was her middle name used, especially after the age of ten. Argh. "How ... how are you? Still in Portland?"

"I am. You're well? Haven't seen you in a long time. Why are you calling?"

Silence. Elenore vacillated between *I want you to love me* and *hey, do you know where my girls are?* But she realized her vulnerability, almost in withdrawal, thanks to Brandon. She felt sad. But if she cried, she might blubber out the whole story. And if she was irritable, Mom might hang up – that'd be nothing new.

Deep breaths.

"I-I wanted to say hello. I'm sorry I've been MIA. How are you?"

"I'm well. Thank you. I moved to a nice duplex. I'm making friends and enjoying being semi-retired. I read and knit. And I like to cook. I have a garden out back. Weather-permitting of course. This is the Northwest, after all. I wish I could at least have tomatoes all year round."

A bit of envy unfurled in Elenore's stomach. Part of her wanted to say, "Can I come to you? Sleep on the couch and eat your cooking? I miss your cooking, Mom."

She didn't. "Well, you could move to California or Arizona and grow all year."

"That's true, Ellie. But my roots are here. And although we aren't in touch much, my only child is here too. I don't think I could leave. Especially now."

Elenore gasped. The past reared over her. Wave after wave. She felt panicky. "Mom, after the car accident ..."

Silence on the other end. When she spoke, Mom sounded tense. "Oh, *that*? I really recommend therapy." Her voice quieted. "Ellie, it's not your fault that Chad and Kelly and the others were killed. It's not. Why can't you accept that?"

A tear landed on the end of Elenore's nose. "I-I don't know. I should have taken his keys, Mom. There'll never be another Chad. Or Kelly for that matter. I-I know I'm at fault here. Why don't you just tell me it's my fault? It is!" She cried in earnest now. Emotions she hadn't felt in years.

Where the heck was Brandon?

"Ellie, you listen to me. Now."

Elenore straightened up on the couch. Pulled her skirt down more toward her knees and sat straight.

Yes, ma'am.

"I'm here Mama." Her voice broke.

"For some reason, your emotions are raging tonight. Hormones? I don't know. But you get that taken care of. Okay? After you do, I want you to get some help. Please. I want you to be a part of my life. And there are other's lives you need to be a part of, too. But not until you can heal … not until you can live the full life intended for you."

Elenore bent over, tears raining down her cheeks. "I-I'm sorry, Mom. I feel … it's all my fault. But you're right, I can't change anything from back then. I'm worthless. And I called you for another reason entirely." She hiccupped.

"You're not worthless, Ellie. No matter what you've been a part of or what you've done." Elenore heard her mother inhale deeply and her voice start to shake. Was she crying? "And I-I haven't always been the best mother. I'm sorry. I want to be better. I'm so sorry."

Elenore slid down off the couch onto the floor, sobbing. "I love you, Mom." She looked up to see Brandon entering the front door *finally*. Without the blonde, thank goodness. She tried, but it was too late to hide the tears streaming down her face.

"I love you, too. There's a better life for you, Ellie. We can't talk about those other things now, but I hold out hope that we can someday. Go take care of *you*, take care of what you need to do to live a new life."

With Brandon glaring at her, she quickly pressed *end* on her phone and lifted her chin. "What? It was my mom."

He quickly glided into the living room and gathered her in his arms.

Well, what do you know? Maybe he cared a little after all. "Just miss my mom and the girls sometimes." She found herself sobbing on his shoulder.

"Shhhh, it's okay. I'm here to make everything better. You have your earnings for the day?"

She nodded at the kitchen table, where she'd laid out the cash and counted it carefully. Twice. It was never helpful to get the numbers wrong.

"Good girl." He pulled her up, helped her to the bed and stripped her down. Then he pulled out his bag with a syringe, powder and needed materials.

The sleep that finally came wasn't restful at all.

Chapter 42
Cienna

Cienna pulled herself to her feet and charged outside. Lou grabbed the phone. Queenie. Her Queenie. Had her bladder not sent a distress signal ... she shuddered.

Betsy must be watching out for her.

She ran over to the side of the store where a hose hung. She unlooped it and cranked the nozzle, but nothing happened.

"Dang it!" She slapped the side of the building.

Adrian's 4x4 squealed into the parking lot. He stared aghast at the flames.

"Adrian!" She ran to him as he opened the door. "I'm here. I was out of the car. Queenie-Queenie's gonna die." A big tear ran down her cheek.

"Oh, thank God." He pulled her close. "Thank God you got out. I'm never letting you out of my sight again."

She smiled into his shoulder and sniffed.

Yeah, that would work.

"I had to pee." She giggled. "And get a drink. Something told me to stop."

"Indeed." His voice caught, and he squeezed her a bit tighter. "I hear the cops."

Two cop cars squealed into the parking lot, with a firetruck and ambulance close behind. Cienna watched, fascinated, as they worked to pull hoses out get the water going and proceeded to drown Queenie.

She sighed.

Elianna approached with her notebook and spoke into the radio on her shoulder. "Ten-four. Hey, Cienna, I'm going to need a statement from you." She raised her eyebrows. "Glad you're okay. Sorry about your car, err, Queenie, is it?"

"Yeah." Cienna pulled away from Adrian and noticed Lou smoking a cigarette outside the store's glass doors. "I took some extra time inside on purpose. Then got ready to leave. We need to go. You guys know Jem and Jade ran away from the hospital?"

Elianna nodded. "Heard that. You think they went back to camp?"

"Probably. We need to go get them. Take them home or something."

She tapped her notebook with her pen. "Statement first. Are you or anyone else injured?"

One of the EMTs approached. "Do you want to sit down?"

Cienna shook her head. "I'm fine. You should check on Lou over there, please."

"How about you let him check you out?" Adrian shifted and stuffed his hands in his coat pocket.

"Oh, fine." Cienna sighed loudly but allowed herself to be walked over to the ambulance, where she sat on the bumper as they took her vitals.

"Anything hurt?"

"I was in the store. Just the car got hurt."

"Well, it's a good thing you were in the store." The man adjusted the blood pressure cuff around her arm and started pumping it.

Cienna slumped. Queenie was a ball of smoke now, blackened, and sad looking. "That's my only car."

The man released the pressure on the cuff and took the stethoscope from his ears. She watched the other EMT walk over to check on Lou and direct her to sit on the curb. "I bet that handsome man over there has a vehicle." He laughed and glanced at Adrian.

"Yes, that's my husband." She smiled. "But his is tall and harder to get into."

"I'm sure you'll figure it out." He made some notes on a clipboard. "Just be glad something told you to get out of the car in time. Your life is more important than a car."

"I know." Boy, did she know. She didn't survive being trafficked only to die in a car fire. This whole "write notes to Cienna and let's blow up her car thing" was getting irritating, for sure. She grabbed her phone and took a picture of Queenie. Sent it to Jazz.

The reply was almost immediate.

OMG, Ci, what the heck?

Queenie's gone. I was in the store when she blew up. You okay?

Cienna shrugged. **All things considered. Gotta get done here and go find the girls. Did you wanna come?**

Nah. You have Ad. I'm seriously getting worried though. Ci, there's a psycho out there hellbent on getting you. I'm gonna go find Roger and kill him myself.

You are not. Cienna rolled her eyes. **And besides, we don't even know it if IS Roger. Gotta go. Talk tomorrow?**

K. Hope you can sleep. And find the girls.

Cienna almost said, "pray my guardian angel leads us to them." Then she shook her head. Jazz would think she'd banged her head for sure.

She completed her exam and walked back to Adrian and Elianna to give her statement. "I was going to find the girls. I called Adrian because I didn't want to go alone in the dark. I had to pee and was thirsty. Something told me to stop right then, I guess, so I asked him to meet me here. I went in, talked to Lou, asked if she'd seen Jem and Jade, went to the restroom, came out to get chips and water, walked up to the register and … boom."

"You mentioned earlier you were intentionally stalling?"

"Yeah, Lou wasn't so nice at first. 'Course I did come in with my mace ready." She shrugged. "I guess that might have something to do with it. Oh, and Jazz called me while I was in the bathroom, so I chatted with her too."

Elianna nodded. "I know we already know each other, but I do need to check your ID and insurance card. You have those?"

Cienna opened her phone wallet and handed them over. Elianna jotted more notes and took a picture of them both with her cell phone. "When was Queenie last unattended?"

"At work today. At the Freedom Center."

"Not the best part of town."

Cienna grunted. "More affordable. Plus, we need to be where the people are."

Elianna wrote on her notebook. "I get that. Was there another time Queenie was unattended?"

"Sure. I was at the hospital earlier." She remembered the conversation with the social worker and then returning to work, only to get a call that the girls had fled. "Um, and I guess technically while I was in there." She hooked a thumb over her back, pointing at the store. "And it was in the driveway at home last night, of course."

Elianna clicked her pen. "A lot of possibilities there." She clicked her radio button. "Dispatch, put in a call to Peters for me, will you?" She tilted her head towards her shoulder, listening via her earpiece. Then to Cienna. "The hospital has cameras and the store might too. We'll check. Any cameras at your place of business or maybe the businesses where you were parked for work today? How about your house or your neighbor's house?"

"Not at the Freedom Center." Although maybe she should get a grant for that. "Maybe around the parking area, although I parked her along the street. Hard to find parking there."

"Not to mention that the homeless people keep pitching tents in the parking lot," Adrian offered.

Cienna shook her head. "It's not one of them. And it's *houseless*."

"How do you know it's not them? They have a lot of mental health challenges."

She frowned at Adrian with a look that clearly said, "we'll talk later." She hated when the houseless people were blamed for everything, and now he was doing it too.

He shrugged. "Just something to consider. We do have cameras at the house."

"We'll be in touch on that. If you want to back up the files for the last few weeks or so and send them over, that would be a good idea. Peters might ask you for more." Elianna shifted and paused with her chin tilted towards her shoulder again. "Any of the houseless people there have issues with you? Or the Freedom Center?"

"Not that I know of."

"Okay. We called a tow for Queenie. Once she's on her way, you can get on with searching for the girls. You know we're keeping an eye out too, right? We're super short staffed right now."

Yeah. That defund the police campaign. Idiots. Cienna wasn't sure who voted for *that* measure. "Okay. We need to get going as soon as we can. It's dark now and they're out there alone. Unsafe."

"I understand." Elianna stepped over to check on her colleague who chatted from Lou. Cienna looked at Queenie. Shivered.

"Come on." Adrian pulled her arm gently and clicked his key fob twice. "Get in. Warmer in the car."

She grabbed the handle and hoisted herself in the warm, leather interior.

"I tried to tell you we should trade cars." Adrian grinned. "This is the comfy one."

Cienna snorted. "I'm not parking this thing downtown when there's only a small space between two cars. Besides, you're closer to work, and this thing eats gas."

He leaned back in his seat. "It has a camera. It would have caught anyone messing around with it."

She sighed. "You just don't get it. No one does."

"Well, then, tell me more."

"It's not Queenie, per se. Well, it *is* Queenie. But it's more what she represents. She's my freedom. I can get in and go wherever I want to. I'm not locked up, tied up or otherwise stuck." She wiped away a big, fat tear. "I think someone is targeting my freedom. They want me to feel stuck again. Helpless. Insecure. Hopeless."

He patted her shoulder. "You may be right. But, Cienna, we can afford another car for you."

She sighed. "Okay. But Queenie saw me through. The first time I got in her and flew down the highway, I felt free. Liberating. She helped me heal."

He nodded. But she knew he didn't really understand. She watched the tow truck enter the parking lot and lower the metal platform. Queenie – a now pitiful lump – still smoked. The tow truck driver hopped out of the truck and walked over to talk to the cops. After a minute, Elianna appeared at the window. Cienna pushed the button to lower it.

"We just need you to sign the title over like you're selling it when you get home and bring it to the station. Queenie will go to the station as evidence after our photographer takes pictures. We'll need to have a look at her. I don't see any need for you to hang out since you're on an important mission. You should, of course, contact your auto insurance company as soon as possible."

"We will. Thank you, Elianna."

She pushed the button to roll up the window and turned to Adrian. "I need to thank Lou. Check on her."

"Okay." As he spoke, a Channel 6 news van pulled into the parking lot. "Uh, time to go."

"For sure. Drive over to Lou first, please."

Adrian drove slowly to the store curb where Lou sat, and Cienna pushed the button for the window again. "Lou, I'm sorry. I didn't know this would happen. Thanks for your understanding."

Lou blew out a steady stream of smoke. "Sure. You better go. News is here."

Cienna stared at her.

"What? You didn't think I knew who you are?"

Cienna huffed. "You hid it well. Anyway, thanks again."

"Glad you stayed extra-long in that bathroom!"

"Me, too. Geez Louise. No pun intended." She shook her head as she rolled the window up. Out of the corner of her eye, she saw a reporter and camera guy approach. "Gotta go, Adrian. We need to find the girls."

He gunned out of the parking lot, and they headed downtown.

Chapter 43
Jem

Jem shivered in the tent. She held Jade tightly. It seemed even colder now after staying in a warm hospital for days. She smoothed Jade's hair back and kissed her forehead. Looked at Jet. "Think we're okay here 'til tomorrow?"

Jet stretched, his fist popping up the vinyl of the tent. He hunched down and looked her in the eye. "Should be. Servio thought so. Get some sleep."

"H-How?" Jem's teeth chattered.

"I got a another sleeping bag. Some company was giving them out. I gave the old one to Zeb. He's skinny and shivers a lot. Here." He rustled around in the dark until she felt a soft lump land on her lap. She let go of Jade and hurriedly rolled it out, feeling for the zipper. "What about you?"

A small flame in the dark. Jet held a lighter. She found the zipper and roused Jade enough to get her inside the sleeping bag – just large enough for Jem to cuddle in behind her sister. Jet zipped them in.

"You, Jet?"

"I'll figure somethin' out." He headed outside. He'd have to move around to stay warm.

She felt bad. Hopefully, one of the other residents could help Jet.

Jem lay wide awake, in tune to the night sounds and the traffic that zipped by not too far away. Noisy! She plugged her one ear that wasn't turned downward to the mat. How would she ever sleep in this racket? How *had* she ever slept in this racket? Despite the sleeping bag, her face froze. She buried it in her sister's hair, trying not to think about the warm hospital, Cienna's cozy home or Mel's fresh cinnamon rolls and cookies. Her stomach growled. She told it to knock it off.

Fortunately, Jade fell asleep quickly.

***

It was a few hours later when Jem awoke to noise outside the camp. Jet was nowhere to be found.

"Jem! Jade!"

She would have sat straight up. But she felt like a hotdog in a bun. She listened carefully.

"Jem!" The voice sounded a lot like Cienna's.

She stilled.

Jade stirred.

Oh, no.

"Jade! Jem! Are you here?"

"Ci—" Jade cried until Jem clamped her hand over her sister's mouth.

"Shh, Jade. No! We gotta be here for a while."

Jade wiggled hard, then bit her older sister's hand. "Ouch! Why'd you do that!"

"Cienna, we're in the red tent!" Jade squiggled and wiggled, trying to get out of Jem's hold and the restricting bag. "We're here."

Jem saw the glow of a flashlight approach the tent, and her heart dropped. Jade had no idea what she'd done. She watched in fascination as the light glowed through the tent, lighting their faces, and then as the zipper slowly moved up, up and around.

"Hey! You wait there! Servio, wake up." It was Mrs. K. The zipper stopped. The flashlight moved back.

"We're here to get Jem and Jade."

Adrian. He'd come along. Why?

Cienna cleared her throat. "It's too cold out here for the girls, ma'am. I'm their official guardian for now, and I need to get them somewhere warm. Jade needs meds."

"Jade needs meds? We didn't know."

Well, shoot. They had the full attention of the camp's nurse now.

"Yes. The hospital was going to send antibiotics home with her, but they left ... they left before getting them."

Jem appreciated that. Sounded less like they'd just ran away. She smiled. She heard Servio clear his throat.

"They don't want to return. They came here for a reason. Surely, you can bring the antibiotics here."

Cienna's voice tensed. "No. Did you hear me? I'm the temporary guardian of these girls, and I can't let them sleep here. They'll freeze."

Were those tears Jem heard in her voice?

Adrian cleared his throat. "We know you take care of them. The best you know how to. But they're kids."

"They're family," Mrs. K interrupted.

Silence from the rest.

"They are family, Mrs. K," Servio finally agreed. "But family also means we want the best for them."

She grunted. "Well, they'd be warm. But still, there's a reason they came back here. Are you hurting them?"

Jem held her breath. Then exhaled deeply. She couldn't let her camp family think that Cienna and Adrian were monsters. They'd been nothing but kind. Nothing like home. A tear dripped on her cheek as she unzipped the sleeping bag. But could she go? Knowing they might get sent home?

A tap on the tent.

"Jem? I know you're cold. Come with us, please. You aren't going to your mom's. At least, we're working hard to protect you both and *not* send you there. Please."

Her stomach growled. Stupid stomach.

"What's going on here?" Zeb called loudly. He must have just woken up.

Jem shook her head. She crawled to the tent flap and unzipped it the rest of the way while Jade rushed around her and flew into Cienna's arms.

"Doesn't look like an unhealthy relationship." Mrs. K sighed. "And she needs medication."

"I want to come. We just can't go home. Ever. Can you assure me of that?" Jem stood with her hands on her hips. "And also, I don't want to leave them all here in the cold."

Cienna sighed. She let Jade go as the little girl pulled away and went to Adrian. "I can't say for sure. But we're working hard on it, I promise. I think your mom ..." She glanced at Jade and seemed to change tracks. "We can talk more later. But I promise we have your best interests at heart. Please come home with us."

Jem sighed. Bed, food and a hot shower called her name. She supposed they could always run away again if it looked like real home loomed in the future. She waved her hand at Mrs. K, Servio and Zeb, who had finally wandered over. "Where's Jet?"

"He went to the warming place," Zeb mumbled. "One warm place, three warm place, five warming places." He shook his head.

"That's it!" Cienna snapped her fingers. "You'll all come home with us tonight. You don't have to stay, but it's too cold out here. It's the middle of winter. Showers, food and sleep. We have room to drive you and an extra bedroom, even with the girls."

Jem tried not to laugh at Adrian's shocked expression. But he quickly adjusted it.

Mrs. K waved her hand at the camp. "Fine for you to say. But we can't leave all our stuff. People will take it. We'll come back to nothing. Oh, dear." She wrung her hands.

Servio stepped forward. "She's right. You guys go. For the night, at least. Help the girls get adjusted. I'll watch camp and keep an eye out for Jet coming back. Zeb? How about a nice hot shower and some dinner? Let these nice people take care of you. And you." He looked pointedly at Jem. "These are good people who seem to really like you. What are you doing here?"

"I-I, *we* can't go home. Ever." Jem stood tall. "If we get sent home, we'll have to leave again quick."

"Jem." Jade pulled at her hand. "What about Elenore?"

"Mom won't take care of us, Jade. Cienna and Adrian care about us more." She noted a tear in Cienna's eye as the woman cleared her throat.

"Well, then, is it settled? Mrs. K and Zeb, will you come along?"

"I guess so. For just tonight." Mrs. K sighed heavily.

"Zeb, we still have yummy cinnamon rolls and stew from dinner. Plenty left over. How about a meal?"

He nodded and went to count things as he placed them in his backpack.

"Jem." Cienna held out her arms and Jem walked over, hugging her tightly. "I'm so glad you both are okay. I was so worried. Won't you come home with us?"

Jem nodded, a lump in her throat. Mom had never even searched for them, as far as she'd seen personally. But here was Cienna and Adrian tromping around camps in the middle of the night to make sure they were okay.

Why?

Were they really worth that much?

Chapter 44
Ruler

Flipping channels, Ruler finally found the only news airing. Good ole Channel 6. Ruler stared in fascination at the blonde woman at the desk, who suddenly held her ear and looked concerned.

"Breaking news." A picture of a burning car and several emergency vehicles flashed on the screen. "A car has blown up at a Portland Wallaby's. Fortunately, no one was hurt. Stay tuned for more information as we learn more."

What? *What?* No one was hurt?

Ruler hurled the remote across the room and jumped up. Wondered what Frenemy would think of Ruler. Then remembered the recent quiet – no note or instructions in over a week. This meant only one thing.

Ruler was the one in control.

Good.

Ruler slammed a fist into the wall. A vase teetered off a shelf and hit the hearth, shattering into pieces. "Dang him!" Ruler put time and a lot of money into the neighbor's simple assignment. Blowing up just the darn car wasn't even the mission.

Shame on Gregory.

Ruler sat and stared at the flatscreen. Maybe the news had it wrong. Or maybe they weren't allowed to report Cienna's death until they informed loved ones.

Ruler could only hope.

Sitting for hours, Ruler waited it out. Hope faded as commercials came on, interrupting the flow and shouting needless information into the world. Then infomercials. Pick up the phone to buy one now, or go online, and the second one is no charge. Ruler mimicked the male host and then laughed.

But what was Ruler doing? Allowing the brain to forget the mission?

Ruler stood and stomped over to the door.

Gregory had to pay.

Chapter 45
Elenore-6 years before

In bed, Elenore raised her head, glancing warily around. Was that a kid crying? Stupid neighbors. She flopped her head back on the pillow. She'd tried to heal on her own, but without Jem she could hardly even get to the kitchen or bathroom. She managed to clean up some and change the sheets – but it took over three hours.

And now withdrawals again kicked her butt. She'd held it off somewhat with pills, but they'd only lasted so long. And these days, they failed to work as well as they used to. When she gained some strength, she searched the drawers nearby for supplies with no success.

The crying grew closer. "Are you okay, Mom?" Elenore saw Jem's horrified look. And by her side, a young girl, with wide green eyes and screaming red hair. The girl stopped crying to stare at Elenore.

"What are you staring at? And who are you?" Elenore frowned, holding her head.

Jem let go of the redhead's hand. "Mom, what happened to you?" Large tears dripped down the girl's face. "Are you okay?"

Brandon entered the bedroom. Elenore squirmed. Her hands twitched. She scrambled to pull a blanket up over her body.

Brandon paused at the bed. "I'll take care of her, Jem. You get the girl a snack, just like Nance showed you."

"What the heck, Brandon? And what do you want from me now?" Elenore saw Jem scramble to grab the kid, who'd ran over to the closet. Thankfully, she left with Jem. "How could you do this to me? And you took Jem!"

He sat on the edge of the bed. She pulled away when he reached out. He patted her knee. "Babe, I don't know what you mean. We talked about it, remember? She wanted to spend a weekend with me. She had a lot of fun. You were looking forward to a weekend alone, remember? You said you wanted to read, take a bath and maybe try that new pizza recipe you've been looking at."

Elenore shook her head fast. What? She certainly didn't remember that. Her head felt fuzzy. And it hurt. Surprise children didn't help with that. "I-I don't know. I don't think I knew any of that, Brandon. And why does Jem have a kid?"

"We talked about that too, hon. She needs a home. She lost her folks." He shook his head. "So sad." He brightened. "You insisted she come live here, and I'm glad for that. You and Jem will take good care of her for a few years."

"What do you mean? Brandon, what are you *saying*?"

"I'm saying she needs a home. When she's six or seven, we can adopt her out maybe. Or send her to boarding school. But you couldn't stand the thought of her going to an orphanage so young since she has no relatives. You insisted." His forehead wrinkled. "I don't understand. Don't you remember any of this?"

She must be going insane.

Elenore plopped her head back on the pillow. It suddenly felt too heavy. "You hurt me. And Len … you said he died. But he didn't. Well, he did. But it was years ago. You kept me at your house, and wouldn't let me leave. That's what I remember."

Brandon shook his head. "Wow. You really did have a weird dream, didn't you? Have you not taken your stuff today? Is that the problem? It must be that, and it's giving you horrible nightmares. I'm so sorry." He frowned. "You sound like I kept you captive. All I wanted was for you and Jem to be safe. Gee."

Elenore gritted her teeth.

"Really, Elenore. Now I am concerned about you for sure. I'm glad I decided to bring Jem and Jade home today."

"Jade?"

"The kid. She won't talk, so we don't know her name. Jem calls her Jade for her eyes."

Oh.

"You didn't beat me?"

He squeezed her hand. Sighed heavily. "Now why in the world would I do that? Oh my word, you think I'm a monster." He felt her forehead, and she startled. "Do you have a fever maybe? El, I'm really worried about you. How long have you been feeling this way?"

"If you didn't hurt me, who did?" Confused, Elenore shook her head and pushed his hand away. She held her head. "This makes no sense."

"We'll have you feeling better soon, I promise. I'm sorry you've been so sick. We would have come back earlier if I'd known. Have you even eaten? Jem!"

Jem appeared at the door quickly.

"Get your mom some soup or some toast. Or crackers. Whatever's in there, okay? She was sick the whole time we were gone, and I had no idea."

Elenore looked warily at her arms. Bruises lined them both.

"She'll be okay." He waved Jem away. "Go. She needs something to eat."

Jem scurried away as he pulled out her bedside table drawer and reached for supplies.

What? No. She swore she'd looked in that drawer.

How was this possible?

***

When Elenore felt better, she stumbled out of bed. Music blasted from the living room. She used the restroom and looked for Jem. What she saw stopped her in her tracks. Brandon and Jem dancing. Brandon saw Elenore and grinned. "Good. Looks like you're feeling better."

She shook her head dumbly.

"Mom!"

Jem broke away. Elenore caught her daughter as she flung herself into her arms. "Yay, you're better. I can help you shower in a bit. Come meet Jade." Her eyes sparkled as she practically hopped up and down. "She's sweet when she's not hungry. Kinda like me, I guess. Haha."

Not a dream at all. Sure enough, this Jade huddled on the couch, her thumb stuck in her mouth. What about the rest? Had she dreamed that, like Brandon claimed?

"I see."

"Mom." Jem pulled at her hand. "You have to say 'hi' anyway. She's new to our family. She's two."

Ha. That kid looked four, if not five. But apparently tiny for her age. "Where did she come from again?" She smiled at her daughter. She'd play along for now.

Jem sobered. "Her mom and dad died. I'm glad you said we could keep her. I'll take good care of her so you don't have to worry. I promise." She tickled Jade under the chin. Jade squirmed and pushed herself deeper into the cushions.

"And ... did we talk about this, Jem? You and I?"

Jem looked puzzled. "Us? About Jade? No, but Brandon said you thought it was a cool idea. Now I have a sister. I always wanted one, you know."

She had a hard enough time keeping Jem safe. Now she had to keep Jade safe, too? She'd seen the way Brandon looked Jem these days. Like he owned her. Like he used to look at Elenore. His eyes appreciatively followed the girl around the room several times. For all she knew, maybe he'd already ...

Elenore shook her head. Now she was being ridiculous. It was jealousy, that's all. Jem was only eight.

Despite everything, she still wanted Brandon to herself. She'd been hopeful when moving to the apartment but realized since he'd just wanted her out of his hair. He required her continued work and absconded with of most of her earnings. But he kept them fed and safe. The power remained on. They even had TV. He maintained privileges, of course, when he wanted them, and he kept her drug drawer supplied. That was no small thing. He complained frequently how expensive supplies were getting. She couldn't afford that on her own.

Brandon touched her shoulder, and she startled.

"Hey, Jumpy. Sorry to scare you. Yes, things have gotten expensive. But we'll make it. We're a family of four now." He smiled broadly at Jade and Jem.

Huh? She said that aloud? Elenore shook her head. And what was this about being a family? She sighed heavily.

"El, go take a shower. Been awhile."

Jem piped up. "I can help you, Mom."

Elenore pictured the bruises up and down her legs. "No, no. Jade would miss you anyway. I can handle it."

She pushed Brandon away and scooted out of the room.

Chapter 46
Cienna

The door clicked shut behind her. Cienna stood silently, observing the familiar lobby. This time they'd administered a more thorough "pat-down." She shuddered. Although given by a female guard, it still wasn't fun. One would think she'd be exempt from search.

She worried. Some guards and administration obviously knew about the wire. What would keep the word from slipping out to Mike? They assured her of confidentiality. But she wondered if she could trust it.

Cienna sighed and sat in one of the plastic chairs. How long would the wait be this time? She closed her eyes, taking a deep breath. When she opened them, the same lady as last time sat only two chairs away. No one sat between them. She smiled brightly at Cienna, and she noted her very pretty light blue eyes.

A coincidence? Cienna narrowed her eyes and leaned forward with her elbows on her knees. "Hello."

"Hello, dear. Another visit today?"

"Yes. And I'm Cienna. You?"

The woman's eyes twinkled. She pulled out bag with a huge ball of yarn and two large knitting needles stuck haphazardly into it. Out came something blue and soft. A blanket? Scarf? Blanket, because it kept coming. Reminiscent of Mary Poppins's carpet bag.

"Whoa. How'd you get those needles past the guards?" If only she could have one of those to visit Mike – just in case.

The woman with the white hair laughed, and it sounded more like tinkling bells. Cienna smiled.

"You can call me Betsy."

"Is that short for something else? Like Elizabeth?"

Betsy paused while pulling her needles out of the yarn ball. Tilted her head. "Hmm, nah. Just Betsy."

What kind of person didn't even know their real name? Cienna smiled again. "You came last time."

"Indeed. Company can be a good thing. Yes?"

Cienna nodded slowly. "Last time you told me I was here for healing."

"And you were, dear. Right?"

"Well, I didn't realize it at the time." Cienna settled back in her chair, listening to the *click-click* of Betsy's needles as she worked. "But yes, it was time to let things go. I felt so much better afterward. Like I finally had some control."

"Sounds like you had some forgiving to do."

"Some ... some things are pretty unforgiveable." Cienna cleared her throat.

"Oh yes! I understand. But look at the result. You've taken your power back. Forgiveness is about you." She huffed a little. *Click-click, click-click.* "He certainly doesn't deserve it. And I'm quite sure he doesn't even care." She paused and raised her eyebrows at Cienna.

"Wait. How do you know? Hey, do you know who I am?" The usual dread settled in her stomach. Of course she did. That explained a lot. Just like the waitress, the waiter, Lou, the receptionist at the counseling clinic ... well, that one was a little more understandable since Cienna's name titled the file – and the appointment schedule.

"I do. You're a precious daughter. Worth more than gold. And now, showing other people their true worth as well."

Cienna laughed. She couldn't help it. Tension seeped from her muscles. "That's not quite what I was thinking." Her mind wandered to Jem and Jade. Those at the houseless camp and others who received help daily through the Portland Freedom Center. Was she showing them their worth? Yes, she supposed she was. Even as she spoke, Mrs. K busied with cleaning Cienna's house, at her own insistence. Zeb returned to camp, but it appeared that the girls would stay, as long as they felt safe and Mrs. K continued to encourage them.

She leaned back in her chair and crossed her arms. Betsy seemed to know things, so why not ask? "Okay, then. I'm valuable." She swallowed. "Then maybe you know why all this happened to me? And to Jazz?" She flung her hand wide, as if the jail was the whole issue.

"Ah." Betsy's forehead wrinkled. "The infamous question. Why are children starving? Why are there natural disasters? Why do things like 9/11 happen?" She glanced quickly at Cienna then back down at her knitting. "And why are innocent children taken? Subjected to atrocious behavior? Sometimes killed?"

Okay. Betsy had a point. Jazz lived. Cienna lived. They'd escaped, with the help of others, of course. And she birthed a beautiful Grace. But what about Penny? And Rose? Her mind flew to Jade once again. The timeline didn't fit for Jade to be Rose's daughter and having an older sister didn't make sense. Unless Jem and Jade weren't really sisters. And unless Jade was actually older than seven. Was it possible? Cienna and Adrian had hired Detective Miller's wife, Private Investigator Mollie, to learn more.

Cienna sighed. "But why does it happen?"

Betsy shifted her knitting project on her lap. "I really wish I could answer that, my friend. I can't. Except to say that there is an issue of free will. We weren't created to be robots, right? We were created to make our own decisions, and sometimes those bad decisions do affect other people."

Cienna snorted. "I'll say."

"Haven't your decisions affected others?"

"Yes, of course." She twisted her hands together. Her voice grew small. "But why me and Jazz? Out of all the thousands of kids. A stupid walk in the woods."

"You're nervous about today."

Cienna nodded, looking around the room.

"It'll be just fine."

Cienna grew warm all over. Perspective, right? Yes, this was hard, but it was needed for the greater good. Why did she suddenly feel like she was in church?

"Will you be here next time?" She looked up to discover Betsy's chair empty. She whipped her head around and jumped up.

No Betsy. Crazy! She shook her head quickly, her curls wrapping around her face and headed back to her chair. On it rested a folded piece of paper. She hesitated. Brushed her hair from her face. The last note she'd received included more threats, and it now rested safely with Detective Peters. Cienna strode forward and snatched it off the chair.

The whys are the most difficult, my dear. We may never know. But be reassured, you are making a great impact on so many lives, and this could not have happened without the experiences you suffered. See you soon. Betsy

See you soon.

Peace filled her. She stuffed it into her pocket, sat and turned to a man a few chairs away. "I suppose your name is Winters. Hey, did you see that lady here knitting?"

He laughed. "I'm Joshua Teek. You must have been dreaming." Then he crossed his arms and closed his eyes for a nap. Or to stop her attempt at conversation. Who knew?

"Rydal-Hower!"

Cienna grinned. Nerves no longer tumbled in her stomach. Confident Cienna. Strong Cienna. She could do this. For Grace, for Jazz, for all the innocent girls and boys who might otherwise be trafficked and killed – unless she moved forward.

***

She stared at Mike, sitting across the table. Once again, chained and handcuffed. Two new guards standing on either side. Again, his brokenness filtered through. And, he sported a large black eye.

Ouch.

"What happened to you?"

"I could say the same to ya." Mike leaned forward as much as his chains allowed. "Why ya even back to see me?"

She gulped. "I heard … I heard you asked for me."

One of the guards gave the other guard a side-eye glance.

Mike laughed.

She pictured him years before, with his red baseball hat, arrogant and charming all at the same time. He was still in there somewhere.

"Don't usually git what I want here." He hunched over and looked at his lap. "So, um, thanks."

Thanks?

That one was new.

She shifted. Wondered if she was truly safe. Hopefully the wire worked, and this project could be completed in as few visits as possible. "You're welcome."

They stared at each other. A memory drifted through her head – a time when they showed politeness to each other. When things seemed somewhat like a real relationship.

But then she'd found Penny under the house.

Cienna quickly rearranged her thoughts. No Penny. Don't think about Penny. "Are you eating? Looks like you've lost some weight."

"Prison mush. Sure. Not the best tasting meal, or even close to half-decent porkchops."

Her breath hitched. He was reminding her of *that* night. She'd escaped. He caught her and threw her back in the barn, where Roger tortured her for days. And later, when she could think with a much clearer head, she'd realized Mike knew all about those days with Roger in the barn. Her jaw clenched. She looked at the guard to regain her focus. Cienna almost rose to fling herself at the door.

Instead, she started one of the grounding exercises learned in therapy. With deep breaths, she thought of things she could see right now. Her chair. Her hands. The jeans she loved. The guards. The dark skin of one and white of the other. The dingy taupe color of the wall. The wooden trim along the bottom. The door, should she need it. If she ran to it, they would let her go without hesitation. The guards stood here, after all, to protect her. She was not stuck.

But no, she couldn't leave. For the sake of Grace and so many others, Roger needed found – as soon as possible.

She blinked and settled her gaze back on Mike. Her breathing normalized. Her heartbeat settled.

He smirked.

Cienna grinned. Strong Cienna. "Smirk all you want, Mike. It was a pretty nice night, actually." Lying Cienna. She continued looking into his eyes. "I did enjoy some of my time there, you know."

Silence filled the room. She winked at him, as he had so often instigated. His jaw dropped.

Yikes.

Adrian would cringe. She almost cringed too. But she had to do this. "Really." Her voice softened. "We had a … a friendship, too. And I felt honored when you told me about your wife and all that. So, why did you want to see me? And what happened to your eye? That looks painful."

One of the guards twitched.

Mike moaned and put his arms up toward his eye. "It hurt. Bastards. They don't like me here."

Cienna's lip twitched. Yes, she'd heard that bad things happened to child molesters and killers in prison. As far as their outcome. Pitiful Mike. Not so big and strong now.

Broken.

She shook her head. Why did that thought keep coming back? Annoying. Mike deserved to be broken. If he actually and truly *was*.

"Yeah, I'm sorry." Maybe she did feel a bit sorry for him. "A fight?"

"No." He groaned. "They snuck up on me. I didn't do nothin'."

One of the guards coughed but couldn't stop a grin. The other guard frowned.

She glanced at them both. Did they hear about the wire? Only a few were supposed to know. Her eyes landed back on Mike. With her brain still protesting, she reached across the table and touched Mike's hand. She saw a guard flinch and move forward. She gave him a reassuring nod and he moved back. She gently squeezed as Mike's eyes flew up to meet hers. "What can I do for you, Mike? I know you're stuck here. Can I put some money on your spending account? Write you letters?"

He grinned. Squeezed her hand back. "Ya can visit me more. How about that, my pretty Cilena?"

She rolled her eyes comically. "Oh, come on. You remember the porkchops but not my name?"

Mike chuckled. "Cienna."

"Uh-huh. Okay. Let me think about that." She didn't want to raise his suspicions by agreeing too quickly. "I mean, it's an okay place to meet, I guess."

Safe for her, that is.

"Sure." He coughed. "When I git out, we can think of better places." He wiggled his eyebrows at her. Shifted in his chair.

An uncomfortable blob settled in her stomach. Well, he was in for life. So not something to focus on or worry about. "It's ... it's a good time to get to know each other in a different way," she managed. "Talking and all that. Like when we talked about Mrs. Mike, remember? And you shared that with me. It made you feel better, right? I know it explained some things to me."

He nodded. Mike seemed a little more agreeable behind bars, for sure.

"So, I'll start." She removed her hand and sat back a little. Ugh. This stuff was *really* none of his business.

Give and take.

"I started a nonprofit called the Portland Freedom Center." It seemed a safe subject.

"Yeah? What do ya do?"

"Help people. Like when they're homeless. Or veterans. People who are addicted, and it's affected all parts of their lives, their relationships, housing and jobs. People just down on their luck." Or taken. Or abused. Or *trafficked*. She bit her lip. "I have a small staff, but a lot of my job is keeping the money coming in. Grants and fundraising and stuff. Of course, I answer the phones a lot too. My receptionist can't handle the volume of people who truly need help. And a lot of organizations use the center to hold their therapy and support groups."

Mike cleared his throat. "That's mighty nice, Cienna." His voice sounded gruff. "And I see ya have a weddin' ring."

"Yes." She refrained from saying more about that. "Now you. What's something I don't know about you?"

He shuffled uncomfortably, then shrugged. Leaned back in his chair. His eyes briefly rested on her ring. He looked up. His lip twitched. "I've been writin'," he announced and looked at a guard as if they might contradict or punish him.

Cienna raised her eyebrows. "Really? Like what?" She smiled.

"A journal is all I have to write in. But stories. I check books out from the library and like to write like them authors do."

"That's great, Mike."

"I been … been reading the Bible."

Woah. And it didn't seem like it was due to a shortage of other books. She nodded, encouraging him to continue.

"And on that note, baby. I gotta tell ya something." He shifted in his chair. "I gotta tell ya I'm sorry. Sorry for how I treated ya. I know it wasn't all *that* good for ya."

Chapter 47
Jazz

Jazz stared at Phil, her boss. "No. I don't believe this." She jumped to her feet.

Phil grimaced. "I know. I'm sorry. It's budget cuts." She sat. And growled. "You're lying. You've wanted to fire me for ages."

Phil shifted uncomfortably. "Admittedly, you're my weakest link. You know that. Not only that incident with your, uh, baton. But now I hear you were screaming at your neighbor's kids and saying you were coming after them. You scared them. You're lucky their folks didn't call the cops. That's hearsay of course, and on your own time, so I'm not disciplining you for that."

"They're *noisy*. Vagrants. I can hardly concentrate. And they give me headaches."

"Well, as you can't get along well with people and resolve conflict appropriately, then this isn't the best job for you anyway. I'm sorry, but our client load is less this year, and I can't afford to keep you. I really think you need some anger management classes and to maybe go back to therapy."

The buzzing in Jazz's head increased as Phil droned on. And on. She flushed. Without understanding how she got there, she suddenly stood next to Phil and started shaking his large shoulders. She moved her hands up to his neck, and he stood, lifting her off the ground and breaking her grip.

"Stop it, Jasmine. Now!" He ripped her magnetic badge off her uniform and removed her baton from the case at her side. He marched her to the door. "And that is assault. Leave now or I'll call the cops. Your last paycheck will be in your account tomorrow. Don't bother returning the uniform!" He pushed her out the door and slammed it. She heard the lock click.

Jazz pounded on the door. "I'm not Jasmine! I'm not! I hate you! All men are the same sick pigs!" She turned and ran out to the street. Tears blinded her eyes as she scanned the area quickly.

Once trafficked. Always trafficked. Once a security guard. Always extra conscious. Or maybe extra conscious ever since kidnapped. Whatever. She pushed the thoughts further back into her brain. Her head whipped back and forth. No bus.

What now?

She took off down the street at a run, her blond hair coming lose from its clip and flying around her. Her phone rang in her pocket. Once. Twice. Wait, that was Cienna's ring tone. The world around her ground to a slow stop as she paused and caught her breath. Ci must be done visiting Mike. She needed to grab this one. Her friend needed her.

She ducked into a store, a busy one. Safer than the curb. "Ci."

"Jazz, what's wrong? You at the gym? Sorry if it's a bad time."

Jazz took a deep breath. Forced a smile onto her face. She'd heard once when working in telemarketing that it made a difference in how your voice sounded. "I was jogging. All good. How are you?" She wandered down the aisles, pretending that she had all the money in the world and could buy whatever she wanted. Cheap clothes and sweatsuits. Handbags and socks hung three racks over. She gritted her teeth, thinking about Phil.

Stupid, stupid man. He would pay.

"I-I'm home." Cienna's voice sounded small. "It was weird this time. That same lady was in the lobby. I feel like she knew everything."

"Nothing new there. Remember the waitress? The endless people, really."

"Yeah, but that's normally when we're together, Jazz. Not on our own. Except for Lou, apparently. This is different."

Jazz paused, trying to think. "Right." She shuffled through a rack of jeans. She needed some but couldn't afford anything now. Not when she had no idea where next month's rent was coming from. She might wind up on the streets and become a client of the Freedom Center because she'd just used the only savings she'd stashed too. "So, what happened?" The middle of winter was a heck of a time of year to end up on the streets. Christmas was only two weeks away.

Silence on the other end. "Uh, we made up?"

Jazz paused. Her eyes widened. "You, um, what?"

"Well, you know I had to, Jazz. They're recording me to get to Roger. Supposedly they're in contact. But I just realized it's going to take a lot more visits than just today to get the info they want. Geez."

"What'd you talk about? Your home life? Your *job*?" Jazz sneered into the phone.

"Not home. Maybe job. What's wrong with you, Jazz?"

"Nothing."

"Okay. Well, you sound weird."

Jazz sighed. "I'm in the middle of the store. And I didn't want you to see him anyway."

"I know. But I gotta, Jazz. You know that. Since Roger's still out there."

Jazz gagged. Covered it with a cough. "You don't have to. The cops can do their own job. And pull in Mollie even, if needed. She told us she made a vow to find him when she saw the wanted poster at the General Store."

"Mike doesn't even know Mollie. It's gotta be me. Roger's still coming after me, and he could start with you and Grace, too. As far as Mike, somewhere, in there, is a heart."

"OMG!" Jazz gave up at the clothing racks and stomped outside the door. "You are joking right now, right? A heart? No, Mike *never* had a heart, and he never will."

"You're wrong, Jazz. He apologized to me. He's been reading the Bible and says that's why."

Jazz felt her blood boil. Mike was going to snag Ci again. At least with his charm. If she could get a hold of him, she'd use her little Ruger, and he'd be out of Ci's life once and for all. And Roger? Him, too. But she'd slice him to pieces first for taking them in the first place. She stomped from the entryway of the store to the street corner. Looked around warily and finally leaned against the wall. "I got fired!"

"You what? Oh, no, Jazz!"

"Freakin' pig. Says I need anger management. Also said stuff that's none of his business. Grabbed my badge off my shirt and snagged the baton. Called me *Jasmine*. Slammed the door in my face!"

"Crap. I'm sorry, Jazz. There's gotta be a plan here. A better job for you where you aren't putting up with all of that." A pause. "Are you telling me everything?"

Jazz flushed. "No! I went around the desk and shook him a little."

"You grabbed him?"

"Take that resource worker hat off, Ci. Yeah, I grabbed him. Stop analyzing me."

"I'm not analyzing. I'm your friend. What else?"

Jazz paused. She could hardly believe the next thing she'd pulled – a first indeed. And Phil was a decent man usually, not a perp. "I-I tried to choke him."

"Hands around his neck?"

"Yeah."

Cienna cleared her throat. "Then the proper term is strangulation. You strangled – tried to strangle him, Jazz."

Jazz kicked a rock off the sidewalk. Glared at a man walking by with his kids. "Well, that sounds worse."

"It is." Cienna sounded somber. "Was he hurt?"

"No. He stood up and took me up with him and then hauled me out the door."

"We better check. Injuries can show up sometimes hours and days later."

"His neck is big. I didn't even get my hands around the whole thing." She looked at her scrawny hands. Clenched and unclenched. Maybe Phil really deserved it.

But had he? He'd only fired her. Not trafficked her.

"Doesn't matter. If you pressed on his trachea at all, it can cause brain damage in 3-5 seconds."

"I wasn't trying to kill his brain cells. Geez."

"I know. Look Jazz, I'm going to call and check on him. Where are you? Going home, I hope?"

Jazz grunted and started walking toward the bus stop. It should come soon. "Yeah."

"Jazz? I might have to report this. I-I have to check into that. But in the meantime, I'm thinking you really need to go back to therapy. You can't let our traffickers win, and every time you're pissed off and do something like this, you're letting them win."

Jazz disconnected the call.

Chapter 48
Elenore-1 year before

Elenore sat at the dining room table, blowing smoke into the room. Her cell phone beeped. She glanced down at it. Hendrick.

Brandon paced in the kitchen.

The girls were in the bedroom, playing some stupid game.

"Who's that?" Brandon inclined his head at the phone.

"A john," she lied.

"Yeah, right." He sneered. "Liar. Your earnings have been half. You aren't even trying anymore. Unless ..." He stopped pacing. "Unless you're keeping the money." He glared at her and tapped his beer can on the counter.

Elenore shrugged. She *was* seeing fewer clients. She felt tired, burned out and sick a lot of the time. Plus, she was getting older, and they liked the younger ones these days. And then – there was Hendrick. A few times with a man who treated her well, and she suddenly realized what she'd put up with almost as soon as she'd entered Brandon's home to take refuge from Len.

Now she felt like garbage when meeting a client. Maybe she always had.

"I'd like to retire," she ventured, knowing the risk. "Really, Brandon. Isn't there another way I could help? Do the books or something? You know I'm loyal. I won't ever turn on you." Her mind wandered back to the times she would wake up with bruises, and he'd insisted she'd had bad dreams.

His loud snarl made her look around for a loose dog. She sighed. She grabbed her phone and texted Hendrick.

Can't talk right now.

Later, baby? Please.

She turned her phone upside down on the table and glared at Brandon. "What?" He was lucky she didn't run away with Hendrick, who treated her right. The few times he'd flown into town, she always tried to look her best. A softer look. Nice pastel or denim clothes that covered most areas. Makeup applied with care that *didn't* say "Come get me. I charge for services." This once-in-awhile-boyfriend cared for her and actually took her out to eat beforehand. Not only that, but he paid for a hotel for a full night or two, not just an hour.

Had Brandon ever even taken her out to eat? She snorted. Only if it counted when she was working at his diner.

"You're not yet fifty, El. And you're still ... pretty. You've just got a mouth on you. You need to sweet talk the men, is all. And go find some at the clubs. The lighting is low, and everyone looks younger." He laughed.

"You don't understand."

Jade came around the corner squealing with laughter. "Ah, come on. I found you already. You can't run away!" She called, then skidded to a stop when she reached the kitchen and saw Brandon glaring at her mom. "Come on, Jade. Where'd you go?" She turned quickly and chased Jade into the living room, pretending not to see her.

"Jem!" Elenore stood up. "Come back!"

Jem sheepishly appeared at the entryway to the kitchen. "I know we're being loud. Maybe I should take her outside to play for a while. Sorry." She lifted her eyes a little to look at Brandon. "I didn't mean to interrupt."

Elenore shook her head. "I don't care. The conversation was stupid anyway. I need you to make dinner tonight. I gotta lay down."

Of course, she couldn't tell her daughter that Brandon kept reducing her supply and seemed to keep her sick as much as he wanted to.

"It's okay, Mom. I can do that, and I'll bring you something."

"Thank you, Jem. Sweetie. Know why I named you that? 'Cuz you are one." She rewarded her daughter with a sweet smile. Jem's eyes glowed.

Brandon tossed his beer can into the recycling bin and looked at Jem, who stared at her feet. He walked over and grabbed her, smoothing her hair. Elenore saw his hand creep further down Jem's back as he pulled her closer.

The man must be crazy.

Elenore saw Jem's body tighten. "Leave her alone. Come into the bedroom with me."

"Oh, yeah? You actually offering this time?" He grinned.

Bastard. He'd planned this.

"I am." She walked over to him and rubbed his arm with her hand. Then she took his hand and placed it on her breast. "Go on, Jem. Find Jade. She's waiting."

Brandon released Jem, and she fled. He yanked Elenore to him and pulled up her shirt. She shook him off. "The girls. Bedroom."

He grumbled as she led him down the hallway. Apparently, he would have been okay with a scene and them walking into the kitchen in the middle of it.

Elenore's heart sank as they neared the bedroom. Well, she would do whatever it took to protect her daughter. Her daughters, she corrected herself. Jade fit in and stayed extremely attached to Jem. They'd obviously decided to keep her – even as her fake seven-year-old birthday arrived.

But Elenore now played double duty to protect them both. Especially since Brandon insisted on home-schooling. They rarely left the house and if they did, Brandon or Elenore always accompanied them.

***

Hours later, with Brandon finally fully satisfied and Elenore sore and nauseated, he pulled out her supply.

"Thank God." She lay back and held out her arm.

"Not so fast." He stretched out her arms, pinning her to the bed, while still holding the small black bag. "We've gotta make an agreement here. You still owe me thousands in medical expenses, and the rent and utilities here both went up too. But you aren't pulling your weight."

She sighed. "Brandon, the girls are requiring more and more time. Especially Jade."

He laughed loudly. "Like you're even her mother. Jem takes complete care of her, and you know it."

"She does a lot. But it still takes a lot of *energy*."

"Shut up. You're worth zero. Even in the bedroom." He tied her arm with the rubber piping and slid the needle into her vein. "You're running out of veins. We'll have to find some creative places soon."

She glowered at him. He'd already accomplished that once.

As her head grew lighter, he helped her sit. "Now you'll feel better. I'm serious though. If you can't work, or you *won't* ..." He paused to sneer. "We'll need another source of income."

"I know. Like I said. I could do the books? Schedule the johns? Put ads out. With the computer, I can do most anything you need right from here."

He laughed. "No, El." He patted her head – like she was a dog. She reached for her clothes. "If you can't keep up with paying customers, Jem is mine without complaint. Well, she's mine anyway. Both of you are. But I'll try to accommodate to help you out. I recognize if I take her out for appointments, you won't have your mini-mother for Jade."

Elenore gasped. "No, Brandon!"

He reached over and grabbed her chin, hard. She winced, suddenly feeling more sober. "You don't understand, El. That's what she's here for. She's already had some practice. Certainly not as much as I want her to have, but enough for now. Didn't she tell you? Why do you think I took care of all of you all these years, with my money? Stupid witch. Anyway, if that time comes and you aren't keeping up expenses, I'll pay a few months' rent for you and a supply of your stuff because you know, that's really the right thing to do. Then she'll come with me. Jem will have to learn what she was truly made for."

Elenore stared at the ceiling as Brandon left. Why hadn't she just died in the car crash along with Chad? Why hadn't she died when Len beat her to a pulp? God was cruel, indeed. She finally rose, pushed both arms into her robe sleeves, and left the bedroom to check on the girls.

It was only late that evening as the drugs wore off and they were watching a movie that she truly understood the calamity she'd caused when she walked into Brandon's house thirteen years ago. And she also knew her arguments would fall uselessly into a black void.

Jem was Brandon's puppet. Just like her. And nothing she could ever say or do would change that.

Chapter 49
Jem

Jem opened her eyes and sat straight. She heard Jade's squeal of laughter all the way from the kitchen.

Christmas Eve Day.

Usually, Elenore lay passed out on the couch. Jem wouldn't have realized the holiday without the increased television commercials and a printed calendar that Elenore faithfully hung on the wall each new year. Jem crossed out each day as it passed.

The holidays were rarely special in the apartment, although Jem tried. They didn't buy a tree and usually didn't receive many, if any, presents like she saw in the movies. She and Jade passed the time making paper chains to hang in the window, coloring, playing games and watching the holiday specials on the TV or computer.

This year, Cienna promised stockings and food and a community theater play that night. The next morning, tantalizing gifts to open – ones torturing the girls now for over two weeks. And the next week, a beach trip.

Sniffing the air, she inhaled the smell of Mel's cinnamon rolls. The scent often floated through the wall. She pulled herself out of bed and felt around for the slippers Cienna had purchased. She yawned as she wandered into the sweet-smelling kitchen.

A fresh pan of cinnamon rolls rested on the counter. Adrian and Mrs. K danced to Christmas music, and Jade sat on the high stool, giggling so hard that tears rained down her cheeks.

"Oh, yeah? That's funny? Check this out." Adrian dipped Mrs. K backward in his arms.

Mrs. K laughed too and rose red-faced. She swatted him with her oven mitt. "Now that's enough, young man. Let this chef get back to work!" She turned to the scrambled eggs on the stove and saw Jem. "Good morning, Jem!"

Jem smiled. "Morning." A lot of smiles reigned in this house. She loved it. She felt safe. And Jade radiated happiness and wellness. Trusting these people paid off. She even thought she loved them all a bit.

"Hi, sis." Jade wrapped her arms around Jem.

Jem held her tightly. Her sister was safe here – even as Jem slept. That meant everything.

"Sleep okay?" She ruffled Jade's red curls.

"Yup! And guess what?"

"What's that?"

"Come look." She pulled Jem to the living room window and Jem stopped, suddenly at a loss for words. Snow blanketed the deck. More flurries circled in the air.

"Wha-at? Oh no! Mrs. K!" Jem covered her mouth with her hand. She felt the very cold air even through the window. She dropped to her knees.

Adrian and Mrs. K hurried out of the kitchen. "Oh dear, child. Oh dear. No, everyone is fine. Don't worry so. Servio packed up camp, and they found the warming shelter last night. Cienna just left to pick them up to bring them here for the holiday."

Jem's eyes widened. "But Cienna ... in this snow."

"No worries with that, young lady." Adrian smiled. "She took the 4x4, and trust me, she's better than I am driving in the snow. Everything will be fine. Let's have breakfast. I'm making hot chocolate. Who wants marshmallows? Gracie! Hot chocolate time!"

"Me! Me!" Both Jem and Jade chorused as they followed Mrs. K and Adrian to the table. Mrs. K hurried to get the hot dishes while Adrian made hot chocolate. Grace ran out of her room to join them, her RC car in hand.

Jem noticed Cienna wasn't home after breakfast. And Adrian checked his phone a lot. She wandered to the window a few times. The beautiful snowfall stopped, and Jade wanted to play. "We don't have snow clothes," Jem cautioned.

"I don't care." Jade ran outside in her t-shirt and stuck her tongue in the air. Jem laughed, got dressed and followed outside with their sweatshirts. Mel chatted with Jade. She heard her sister laugh.

"Jade, put this on." Jem tossed a sweatshirt at her. She noted Grace off to the side pulling a board from the side of the garage.

"Oh, there you are dear. I was just telling Jade she needs to eat three more cinnamon rolls and put some weight on."

"We'll have to work on that. We have stockings, so maybe there's goodies in there, too."

"What are you doing out here then? You should be opening your stockings." Mel patted the ball of snow Jade scooped up from the ground. "Too early to make a snowman. Tomorrow it'll stick better."

"It could be gone tomorrow." Jem smiled and pulled a knit hat over Jade's head.

"Hey." Jade protested.

"Hey, yourself. Heat escapes out of your head the most." She remembered the cold nights in the tent and shivered. She straightened up to see a funny look on Mel's face. "What?" She shook her head in confusion. Had she done something wrong?

"Nothing dear." Mel answered absently and blinked a stray flurry of snow off her eyelashes. "It's just for a minute there …"

Jem waited for the older woman to say more, but she didn't. She tried to cover the awkward moment. "Stockings are waiting till Cienna gets back. She went to pick up our camp family for the holiday."

"Is that right?" Mel smiled broadly. "How kind of her. Yes, I remember them. Zeb, I recall, was counting all the trees in the yard."

"Amongst other things. He was introduced to me as the Number Man. I guess that's how he understands life. He's nice though."

Mel nodded. "He is indeed. They all are. And what about your young man? Is it Jet?"

Jem blushed. "I think Jet's coming this time. He's just my friend."

They watched as Jade ran over to Grace, grabbed her hand, and giggled. Grace dropped the board, and they ran to tumble in the snow.

"Wooohoooo! Come play, Jem!"

Laughter bubbled from Jem. Happy Jade – with a friend in Grace. Smiles before leaving home were so rare.

"Jet's just our friend." She rubbed her hands together. "But we actually wouldn't be here without him."

"Oh, do tell. I love a delicious story."

Jem paused. "Well, not delicious exactly. You see, Jade and I ran away from home. It … it wasn't safe."

Mel frowned. "Are you … were you hurt?"

How to answer that question? Jem shaded her eyes from the sun peeking from behind the snow clouds that seemed to follow Jade, who moved further away.

"Hey, come back!" Jade suddenly had an acre to run on after mostly being cooped up in an apartment her whole life. That and a parking lot to play in when she was lucky. She'd better keep a closer eye on her. She turned to Mel. "We had to go. Jade could have been hurt, yes. I wasn't going to let that happen. We came here and had nowhere to go. Jet saved us. I'm grateful."

"I am, too. I'm glad you're here and that you're both safe. But I heard you came from Seattle. Why did you come here?"

"My grandma's here somewhere," Jem admitted. "I had her phone number, but my phone … we lost my phone. So, then we were stuck at the bus station until Jet insisted on taking us to the camp."

A funny look crossed Mel's face again. She turned and wandered back to her side of the duplex.

Well, that was weird. Not even a goodbye. Jem shrugged and ran after her little sister and Grace.

Chapter 50
Cienna

Cienna navigated the slick streets while admiring the snow. Pretty, but it potentially deadly for anyone houseless. A ball of guilt rolled in her stomach. She should pick these guys up, take them home and open the Freedom Center. Surely there were people that needed her help on Christmas Eve.

She shook her head. She'd promised Adrian, and they planned for a houseful of people. This was a holiday to truly enjoy. Her phone rattled in the cup holder, and she glanced at it. Her dash cell phone holder burned up with Queenie. She needed a new one.

Jazz. Well, she could wait. In fact, for the first time in her life, the thought of her best friend created irritability. What was Jazz thinking attacking Phil like that? He could have pressed charges. Instead, he assured Cienna that he'd see a doctor and asked her to please get Jazz the help she needed.

Cienna shook her head. If only she could. Jazz continued to escalate. She bit her lip. Should she call her friend's parents? Jazz would be livid. But she'd moved from somewhat suicidal to maniac territory.

Cienna mumbled as she pulled into the community center. Only ten miles took an hour and a half to drive. Even with Adrian's 4x4, the fastest, safest speed remained 25 miles per hour. Those without a 4x4 or insisting on a higher speed slid all over the road and many now rested off road. Stuck. She pulled into a parking spot and breathed a sigh of relief.

Now she just had to find everyone and drive them back home. Hopefully, Zeb would stay for a while this time. Mrs. K missed him. Last minute presents waited for each of them under the tree.

She opened her door and entered the warm building. Cots lined the entire gym – a side room filled too. An unpleasant body odor reached her. She saw several people exiting the locker rooms with wet hair. Hopefully everyone desired cleanliness today. Servio picked up plates and garbage from breakfast, so she headed over.

"Hey, Mrs. Cienna."

"Hey, Servio. Cienna's fine."

"Alright then." He nodded. "I gotta finish my chores. Zeb's by the drinking fountain. And we need to make a stop to pick up Jet if that's okay."

"Of course. But I hoped he was here staying warm last night."

"He was. Only left a couple hours ago. I get it – not too big into community living myself."

She hoped they wouldn't mind living with the rest of them at the house for an overnight or two. "I understand. I'm the dark blue Explorer in the parking lot. See you there."

As she wandered through the crowd, a few clients waved or came to say hello. Gratefulness filled her. They were safe, warm and off the streets – for now. Several of them she'd previously attempted to get into shelters or transitional housing … to no avail. Well, a few claimed success. The others chronically landed back on the streets.

Elianna waved at Cienna.

Cienna smiled. "Security duty?"

"Just making sure everyone's safe." She grinned. "How're you holding up?"

"Doing okay. I miss Queenie." She almost said "I miss Jazz too" but caught herself. "Is she still in the evidence yard?"

"I think they've about wrapped that up."

"Any clues?"

"Peters will be calling you about that. Probably after Christmas. Or maybe the new year. Any more notes? Weird stuff?"

"Been quiet. Maybe they're getting tired of trying to scare me."

"Don't let your guard down, Cienna. Did you see Mike?"

"Twice now." Cienna nodded. "I'm okay though. Made a friend there. She's pretty encouraging before I go in."

"Glad for that." Elianna's adjusted her earpiece. "Oops. Gotta go. I hear you're picking up a few for Christmas?"

Cienna nodded and continued forward. She waved to the local DA's office assistant, who was on the monthly domestic violence community board with her. Saw the director of the local women's shelter, too, and the man from a church who passed out bedding and coats at the local parks. Her people sheltered here – smelly or clean. She briefly smiled remembering Betsy's words that she made a difference. She truly hoped so.

Now, if she could only help her best friend.

Cienna smiled at a woman trying to herd her kids into the locker room for showers. She found Zeb. He wandered about, pointing at each cot.

"Zeb!"

He finished counting and wandered over. She motioned toward the outside door. "I'm in the dark blue Explorer out there, okay? Can you come soon?" She wanted dignity for them – not to escort them out or to force them. Anyone could change their mind.

But she hoped they wouldn't.

"Hello, Miss...miss..."

"Cienna." Had he even heard her?

Zeb grinned. "There are twenty-five cots in that row."

"I see." She laughed. "I'm out there. Blue Explorer. Same one you rode in before, okay?"

"Yes, ma'am."

After Cienna finished saying hello and a quiet "Merry Christmas" to more colleagues, she pushed out the door and clicked the key fob.

When Zeb and Servio clicked into their seatbelts finally, she pulled out of the parking lot. They smelled clean – thank goodness. They seemed happy and calm. A great holiday awaited.

She clicked Adrian's icon and voice messaged him. **On the way back.**

"Where to?" She glanced in the rearview mirror. They both chose the backseat. Maybe they were saving the front for Jet.

"River Park. There's some building. Old barn-looking thing I guess they store landscape supplies in." Servio stretched his arms above his head and yawned.

"Why's he there?"

"Dunno. Someone just told me he wanted us to pick him up there. Maybe someone he's checking on?"

"Gordy stays down there sometimes." Zeb turned to the window. "One building, two buildings, five buildings …"

"Okay." Cienna ignored the stirring in her gut. A bit strange, but then again, people on the streets sometimes did strange things. Heck, even Jazz could claim strange. Cienna too. But she also knew Jet took care of a lot of the houseless people. So, it made sense.

Servio directed her as she cruised the streets slowly. It looked like it might snow again. Well, that's all Portland needed. They owned very few snowplows and rarely pre-sanded the roads. She peered through the windshield as white flakes started floating down again. "I'm glad you're coming for Christmas. We're having clam chowder and fresh rolls from Mel for lunch. Turkey tonight." The delighted groans from the back gave her a smile. Zeb even stopped counting.

"The girls have stockings to dig into but are waiting for us." She glanced in the rearview mirror again.

Servio grinned. "They deserve a warm Christmas. Thanks, Cienna. I promise we tried to take good care of them at the camp."

"I know you did." She reassured him and turned her blinker on. "I have no doubt of your care for them."

They pulled up to the building finally, and Servio hopped out. "Be right back."

Ten minutes later, Cienna tapped the steering wheel impatiently and restarted the engine for heat. Zeb counted the statues in the park. She rolled her eyes. There were only a few. He started over again several times. "Zeb, how about the trees?"

"Sure. Why not?"

She breathed a sigh of relief.

Twenty minutes later, she gritted her teeth. What in the world was taking so long? "I'd better go in."

"Okay." Zeb yawned. He stopped counting.

Cienna hopped out of the car with her keys and mace. She opened the door that Servio had entered. "Jet? Servio?" No answer. She saw a flickering light further ahead so she strode in. Hmm, if Gordy was hanging out here, he sure shouldn't be making a fire in this old building – even to keep warm. "Jet!"

The door slammed behind her.

She heard a click and a heavy scraping as a board slid across the outside. Cienna knew that sound. She opened her mouth to scream.

She was back in the barn.

Chapter 51
Jem-3 months before

Jem rarely left her bedroom anymore. She still fought nightmares about Brandon turning up to fix Mom's sickness. Wait. She herself had called him for help. She shuddered.

"Go. Be a good girl. I'm sorry." Mom had gasped on the bathroom floor as he pulled out cash and drug supplies, reminding her of "the deal". Then just as quickly, Mom begged Brandon to hurry up with shooting drugs into her arm and sent Jem to Brandon's truck.

"Someone around here has to work." Brandon remarked snidely when he got into the truck, and in the next few days, Jem finally understood. They returned to the blue trailer, and although she tried to run three times, there was always some lady at the house forcing her to stay. In her and Mom's room in the den, she trembled as Brandon came in first and hurt her. She hauled off and hit his nose straight on once. He swore, called her a witch and punched her in the chest. For hours, he became a stranger as she cried and finally disappeared into a numb ball.

"Gotta break you in. But I'll still keep you fresh. More money for your mom's rent that way."

She refused to eat the next day, although both Nadine and Mynx encouraged her. Nadine even shared funny stories about when Jem had been born in that very room. And a few hours later, the first "gentlemen caller" entered her room. He was worse than Brandon, and it felt like someone rubbed a fresh scrape raw as he sweated over her.

She couldn't help the tears as he hurt her. She'd never felt so much pain, except maybe when Brandon visited the night before. But the pain differed now. She could no longer remember. The man shoved her over and looked at the blood on the sheets. And as he dressed, she saw the gun he tucked into his waist. In fact ... wait, wasn't that a uniform he was putting on?

The dude was a cop!

She grabbed a blanket and huddled in the corner of the bed against the wall. Her whole body shook.

He laughed. "Worth it, little girl. Are you twelve? You look thirteen maybe. Either way, you made my day. Brandon saves the freshest for me, and for some other comrades. Guess you'll meet them soon. He was pretty quick to text. I pay triple for fresh. Now if he'd just get some younger ones. Yeah. See you later, chickee."

The door slammed as he left.

It was quiet for a bit, and Jem bit her lip as she huddled on the bed against the wall. Would someone else come now? She cleaned herself up with tissue from the Kleenex box. Limped to the door and peered out. The rest of the girls busied themselves behind closed doors. One man leered at her in the hallway. She pulled on her clothes. Scooted to the front door. Where did that nice lady live? The one they visited while moving out? Jem remembered her kind eyes – even though she apparently gave Mom news that Mom frowned at.

A hand appeared above her and slammed the front door. "Where do you think you're going?" Nadine glowered at her.

Jem shrank back. "Fresh ... fresh air. Actually no. Nadine, I can't do this. I gotta leave."

Nadine frowned at her. "Actually, honey, you can't. You see, you owe your mom. She ain't so great at this work anymore. Maybe she's really sick or something." She laughed. "Anyway, Brandon says rent is still due. Overdue, actually. You leave and you and your mom and Jade have nowhere to live. No food either. You'll starve on the streets."

Wait. Mom sick? Other than drug withdrawal? And no way could Jade survive on the streets!

She stood tall. "Mom can get a real job." Surely she would – if she knew the truth.

"No, she can't. She has pain issues. And addiction issues, as you know. Ain't no one going to hire her anymore."

"But ... but what about Brandon's diner?"

"He closed it. Trust me. No one will hire your mom. She's washed up and been refusing to work fulltime as it is. This is on you. *You're* the adult now."

With a sickening feeling in the pit of her stomach, Jem looked at the carpet. Her face flushed. Taking care of Jade *was* her job. She gagged, trying not to throw up. "What do I need to do?"

***

When Brandon dropped her at home a few days later, he grinned. "Be a good girl. Tell your mom rent is paid for a bit, but I need to pick you up next weekend probably. She'll be so relieved you can start help providing. I'll bring her stuff by later if she's sick again."

Jem glared at him and gathered her things. She slammed the door of his truck and stomped upstairs to their apartment. She and Mom needed a serious talk.

She found Mom dozing on the couch and Jade playing with Legos. Jade squealed and threw herself into Jem's arms. "You're home! Did you have fun? Mom said Brandon might take you to a carnival! I want to go!"

Tears gathered in Jem's eyes as she smoothed her sister's bouncy red curls. A carnival indeed. She could barely walk. She forced a smile. "Sure. It was fun. Mom been sleeping for a while?"

Jade nodded seriously. "I got cereal for breakfast. She didn't even notice!"

Hmmm. Jade went to the couch and stared at Mom. She wanted to slap her. Instead, she took a deep breath and felt for a pulse. Still there. Mom's chest rose and fell. She briefly thought of Nadine's comment and wondered if Mom was sick for real. Could there be something else going on?

She fought the bile rising in her throat as she turned away. Nonetheless, Mom had pretty much sold her daughter. What kind of excuse was there for *that*?

***

Jem pulled a protesting Jade into their bedroom when Brandon's boots pounded up the stairs. Her heart beat wildly against her chest and drops of sweat rolled down her sides. Was he there to pick her up again? Who would watch Jade?

She pulled out a puzzle for her sister. "Work on this. I'll help you in a minute." Then she skittered over to the door, trying not to breathe too fast and give her position away. Her heart pounded as she slid down against the door. Mom and Brandon argued, and their voices grew louder.

"This is the way it is, El! You don't have a choice." Brandon's voice boomed. "You obviously can't keep up with the work, and you made an agreement when we got you the apartment. Fulltime work – which you stopped. Other option is you're homeless. You know, I'm starting not to care whether you are or not! Good golly! You're more work than you're worth! I'm sorry for the day I found you in that trailer park!"

"No, Brandon! No." Mom's voice shrilled. "I didn't mean to get sick all the time. And I'm getting older, you know. Like I said, most clients like the younger ones more. Do you see my wrinkles? Oh, my gosh!"

Jem pictured Mom examining her flushed face in the entryway mirror.

"But I still love you!" Mom exclaimed. "I want this to work! I know we can't see you all the time but, please, I know you care for us. I've got two girls who depend on you, too, and they even see you as a dad, Jade especially. Please. If you can just float the expenses for a few more months. I've been exploring work-at-home jobs. There're some good ones available in customer service!"

The slap echoed loudly. Jem pictured Mom cowering in the corner.

"Um. No." Brandon's voice grew extra loud. "That's not how it works, *Elenore*. Now here's the deal. I need Jade too."

Mom wailed.

"I know." His voice quieted. Grew more soothing. "It's not your fault, El. You've done the best you can. And Jem working is helping, for sure. But I should have started her earlier. Jade is really the goldmine here! It'll help you too. What about some extra money for you, too? You could take that trip to Hawaii you've always wanted? Come on, El. I'll take her anyway. You know that. You're not in charge. But I'll keep providing everything that you need if you give me a break here. You won't have to worry ever again about rent or food or utilities. You're absolutely worthless at this point. What else are you gonna do?"

"I-I don't know," Mom whimpered.

Jem heard their voice come closer. Brandon was taking Mom to the bedroom. She plugged her ears to drown out the noises after that.

***

Brandon roared away in his truck. Jem checked on Mom, now passed out on her bed, her arm thrown out. Jem noted the fresh needle marks. She soothed Mom's bangs back. "You don't have the strength to say no, Mom. But I do. I can't believe you let him take me and now … Jade. I can't. We can't. Take care of yourself."

With their backpacks, Jem and Jade crept out the front door, never to return.

Chapter 52
Cienna

Cienna scrambled to check her pockets. Oh, that's right. Her cell phone still rested in the Explorer's cup holder. She only had her keys – and her mace.

When had she ever left her cell phone in the car?

Surely a sign she'd been feeling more comfortable. Time to change that for sure.

Her heart pounded as she crept along the wall, feeling things out in the almost-dark building. She heard the woosh of water below her as a small wave splashed and broke. That's right. This building was built over the water. And even though it was a river, often wakes came when boats made their way through.

And then, white shone in the dark. A note.

She grabbed it with trembling fingers. Enough light from a window far above poured in to read it. She tilted it and brought it closer to her face.

> Hey now. Don't be too worried.
> But don't you wish you had listened?

Oh, my word. She shook her head. Listened to the garbage of a deranged monster? Okay …

But then again, had she done everything she could? Doubt crept in. The local police departments and Detective Peters and Miller were all aware.

But they certainly hadn't protected her.

Was Roger in the building? Watching her now?

INNOCENT VOICES

She crammed the note in her jeans pocket. "Servio!" But then, a brief thought. She didn't know Servio that well. Could he behind this?

"Okay, okay." She practiced a grounding exercise, even as her heart tried to pound out of her chest. "Roger? Are you there?" She'd rather meet him face to face than be surprised.

She stepped forward. Silence met her. Okay, no Roger then. Hopefully. And with Mike secured in prison, who else could it be?

Servio. Gordy. They were here somewhere. Surely, they were the good guys? She pointed her mace and focused on the flicker of light ahead, taking a deep breath. Walking to safety ... or into the bowels of hell? But nothing was worse than what she'd already suffered, for sure.

Strong Cienna. Brave Cienna. She could do this. *Hey now, don't be too worried.* Huh. When she focused on that part of the note, it didn't seem like it was someone who really meant harm. More ... *motherly*.

She almost slouched against the wall and slid to the floor to hide her head in her arms, but instead took a deep, steadying breath. She hoped Zeb understood enough to pick up her phone and activate the emergency feature. He wouldn't need her passcode. Or maybe set the alarm off on the SUV.

She crept toward the light. A board loosened beneath her. She caught a nearby pole. Yikes! Cienna stepped more carefully after that.

Bang!

She stilled. Pressed herself against the wall. A tickle on her shoulder. She raised her hand and turned quickly, brushing her shoulder with one hand. A large spider fell off and scuttled away. She shuddered. "Oh my gosh, I can't do this. I can't."

She leaned against the wall, looked upward.

And who came to mind? Sweet old Betsy. Betsy suddenly filled her thoughts.

You can do this.

Cienna gasped. "I can't."

INNOCENT VOICES

You can! You visited your trafficker in prison, Cienna. The man who both wooed and raped you. Tied you up and even starved you in the early days.

Cienna paused. "How did you know that?" Was she sinking into delirium? "I-I was a different person."

Yes. And now you're stronger. My girl, do not let him do this to you. Do not let him set you back. You've come so far.

"Argh!" Cienna changed forward and slammed her body against another wall on the opposite side, making her way down the hallway. More white. Another note. She grabbed it, her eyes hard and eyebrows furrowed.

> Haven't found a way out yet?
> Ci, I'm a little disappointed.

Something familiar stirred in her brain. She crammed the note into her jeans pocket. She felt her way along the hallway. No windows. But then, a doorknob. She pushed the door open and almost fell in as it gave way. She landed on the floor and hopped up. Even darker in here. But there must be windows. She started to her right and felt around the room. At her height, slightly above and below. She found two, both boarded up.

Okay. She nodded. Keep going to the light instead of getting sidetracked. That was the message. Don't focus on getting out, as hard as that was. She slammed the door on her way out. Oh, yes – they'd know she was coming.

"Servio! It's me!" She called out as she again felt her way down the long, dark hallway. "It's Cienna! Where are you? Jet? Zeb's waiting for us in the car! Roger, is that you? Show yourself!"

Eerie silence greeted her. She shook her head and pictured the fear, a dark cloud, flying out of her head. Pictured peace. Her river. Betsy sitting next to her, knitting. Her heartbeat slowed, and she suddenly could breathe well again.

She recited, "nothing has changed but my attitude, and that changes all. Everything behind me and everything before me." She gritted her teeth and charged forward toward the light.

She stumbled through an archway and stopped. The room boasted a fireplace, a large fire aglow. She thrust her mace forward and started circling it around the room. Servio sat in an upholstered chair. Jet smiled thinly at her from behind a desk.

"Oh, my gosh. What the heck is going on? This was like the worst game of *Clue* ever!" She stepped further into the room.

"Cienna, don't!" Servio leapt forward.

She dropped her mace and turned. There was Jazz, holding her gun with shaking arms. She slowly circled the room with it, pointing it at each person.

Cienna's jaw dropped. "Jazz." She breathed out her name.

But Jazz looked different somehow.

"Wait." She stepped toward her friend. "*Bay?*"

Chapter 53
Elenore

Elenore clicked her phone and answered Hendrick – he'd waited several hours until she finished her jobs for the day. **Sorry love, I'm here. When you coming? Would love to see you.** She texted a picture of her pouty lips. She grinned and tossed her phone on the couch. Then sighed.

She missed the girls.

But what would their life be like if they'd stayed?

Something like hers. But worse because they were so young.

A weird stirring churned her gut. Could she be sure that Brandon hadn't already hurt her girls, especially Jem? No, she honestly couldn't be sure at all. She remembered awaking on the couch after Jem returned from the long weekend with Brandon. Jem and Jade stayed busy in their bedroom. Brandon said they enjoyed a carnival, but funny, she didn't remember Jem showing her any oversized stuffed animals or even talking about the roller-coaster. No smiles. In fact, if she remembered correctly – Jem and Jade refused to leave their room even for macaroni and cheese.

For a moment, she allowed her thoughts to drift back. Way back. To Chad, who loved her sweetly and fully. Who protected her. To Kelly, who truly heard her and seemed to care. To a brick wall that took the final turn for all of them except her.

Why the heck did she deserve to live?

Her phone pinged.

Yeah, about that. I really like you but the wife moved back in. So, I shouldn't be texting you anymore.

Elenore sniffed. Now even Hendrick didn't want her. Stupid wife.

Maybe she'd lived only to parent Jem. Was Jem here to make a difference in the world, unlike Elenore? And what about Jade? Brandon brought Jade – but it was obvious that Jem needed Jade and Jade needed Jem. And she, Elenore, had failed to protect them.

A sick feeling filled her stomach as she realized what she'd allowed by getting addicted to the drugs Brandon provided. And by not paying attention to the red flags. The black cloud crept into her soul and darkened, until it overwhelmed her whole body. She curled on the couch and tightened up into a ball. Yes, she was due for her stuff again, but she didn't expect to hear from Brandon – he kept his own schedule these days. She managed to dial her mom through her tears.

"Mom? I-I've done horrid things. I need to just leave the world. Get out forever."

"Oh no, Ellie. No. Especially now. My darling, there is more here for you. You're *needed*. Please be safe. Are you planning to hurt yourself?"

"I-I need to. I've done horrific things." She gulped. "I've loved a man who's a monster and has probably hurt Jem and Jade now. They're gone, Mom. They left. I think they were looking for you. I think Brandon hurt them, and it's all my fault."

"No, no, dear. Not your fault. Listen to me. The drugs have you all mixed up. And so does Brandon. You need to leave. There are people to help you."

"You don't understand." Elenore sobbed. "I'm stuck here. I'm stuck forever. And now the girls are gone. Forever maybe. I need drugs. I need my stuff. Mom, how did I get here?"

"I don't know." Mom's voice caught, and she sniffed. "But it doesn't matter anymore, Ellie. You can move forward and make better decisions. You can get rehab and healing.

Leave Brandon. There are men who are worth your time. Brandon is not!"

Elenore paused. Like Hendrick? He was nothing like Brandon.

But Brandon brought her the drugs she needed. Hendrick wouldn't do that.

"I'm ... I'm in withdrawal." She admitted finally. "I-I can't do anything. Anything until I get that. Maybe I can think clearly after that."

"I know." Her mother's voice gentled. "I get where you are. I was there at one time, too. I never told you. But I struggled with pills. That's why I was so cheery most of the time. And actually, pretty skinny too." She laughed. Then sighed deeply.

"What? I never knew."

Mom grunted. "I was careful and pretty functional. It runs in our family, Elenore. But you have more serious issues now, and that's why the girls ran."

Elenore shook her head. "How do you know why they left?"

"Never mind that. Will you get help? There are resources. How about you come to my home?"

Elenore paused. A foreign concept.

"Yes. I want you with me."

Elenore's brain started an instant battle. "Why-why would you want me?" She realized her voice sounded quite icy. And for good reason. "I called you, Mom. Pregnant. I didn't know what to do. Just because you visited once since then doesn't erase the fact that you never wanted me." She paused to wipe the sudden tears rolling down her cheeks.

"I always wanted you. I always loved you." Mom sounded choked up. "Ellie, I know I wasn't the best mom. I took pills to deal with your dad leaving. I didn't make the best choices after that. But I'm clean now, and I love you. You're my one and only. I will never love anyone else more. Please, just come. I live near Portland now, but I have room for you.

You don't need Brandon. But I do have other things you need, things that are important to you."

Elenore's breath hitched, and she wiped her eyes with her sleeve. "What? What, Mom? Stop it. If I come, you need to be straight up with me right now. What is there that I need?" She heard the pause on the other end of the phone. Hesitated. Had she gone too far? She held her breath. Was there a reason she needed to get out? To get clean?

"Ellie, I know where your girls are. They're safe. If you can get yourself straightened out and get away from Brandon, they'll want to see you."

Chapter 54
Jem

Delicious smells permeated the air. Jem sniffed appreciatively. She couldn't wait to dive into the clam chowder. Why were Cienna and the others taking so long? She wandered over to the window to check on Jade and Grace playing. Back outside, Mel played again with the girls. Jem should bring Jade in soon. She saw her red hands from the window.

"They should probably come in soon."

Jem jumped.

"Sorry." Adrian stood next to her, wiping his hands on a dishtowel. He eyed the sky.

"I'll get them." She recovered quickly, smiled and went to open the door. "Time to come in Jade! Grace! And Mel!" She laughed.

"Look at that. Like I'm a *child*," Mel exclaimed loud enough for Jem to hear as they stomped the snow off their boots and shoes on the porch. Jade and Grace giggled and Mel grinned. Jade opened the door widely for them to enter and closed it behind them. "Just kidding. It is rather cold. Time to warm up. Soup ready yet?"

"Pretty much. But still no Cienna." A frown crossed Adrian's brow. "She texted that she was on the way back, but that was over two hours ago." His phone rang and he darted over to it while Jem herded Jade and Grace down the hallway. They passed a sleepy Mrs. K, just awakened from a nap. She smiled at the soaking wet, but smiling, girls.

When Jem headed out of the bedroom with an armload of wet clothes and Jade trailing behind her, she heard Adrian

Elenore sniffed. Now even Hendrick didn't want her. Stupid wife.

Maybe she'd lived only to parent Jem. Was Jem here to make a difference in the world, unlike Elenore? And what about Jade? Brandon brought Jade – but it was obvious that Jem needed Jade and Jade needed Jem. And she, Elenore, had failed to protect them.

A sick feeling filled her stomach as she realized what she'd allowed by getting addicted to the drugs Brandon provided. And by not paying attention to the red flags. The black cloud crept into her soul and darkened, until it overwhelmed her whole body. She curled on the couch and tightened up into a ball. Yes, she was due for her stuff again, but she didn't expect to hear from Brandon – he kept his own schedule these days. She managed to dial her mom through her tears.

"Mom? I-I've done horrid things. I need to just leave the world. Get out forever."

"Oh no, Ellie. No. Especially now. My darling, there is more here for you. You're *needed*. Please be safe. Are you planning to hurt yourself?"

"I-I need to. I've done horrific things." She gulped. "I've loved a man who's a monster and has probably hurt Jem and Jade now. They're gone, Mom. They left. I think they were looking for you. I think Brandon hurt them, and it's all my fault."

"No, no, dear. Not your fault. Listen to me. The drugs have you all mixed up. And so does Brandon. You need to leave. There are people to help you."

"You don't understand." Elenore sobbed. "I'm stuck here. I'm stuck forever. And now the girls are gone. Forever maybe. I need drugs. I need my stuff. Mom, how did I get here?"

"I don't know." Mom's voice caught, and she sniffed. "But it doesn't matter anymore, Ellie. You can move forward and make better decisions. You can get rehab and healing.

Leave Brandon. There are men who are worth your time. Brandon is not!"

Elenore paused. Like Hendrick? He was nothing like Brandon.

But Brandon brought her the drugs she needed. Hendrick wouldn't do that.

"I'm ... I'm in withdrawal." She admitted finally. "I-I can't do anything. Anything until I get that. Maybe I can think clearly after that."

"I know." Her mother's voice gentled. "I get where you are. I was there at one time, too. I never told you. But I struggled with pills. That's why I was so cheery most of the time. And actually, pretty skinny too." She laughed. Then sighed deeply.

"What? I never knew."

Mom grunted. "I was careful and pretty functional. It runs in our family, Elenore. But you have more serious issues now, and that's why the girls ran."

Elenore shook her head. "How do you know why they left?"

"Never mind that. Will you get help? There are resources. How about you come to my home?"

Elenore paused. A foreign concept.

"Yes. I want you with me."

Elenore's brain started an instant battle. "Why-why would you want me?" She realized her voice sounded quite icy. And for good reason. "I called you, Mom. Pregnant. I didn't know what to do. Just because you visited once since then doesn't erase the fact that you never wanted me." She paused to wipe the sudden tears rolling down her cheeks.

"I always wanted you. I always loved you." Mom sounded choked up. "Ellie, I know I wasn't the best mom. I took pills to deal with your dad leaving. I didn't make the best choices after that. But I'm clean now, and I love you. You're my one and only. I will never love anyone else more. Please, just come. I live near Portland now, but I have room for you.

still talking on the phone. Grace zoomed her RC car up and down the hallway. She was in her pajamas. "Where are your wet clothes, Miss Gracie?" Grace laughed and darted into her bedroom.

"Really?" Adrian paused and then got up from the table and started pacing. "Boy, that does add a twist, doesn't it?" His eyes briefly rested on Jade, and then moved to Jem.

Jem sighed. Maybe Mom and Brandon had finally showed up. She carried Jade's wet clothes to the laundry room and started a load. Grace brought her clothes and Jem added them to the washer. She returned to the dining room and sat, watching as Jade gazed at the twinkling Christmas tree and explored the packages underneath for at least the tenth time.

Adrian disconnected the call and stroked his chin. His eyes met hers.

"You might as well tell me." Jem shrugged as Adrian sat across from her. "They've found us, huh? Mom and Brandon?"

He shook his head no.

"Then what?" She lowered her voice, conscious of her sister in the next room. "Tell me, Adrian."

"Here it comes!" Grace yelled and sure enough, the car zipped under Jem's feet.

"Grace." Adrian seemed slightly irritated.

"Sorry." She mumbled and crawled under the table to clear a path from the chair legs.

Adrian met Jem's eyes. "They got a match on the DNA for Jade."

Her heart plummeted. Jade deserved to know where she came from and who her folks were. But each time she thought about it, a bitter taste coated her tongue. If Jade did have a real family, and of course she did, where did that leave Jem?

"Is it Brandon? Is he her dad?" She sniffed.

Adrian shook his head. "He's not. But I'm not sure the answer's any better than that. See, once they found ... Rose's body, at the farm, no one claimed her. So she ... she was cremated. Do you know what that means, Jem?"

Jem nodded quickly. But she appreciated Adrian's caution. "Yes, I understand."

"They were able to get Rose's, er, remains, but there wasn't enough left of the bone or teeth to extract DNA from them."

Jem's shoulders slumped. "So, no way to track if Rose was her mom?" She knew a little of the story of how Cienna's friend Jazz, apparently the crazy blond lady they'd met at the Freedom Center, was trafficked and worked at a farmhouse as a hooker. Hmmm. Kinda like herself. Her cheeks flushed. Jazz befriended Rose and promised she'd find her daughter. And when Jazz saw Jade, she became convinced that this Rose was Jade's real mom.

Jem corrected her thoughts. Jazz was apparently Cienna's best friend and, it turns out - they'd both been trafficked and survived.

She wasn't crazy, Cienna had explained. Just very *traumatized*.

Jem got that.

She wanted to tell Cienna what Brandon forced onto her. But she couldn't. They would see it as Jade living in a dangerous environment. Jem hadn't done enough to protect her. She sighed heavily.

"They matched her DNA to a father."

Jem leaned forward, then placed her head in her arms. "Is Jade going to have to leave me now?" Her shoulders shook. She heard Adrian get up and felt his arm on her shoulder. She shook it off. "Well?"

"I don't think so. It matched to some man named Roman, and he's locked up."

She popped her head up, hope flooding her heart. "For what?"

"Drugs. Trafficking. He sold Rose and Jade. He'll be locked up for awhile."

Her heart pounded, vibrating in her ears. Grace's car started racing up and down the hallway again and then into the living room, coming to rest against some packages.

How did Brandon play a part? Had he purchased Jade later on?

Her head spun. "OK. Can we still stay here for now?"

"Jem, you are both always welcome here." He stood and she let him hug her briefly as Mel waltzed by and into the kitchen.

"Hey." Mel called out cheerfully. "I was going to stay for lunch but it turns out I need to go pick up someone for Christmas. I'll be back late."

"Maybe you should wait until the 4X4 gets back? Take that?"

Mel waved her hand dismissively. "My Subi can handle it. No worries. The news just said it's warming up now anyway."

Jem hugged Mel goodbye, and it seemed that Mel wanted a longer hug than ever before. "Back tonight, precious girl. With a gift for you."

"Okay." She smiled and watched Mel give Jade a long hug too. "And for you, as well!" She practically ran out the door.

"Well." Adrian raised his eyebrows. "Guess she's the Santa this year. Suppose that'll be the best gift ever?"

No. The DNA test that meant Jem and Jade still had time together was the best gift of them all, no matter what Mel brought back or whatever rested under the tree.

Adrian's phone buzzed on the table, and Jem glanced at it. Detective Peter's name flashed across the screen.

Chapter 55
Elenore

Elenore stepped out of her room of Portland General Rehab with her bag by her side and walked to the lobby. She smiled at the receptionist and sat by the window. Snow lay on the flower beds around the parking lot.

A fresh beginning indeed.

Her stay here, so far, remained difficult. Not that things were easy before. But she'd accepted The Life as inevitable until Mom stepped in and convinced Elenore that she was worth more than what she built – a life Brandon lorded over.

A new gal sat in the lobby. Her hands shook – her thin dark hair clung to her face. A good extra twenty pounds would benefit her, for sure. Elenore remembered checking in. Without Mom by her side, and especially without Mom sweeping in and driving her four hours away, she might have fled.

Now she was glad she hadn't.

Fleeing obviously hovered in this gal's brain.

"Hi. I'm Ellie. Are you new?"

The girl nodded fast. "I-I don't really want to be here."

"I didn't either."

"Why'd you stay?"

Elenore considered. "I was screwed up. My mom helped me get it straightened out. I-I even had a pimp."

"Oh? Wow." The girl sat straighter. "That would be hard, I think. Where's he?"

"Not sure. As soon as my mom drove me out of town, we called the cops. They let me know he was arrested. Hopefully, he's behind bars." She briefly allowed her mind to settle on the handsome Brandon and wondered how he fared. But then she shook her head. In one of her many therapy sessions, she realized her tendency to choose unhealthy men. Len, Hendrick, Brandon … and really, Chad too.

Their abusive tactics weren't her fault. Neither were their substance abuse and mental health. But when red flags popped up, she could have left. And called the cops. But by then she'd been so absorbed – "in love", and addicted.

The payoff sucked.

Elenore wiped a quick tear from her eye. Was she worth a better life? Her counselors seemed to think so. Working on these new concepts might require commitment until her dying day – as well as staying off substances.

The gal stared. "I'm Rebecca." She clenched her hands together and crossed her ankles. Lifted then recrossed them again. Itched her scalp.

"Coming down, are ya?"

"Yeah."

"They'll help you. Did someone help you come in? A friend?"

"N-No. Just me."

"You just walked in?" Elenore raised her eyebrows. "I'm impressed."

The girl sighed, then crossed her knees. She itched her arm. "I don't think anyone's been impressed with me before."

Elenore knew Rebecca wanted to walk out the doors right now. Elenore might be the only reason Rebecca still lingered. "I don't think anyone was impressed with me either. But look at us both. Here we are."

"Looks like you're leaving."

"Yeah. Mom's coming to pick me up for Christmas. Merry Christmas, by the way."

She snorted. "Christmas indeed."

"Really, Rebecca. Sobriety will be your best gift." She closed her mouth. Geez, these days she sounded almost preachy. But if she could stop Rebecca from leaving this room, it was worth it. Regretfully, she thought of Nadine, Mynx and the other numerous ladies. Where were they? Probably arrested for prostitution. Elenore might land with some minor charges too, but they'd promised to go easier on her since she ratted Brandon out.

Law enforcement didn't understand that these ladies felt they didn't have choices. That somehow, someone else held all the power, and, in Elenore's case – the drugs became the most important partner of all.

She sighed. Maybe it was time to increase the education around prostitution. She giggled. Super-Ellie to the rescue! But not now – she still had so much work to do on herself. And of course, her first priority was to find her girls and somehow make it up to them.

"I'm glad you came. They'll help you if you let them. Do me a favor, huh?"

"Rebecca Yeager!" A lady called from the desk. Rebecca jumped up – her eyes wide. Then turned to Elenore. "What's that?"

Elenore smiled. "Stay at least 'til I get back. I could use a friend. See you in a few days?"

Rebecca seemed to consider, then nodded as she hurried over to the desk. Elenore watched her sign her name. When Rebecca looked back at her, she gave her a thumbs up.

She could do this. Elenore gave her new friend a big smile and leaned back in her chair. And for once in many years, felt proud of herself.

***

Mel pulled into the slushy parking lot and found a space fairly quickly. Maybe not as many visitors came on Christmas Eve. Her heart lifted as she opened the door and stepped out.

This was a day she'd waited for – for many years. Elenore and she had talked daily on the phone for the past few weeks. Managed several in-person visits. And finally, finally, they'd held some deep conversation and apologies on both ends.

She'd missed her.

The sliding doors to the building opened, and she stepped into the warmth.

"Hi, Mel." The woman at the desk waved. Greeted her with a big smile.

"Hey, Rhonda! Merry Christmas!"

Rhonda glanced at Elenore, who stood and picked up her bag. "Happy for you both. Have a wonderful holiday. Elenore, we'll need you to sign out, please."

Elenore nodded and went to the desk, signing her name with a flourish. "Merry Christmas, Rhonda. Thanks for what you do here."

Mel straightened and held her shoulders back proudly. Ellie was coming back. A slow road indeed – but paying off.

She hugged her daughter and led her to the car.

"What the heck is it with 'Mel'? I think Joy suits you better." Elenore tossed her bag into the trunk.

Mel raised her eyebrows. "I happen to love our middle names. I have my own story." She admitted. "Hop in. I'm so glad to see you for Christmas. And I have a great surprise for you." Ellie tossed her a worried glance. "I promise it's a good surprise."

As they made their way out to I-5, Mel gripped the wheel a bit tighter. "My story? His name is Joshua. Josh, for short. We had a decent relationship at first." She glanced at Ellie and caught her surprised look. "Yes, your mom has a life." She laughed. "I didn't date for a many years after your dad left and I received those divorce papers. You remember that day. I cried and cried."

Elenore nodded, remembering. "Yeah. That's the day I found his booze stash in the garage and started drinking. Dad was gone forever. Did I do something?"

"Oh no, Ellie. No, it wasn't you at all. He was broken with his own trauma. I'm sorry I didn't realize you found his cupboard. But I'm glad you feel you can tell me now."

"I think I have to. Accountability and all that. Making amends. All that goes together, and I'm only going to hurt myself if I don't tell the truth. There's a lot more I must tell you … someday … but yes, I remember the day the papers came." Tears dripped down her cheeks. "Sorry." She reached back and grabbed a tissue box from the backseat. "I cry all the time now. The counselors say it's a good thing I'm finally feeling things and I need to feel them to get through them. But it sucks."

Mel glanced at her with a worried expression. "Yes, it's important to feel. Want me to stop?"

"No, no. Go on." Elenore blew her nose loudly. "Mel." She laughed.

"Okay. So, there was Josh – I met him online. But oh, my word, he became abusive. I had no idea. He'd been married twice and said both ex-wives were crazy. I believed him. There was even a restraining order with one because she accused him of some stuff that I knew he could never do. Not the sweet Josh I knew. Anyway." She took a deep breath and turned her blinker on. "He'd been … not being very nice. A lot of verbal and psychological abuse. He would do things like yell and rage at me one day and then two hours later, act like nothing happened and look at me like I was nuts if I brought it up. I decided to look a little more into his past. I-I called his ex-wife."

"You what?"

"I called her. She didn't seem crazy at all. Super reasonable. Happy to chat and had some serious warnings for me. He choked her and then tossed her down the stairs because she got home late from work one night."

"Wow."

"Yes, wow. I started believing her story. Then we met for lunch to talk more. But when Josh found out, all heck broke loose. He came after me …"

"Oh, my gosh, Mom." Elenore sat on her suddenly shaking hands.

"I'm fine. But there was a gun. He threatened my life. Already black and blue, I called the cops. They arrested him and took me to a shelter. But he got off. Charges didn't stick. He was out of jail the next week, and that's when I decided I'd better move and change my name, too. I'm careful now with who I let into my life." She took a deep breath. "And of course, who I let into my family's life."

Elenore raised her eyebrows. "Do you mean … Jem and Jade?"

"I do. Ellie, Jem and Jade were homeless for a while. But they're safe now. And they're staying with my neighbors."

Elenore slumped back against the seat, her face bright red.

"It's okay, Ellie. You've changed. It's time. Time for them to come back into your life."

Chapter 56
Cienna

Cienna stepped closer. "Bay," she whispered.

Bay waved the gun recklessly. Servio and Jet both advanced. "Get back!" Cienna shouted. "I know her. She's my best friend." She choked out the last word. Saw the men back up slightly out of the corner of her eye. Jet mumbled something about recognizing Jazz.

Jazz/Bay started mumbling too. Something about Frenemy never understanding and how Ruler must take over due to this.

Ruler. Was her name now Ruler? Cienna took a deep breath. Great. More personalities than ever before. "Ruler!"

Jazz's head snapped up, her eyes piercing. "What?" She gritted her teeth.

For gosh sakes, the voice didn't even sound like Jazz.

"Who ... who are you now? Are you Ruler?"

"You!" The gun came closer to Cienna. Both Servio and Jet stiffened, and Cienna waved them away. If they dared make a move, Jazz might discharge the gun. "You're the stubborn girl on the wall. I must hurt you. I must see that you help no one ever again. You broke a promise that hurt someone's heart ..."

A promise? The only promise she could think of was the promise Jazz had made to Rose to find her daughter. And it was after Rose died, for gosh sakes. Although Cienna had stopped helping Jazz pursue it when Jazz seemed to be going backward again.

Bingo.

"I-I'm so sorry. I didn't mean to break a promise. I know Rose meant a lot to you."

The gun waved wildly. "Rose meant a lot to *Bay*," Ruler hissed. "I could give a crap. Frenemy seemed to care, though."

Cienna nodded. Her heart threatened to beat out of her chest. A bead of sweat rolled down her forehead.

She wanted to flee.

No, no. She couldn't. River, bare feet, Betsy. Strong Cienna. Getting them out of this alive – the ultimate priority. "I think I understand." She tried to soften the panic in her voice. "Frenemy is Bay, right?"

Ruler growled. "I don't know so much. We pass in the night. She leaves me instructions, and I do them. I'm a good worker."

"I'm sure you are." Cienna blinked. A good worker with boards, threatening notes and fake bombs. And then a real bomb.

But this was Jazz – her best friend.

She pulled the two notes out of her jeans pocket and waved them. "These are from you?"

"I follow instructions."

She bit her lip. Even to blow up Queenie and Cienna, her best friend?

Thoughts crowded in, confusing her mission. How could this even be possible? Damaged Jazz. Ugh. Tears threatened. She shoved them away.

"Look, uh, Ruler, we aren't getting very far here. Maybe you could put the gun down? We can talk better if you do ..."

"No. I'm supposed to kill you." The monotone and low-pitched voice chilled Cienna. The look on her friend's face intensified.

A panic attack started. Cienna saw Servio shake his head and move forward again, while Jet sat much straighter – his eyes moving quickly back and forth. "No, Servio! It's okay, Jet!" She sighed. Turned back to Ruler. Progress seemed slow – but was essential before the guys made a move.

How would they ever get out of this alive?

"Tell me more." She tried the technique Adrian taught her and she often used with clients. "Why does Bay, uh, Frenemy want me dead? How will that help her?"

The gun wavered. "I do as I'm told. She pays the rent. Otherwise, I'd be on the streets. But then Gregory really screwed it up. You were supposed to be dead along with Queenie!"

"Who's Gregory?"

The voice hardened. "A very stupid, stupid little neighbor man. Took care of him though."

"A neighbor in … in your apartment complex? Ruler, did you shoot him?"

Ruler laughed. An evil, grating sound new to Cienna Who was this … this evil person? A demon? She gritted her teeth. It didn't matter. Keep Ruler talking. Get Ruler to relax so one of them could dive for the gun.

Ruler paused, as if really considering the question. A mix of emotions played across Ruler's face. "I don't think so. Not yet. But then again, he has been a bit, shall we say, restrained? For a while now."

Cienna took a deep breath. "Does Gregory have access to water?"

"Oh, yes." Ruler laughed. "I left him a bucket. Of course, he might have to dump that and use it for … the facilities."

There.

It was an awful reminder of Cienna's time in Mike's barn. Only Jazz and Adrian knew *all* the details. Jazz was in there somewhere. Hope made Cienna's heart bump wildly in the almost-quiet room.

"Jazz." She whispered and let the tears flow. She backed against the door and slumped. "You remember what happened to me. To Cienna. *Me.*"

Ruler's face contorted. It went from sheer anger, to confusion, to angst, to a softening. Cienna watched the transformation with her mouth wide open.

Jazz turned the gun and looked at it. She started sobbing as she leaned forward, her blond hair sticking to her face. "I-I was going to shoot you all. I-I can't believe I was going to shoot my best friend."

Cienna straightened up against the door. Stepped closer. "Jazz, I love you. Give me the Ruger please."

"No." Jazz looked up. "That's not the answer. This is the only answer to get rid of them all. I love you too, Ci."

And she turned the gun toward her chest and pulled the trigger.

Chapter 57
Cienna

Sobbing, Cienna ran to Jazz as blood spread on the floor. She soothed back her best friend's hair. "No, Jazz. No."

This couldn't be the end. She couldn't let it be the end.

They'd been through far too much.

Jazz breathed. Still had a pulse. Cienna ripped off her jacket and pressed it against her friend's chest to try to stop the blood. Jet ran out through the archway of the room. Within moments, voices echoed down the hallway and lights flashed as law enforcement came near. They burst into the room with guns drawn.

Cienna threw herself on top of Jazz. "No! No, don't shoot!" Tears poured down her cheeks.

"Ma'am, we're here to help. We need you to move."

Cienna slid off her friend and scrambled backward on her butt with her hands propelling her. She saw Adrian enter. Felt him kneel next to her. Heard his voice from a great distance. She was too numb to feel his chest as he pulled her close and then she fought him anyway. With her fists, she pounded at him as she cried torrential tears. She saw that she was leaving bloody marks on his shirt and stopped. "I-I'm sorry."

She saw other officers enter the room, Elianna searching every corner with her flashlight and gun. "No … no other bad people." Cienna tried to explain, gasping through tears. "It was Jazz all along. Another personality. Please help her. Please don't let her die."

She barely felt Adrian pulling her off the floor and carrying her to their SUV. He must have grabbed a car service to get there. She watched numbly as he offered the backseat to Servio and Jet, who looked as stricken as she felt. They climbed in, and she felt one of them touch her shoulder, trying to comfort her. She pulled her legs up and wrapped her arms around her knees. She watched for the gurney to come out and breathed a sigh of relief to see Jazz's face exposed instead of covered in a body bag. An oxygen mask covered her face.

Would she make it through?

Jazz *had* to make it through.

She fumbled for her phone. Servio handed it to her from the backseat. Zeb was AWOL now but apparently had figured out her phone's emergency feature to call for help.

Someone needed to let Jazz's folks know.

Jazz's mom picked up on the second ring. "Cienna?"

"Yeah it's me. Hey, I'm so sorry." Her voice caught and she gulped. "Uh, Jasmine's been going a little downhill with the personality thing. I …, uh, *she* shot herself tonight."
She heard the gasp and wail on the other end and scrambled to comfort Mari. "She's alive. Call Ken, please. I'll text you when I know where they're taking her. I'm so sorry, Mari." She ended the call on a sob and leaned forward.

Did she see what she thought she was seeing?

With the ambulance doors wide open, the EMTs performed CPR.

Cienna scrambled for the door handle, her hands still bloody. She slipped through the open door, almost falling to the ground. She pushed to her feet and ran to the ambulance. "Jazz! Wake up! Wake up Jazz! You can't go. I need you. You can't go yet. Breathe, Jazz! Tell your heart to beat! I need you, my friend. I need you …"

One EMT started to roll his eyes, but the other put up his hand. "We have a rhythm. Let her talk."

Cienna scrambled up into the ambulance and practically pushed the other EMT aside. She grabbed Jazz's hand. They increased her oxygen.

"Stable for now." The EMT announced. "I think she heard her friend."

Cienna breathed a sigh of relief. Bent down to her Jazz's ear. "Jasmine Leah Jenkins, we've been through far too much for me to lose you tonight. Fight for me! Fight! You can do this. Don't leave me yet. We need to grow old together. And knit blankets …" Hmmm, she couldn't imagine knitting blankets. "Write books, walk in the park, play with Grace and her kids. Take them to the carnival …"

The machine monitoring her friend's heart beeped, beeped, beeped.

Then paused.

"No, Jazz! No! Gosh darn it! Ruler? Bay? Frenemy? Whoever can hear me-"

"We need to go. You coming along?" The EMT's eyebrows furrowed. He shook Jazz's shoulder, and her heart monitor started beeping regularly again. "You say her name is Jazz? Or something else? Keep talking to her. She needs to hear you right now."

"Yes! It's Jazz!" Cienna glanced out the door and saw Adrian's worried face. "Call Mari! They said we're going to Emmanuel." Somehow in the ruckus she'd heard that on the radio traffic. "They can meet me there. I-I love you."

"I'll take the others home. I love you, Cienna."

She couldn't be sure, but it appeared that Adrian also wiped tears away.

The door slammed, and they headed to the hospital.

Chapter 58
Jem

Jem paused at the doorway. Christmas morning, and Cienna sat by the tree, weeping. The news droned on. Adrian had returned home last night. Jet gave Jem the rundown. Servio and Jet slept in the basement bedroom.

Cienna returned home sometime during the night, late, via a car service. But Jem was quite sure she'd rather be at the hospital.

Instead, Jem suspected she'd come home to make sure that everyone here actually had a Christmas.

Sorrow bloomed in her chest. She went over and sat next to Cienna, wrapping her arms around her honorary mama. "I'm sorry about Jazz," she whispered. "Will she be okay?"

Cienna sniffed, wiped her tears on her sleeve and squeezed Jem back. "They think so. She's … she's critical though. I'll head back after we all open gifts and have some lunch."

"Did you get some rest?"

Cienna nodded. Managed a little smile. "A couple hours. Guess my body was tired. Tears wear me out too." She wiped her face again and turned toward Jem. "I'm so sorry. This was supposed to be such a special Christmas for the two of you. Boy, did that turn upside down."

"It's okay. Most of my holidays seem to turn upside down."

They laughed, thinking of Thanksgiving spent in the hospital. But at least Jade was healthy now.

"You know what?" Cienna whispered. "You never did open your stocking. We were gonna do that yesterday."

"A lot's happened. And Adrian said the clam chowder burned."

Cienna poked her in the ribs. "Yeah. Chowder for the new year maybe instead. How about you open up your stocking?"

Jem giggled. "Yeah? What about Jade?"

"Let her sleep. Come on. I want to see what Santa brought. There it hangs. Lonely." She looked at the fireplace and shook her head mournfully. "So sad."

"We don't need things to be any sadder here!" Jem jumped up and ran over to the fireplace. She carefully unhooked her stocking and brought it back to sit near Cienna. "Are you sure?"

"Yes! Do it!"

Jem turned her stocking upside down and shook some things out on the carpet. Then she paused. "I-I don't know how to do it. I've never had a stocking."

"Well, you're in luck. There's never been a correct way. It's a very individualized process. But hey, something is stuck." Cienna reached over and flicked the stocking.

Jem shook it again. Cienna smiled. "You're gonna have to reach in."

Jem giggled, then reached inside the large stocking. When she pulled it out, her face glowed. "A phone! A new phone! Thank you!"

"What?" Cienna smiled. "Are you sure?" She pulled the stocking away as the box was fully revealed. "They say to not trust boxes, you know."

Jem laughed and tore it open. "It is! A new iPhone! Those cost … so much! I can play my music on it!" She pulled it close and hugged it.

Cienna smiled. "Every girl needs a phone, you know. And it's on our plan. We have unlimited messaging and minutes. I put all our contact information into it already."

"Wow!" Jem started to cry. "But what if we can't stay here?"

"Well, we're working on that. But that won't change anything. Once you're on our family plan, you're there to stay. I want you to always have a way to contact us, no matter what happens. Unless of course, you get a new family, and we need to transfer it to their plan. That's okay. And hey, you have chocolate!"

They dove for the mini chocolate bars and gold coins. Managed to find their favorites and soon popped them in their mouths. Jem found an orange at the toe of her stocking and a gift card to a clothing store at the mall. Not that she'd ever been, but she'd heard about it on TV. And she couldn't wait to find the store and learn more.

Epilogue
Jem

They were in the middle of Christmas turkey lunch when a noise alerted them to new arrivals. Cienna jumped up. "Welcome, Mel! I'll get another plate!"

Mel hesitated at the dining room entryway, then motioned behind her. Sheepishly, Elenore appeared at her side.

"Elenore!" Jade cried and jumped up. She ran to her, and Elenore caught her in a big hug.

"Hi, honey. You look like you're having a nice meal. I'm glad for you. Is that mashed potatoes I see?"

Jem dropped her napkin and stood. She crossed her arms. Anger simmered. "So, you found us. Where's Brandon?" Her heart hammered. They'd finally come to take them both back. But a surprise awaited them. Jem had prepared – with a kitchen knife tucked under her mattress. She glared at Elenore. Oh no. She and Jade would never return willingly. Never. Memories flooded her brain, and she pushed them away.

"No Brandon." Elenore put her arms out. "Just me. I'm sober, Jem. We called the police on Brandon. Mom brought me …"

Mom?

"Wait!" Jem shoved her chair back. "You're my … you're our …"

Mel smiled. "I'm your grandma, honey. I'm Joy Stevens. I go by Mel now. But I knew you as soon as I set eyes on you, and I'm not gonna let you out of my sight ever again …"

Servio coughed. Jet cleared his throat. Mrs. K harrumphed.

Yeah. Okay. Some grandma she'd been.

Jem sat suddenly, but perched on the edge of her chair, her appetite ruined. "Sit down, Jade." She ordered, but the girl continued to hover around Elenore.

"Wait." Cienna lifted her hand. "We can talk later. I heard something." She threw her napkin down and ran into the living room. Jem rudely brushed by mom and followed Cienna.

Breaking news filled the screen. The newsman brushed his bangs aside. "I'm sorry to bring this news on what should be a happy holiday. There's been a prison break. I repeat, a prison break and escape by several prisoners at Portland Penitentiary. These men are considered armed and dangerous. Do not let them into your homes. Again, there has been a prison break. They are armed and dangerous ..."

Jem saw Cienna gasp and cover her mouth as the mugshots of the escapees scrolled across the screen.

"Mike," she whispered.

This day I call the heavens and the earth as witnesses against you that I have set before you life and death, blessings and curses. Now choose life, so that you and your children may live. -Deuteronomy 30:19 (NIV)

THE END

Enjoy a couple of chapters in the next book: "Innocent Hearts: Guardians of Grace Book 3".

Innocent Hearts: Guardians of Grace Book 3

Prologue
Lynn

Lynn heard the patter of naked feet before she saw her. Slowly the fridge opened, casting an eerie light into the kitchen and the dining room beyond where Lynn sat, the open, empty pizza box before her. Her stomach rumbled uncomfortably as she watched her seven-year-old daughter poke her head into the fridge and heard her moving the pickle jar, the milk, the bag of shredded cheese Lynn needed to toss.

Oh dear. She wasn't the only one with the munchies tonight.

Lynn barely moved. But the kitchen clatter increased. The open refrigerator door suddenly slammed against the wall. Ashlynn banged her head backing out of it, only to ram into the large dark figure standing there.

Levi stood there. As Ash looked up with large eyes, he pushed her shoulder, and she stumbled back against the counter. "There you go again, piggy. Just like your mother."

Lynn shriveled back against her chair.

Levi peered into the fridge. "I see you ate all the pizza already. How long have you been up?"

Ash hurried over to the sink and grabbed a glass from the cupboard. She rubbed the back of her head with her other hand. "I didn't eat the pizza, Daddy. I was ... was just thirsty." She turned the faucet on and filled the glass. "I'll go back to bed now."

"Not yet you're not. No wonder you've gotten chubby over the last few months. You know, when you eat at night, the calories add up. This explains things now."

Lynn shrank even further in the dark dining area, feeling every inch of fat around her waist she'd gathered like the dandelions in the front yard. Ever since the boys were born four years ago.

Ever since Levi developed a mean streak.

Levi slammed the fridge closed and headed to the sink. Lynn saw just well enough to see her daughter shrank against the counter. The small light above the sink flicked on and the light illuminated Ashlynn's scared face. She placed her glass on the counter. Good girl. Safer to not have glass in her hand. Lynn should get up now, tell Levi who really ate the pizza and tell Ash to get back to bed.

But she sat, frozen.

Levi poked their daughter in the chest.

"Ow, Daddy." Ashlynn crossed her arms in front of her and looked at the floor. She wanted to run. Lynn read her face clearly – fear.

Levi poked her in the stomach.

"Stop, Daddy. I want to go to bed now." Ashlynn slid along the counter to her right and grabbed her glass. She chugged it.

She really must be hungry. Lynn hoped the water would fill her up, but she doubted it. It never worked for her either.

Ashlynn set the glass down. "Can I go now?" She yawned.

Her father glowered. Raised his hand and shook his finger at her face. "Just remember what I said. Keep eating at night, and you'll be a fat pig like your mother."

"Okay, okay." She brushed by him, and he swatted her butt as she passed. She ran out of the kitchen, and Lynn heard her quick feet pounding upstairs as fast as she could go.

She took a deep breath. Her heartbeat quickened. Of course. It had to work much harder with the extra fifty pounds she'd added.

A fat pig indeed.

She groaned softly and put her head down on her arms.

Drowsiness washed over her. She should have said something. Oh, well. At least Levi hadn't hurt Ashlynn. He poked at her playfully, for sure. And she'd hit her head in the fridge – but that wasn't really his fault.

Lynn's mind wandered as Levi scrounged around the kitchen.

Who was night eating now?

He plopped a packet of ramen on the table and took a pan from the hanging rack. "Did you think I'd miss the fact that your side of the bed is empty?"

Lynn snapped her head up. So much for staying quiet. But it was still dark in the dining room. She inched the pizza box farther away with her finger. Grabbed a napkin to scrub at her lips.

"Of course not." She managed to keep her voice cheerful, although her hands shook. "But ... but it wouldn't have done any good to let her know I was here. You were already taking care of it."

Levi added water to the pan and turned the burner on. "Indeed. Although I should have whipped her for it. That entire pizza is gone. Just gone!"

A shiver started at the base of Lynn's spine and moved to her neck. A lump crept into her throat.

The problem with her husband was that she could never quite tell when he was being serious or whether he was playing with her mind.

The water in the pan started steaming, and Levi dumped the noodles into it. "Well, since you left bed, I guess I can come eat with you at the table, then." He raised an eyebrow as he stirred the noodles, then grabbed a strainer from the cupboard above the stove.

What? Oh no!

Lynn grabbed the pizza box as quietly as she could and closed it, setting it on the chair next to her. She pushed the chair in as far as it could go. The chair feet squeaked as they moved. She stilled. She tucked her foot around the chair leg. Levi needed to choose another chair. Should she ditch the box and leave the other way – go around to the living room to head upstairs? Just because the box was there didn't mean she was guilty. But then, it looked like Ashlynn truly was.

Lynn yawned loudly. "I'm probably going to head back to bed. I'm pretty tired."

Levi's sudden whistle filled the kitchen. Was that the Andy Griffith tune? He quieted as he took the pan of noodles to the sink and drained them through the strainer. "Carbs will do that," he said evenly. He grabbed a bowl from the cupboard and dumped the noodles in. Found the sauce packet and sprinkled it over the bowl.

Lynn shuddered. He was the only person she knew who liked it so strong. When she made it for her and the kids, she added the sauce to the noodles and the water and then strained them out.

"Oh, I'm not hungry." She shifted her legs under the table. Well, that was true anyway. Her stomach actually hurt from all the pizza.

Levi laughed. He entered the dining room and light flooded the table. She blinked. "What's the matter? You look like a deer in the truck's headlights. What? You don't think our daughter needs discipline? Some mother you turned out to be." He snorted.

"I-I'm fine with discipline. I-I think you maybe were a little harsh with her. Maybe she really was hungry."

He sat at the table, fortunately across from her. At the same time, both their gazes fell on the wadded-up napkins stained with red sauce. He looked at her, so she cast her eyes downward at the table. "Speaking of needing discipline … where's the box? Did you think you could hide it from me? I can smell it."

Lynn's face flushed. She yanked the box out from its hiding place and threw it on the table. Unfortunately, it slid over and pushed his fork off the table. "Sorry." She quickly apologized.

He sneered. "Disgusting. You ate *all* the leftovers? There was over a half left. So much for me packing lunch tomorrow." He rolled his eyes, grabbed his fork from the floor and stabbed the noodles with it.

"I-I shared some with the dog?" They both glanced at the blonde mutt stretched out happily on his bed near the wall.

"You're lying. And there's really only one way to fix this, you know. You'll sit here with me while I eat, and then we'll have to figure out a way to burn all those calories you took in. I guess the other option is to make yourself throw them up before they hit your waistline." He crammed noodles into his mouth.

Lynn groaned and covered her face with her hands.

Chapter 1
Jazz

Jazz opened her eyes and stared at the ceiling tiles dotted with holes. Moved her eyes around the room. White, all white.

A hospital. Why the heck was she in a hospital? She struggled to sit but large, thick bandages covered her torso. And her chest felt like it was on fire. She settled back on the pillow. Tears leaked down her cheeks. She turned to look at the open door – surprised to see cops. Two in the hallway in deep discussion.

Guarding her?

A brief memory hovered. She quickly pushed it away. She glanced at her button to call the nurse. Screw them. She didn't need anybody.

But a nurse bustled into the room anyway. "Well, good morning, Jasmine. Is that what you would like to be called today?"

She groaned. "I go by Jazz."

"Good. I have your sister calling your room here in a minute. But she for sure wants to talk to just you. Jazz, that is. We gave her your room number."

"Amelie?"

"Yes." The nurse nodded as if satisfied and pushed over a small side table that held a phone and a menu.

"Where am I?"

"You're at Emmanuel Hospital. Don't move now. We need to limit your movement until you heal more. We performed emergency surgery."

Why?

The phone rang.

"There she is!"

The nurse's cheerfulness churned Jazz's stomach. The woman picked up the phone and introduced herself. Then handed the phone to Jazz, who snatched it from her.

"Am?"

"Hey, Jazz." Relief filled Amelie's voice. "How ... how are you? I'm on my way. Mom and Dad are out of town, and their flight got delayed, but they're trying to make it back."

Jazz laughed. Was everyone crazy here? "Mom and Dad are divorced. What are you talking about?"

"I know, sis. But they did a trip together. Uncle Brad is on hospice, I guess ..."

"Oh. That's sad. I didn't know. You driving from Seattle? What about Mitch and the kids?"

"They're staying here. Too hard to load everyone up, disrupt their school and sports." She laughed but sounded tense.

Jazz laughed too, picturing her sister piling her brood into their red minivan. In nine years' time, Amelie had managed marriage, finishing her degree and popping out three kids.

A life foreign to Jazz.

"I called Seth. He can come if you want him to."

Jazz considered. Her little brother towered over her these days and had just enrolled at the local community college, volunteering as a police reserve in his spare time. Luckily not in Portland. On the west side of the county instead. "Tell him I'm okay."

"Okay. I will. See you in a few hours."

"Amelie, I don't understand why I'm here." Jazz felt tears again. Sheesh. She was an emotional yo-yo.

Amelie sighed. "You don't remember?"

"Remember what?"

She groaned. "I guess it's true then. Jazz, Bay came back for a while. Under ... under some other names, I guess. And she hurt you."

But Bay *was* Jazz.

Jazz groaned. "How? What did she do? I hadn't heard from her in a long time. I-I thought she was finally gone."

"She, uh ... uh, shot you in the chest. We could have lost you, Jazz. Had that bullet been even a couple inches higher, it would have hit your heart."

Now Jazz heard tears in her sister's voice.

"Anyway, you're okay. We'll talk more when I get there. I'm so relieved you're alive. We all are. Cienna was a complete mess."

"Ci was there?"

"She was. No, you didn't hurt her. I mean, Bay didn't hurt her."

Jazz turned over on her side and tried to pull her knees up, but pain shot through her ribs. "Ow. Dang it. Okay, get here soon." She eyed the cops in the hallway. "Otherwise, they're probably gonna take Bay to jail and put her on the Trouble Couch."

After hanging up the phone, exhaustion set in. The nurse inserted meds into her IV, and she felt sleepy. With her history they'd limit her pain medication and remove her from them as soon as possible.

That was the only option for Jazz.

As she was falling asleep, she heard Ruler jeering. "Couldn't even kill yourself, Frenemy? Can't do much right at all, can you? Guess you better figure out how to finish the job."

To be continued in "Innocent Hearts: Guardians of Grace Book 3." More information at the author's website: ***www.juliebonnblank.com***

Want to learn more about Rose's and Penny's stories? As my gift to you, these are available in two free eBooks that you can download at **www.innocentjourneys.com**

A Note from Julie

Hello friends! Wow, you've made it through Book 2 and I'm so appreciative of your support and love. And yay! I made it through Book 2 as well! Ha ha. As you can see, I've already started Book 3, "Innocent Hearts", and I'm hoping to release it this year so that you don't have to wait a full year for the next segment.

As I'm writing this, I just received word that "Innocent Lives: Guardians of Grace Book 1" is a finalist in the American Book Awards! And literally another email just arrived about the American Book Fest Awards! Very exciting and I am so grateful to Jesus as well as my team members and supporters for helping me get these words out of my head! "Innocent Lives" also won a BookFest Award and a "Human Trafficking Awareness" award from Hope PYX Global within the past year.

As you might have guessed, I decided there was WAY too much story to make it all happen in three books. Plus, I needed to stretch out the timeline a bit (you will see why later). So, at this point, I am planning on a 4-book series and the fourth one will be called "Innocent Souls". Yup-I started with lives at stake in "Innocent Lives" and they are also at risk in the next two books, but that is not the true ending. We still have souls that live eternally – even when we die.

What's next for me, you wonder? Well, I still want to finish that devotional healing journal for ladies looking to heal from abuse and trauma. It's about halfway done but I've been so busy with this series and full-time work (plus speaking, teaching, DV coaching and designing websites), that it's been put aside. And there just might be another fiction series percolating in my brain – a never-ending joy but curse as well since it sometimes prevents sleep and other important activities.

As always, I am thankful to my Heavenly Father for creating me, for giving me the desire to write and for making it possible to go to conferences, take classes, have mentors and to truly hone this craft of writing. I'm grateful to my husband Bill who puts up with my endless typing and often filling my "official days off" with writing and writing-related activities. Yes, we still make time to get to the beach, as though not as often as we both want. I'm grateful to my parents, who have supported me and my gifts since I was born. I will never, ever find greater cheerleaders and I am so very grateful. Thank you to our four kiddos and especially the kiddo who gave my first grandchild this past year (I'M A NANA!). I deeply appreciate the assistance of my editor, Louise M. Gouge, who makes all my writing better. We are a true team. And I am thankful as well to my beloved friend, Cathie Blackstock, who is my wonderful proofreader and "finalizer" and in this book, caught a MAJOR miss I didn't catch, and my editor didn't see either! She also catches names that should have been changed, characters that should have been included in certain scenes and more! Thank you, Cathie. I am so grateful for you. Thank you to high school friend, Carlea Dill, who reviewed some parts of the book regarding the 911 dispatching as she was an amazing dispatcher for years. I'm thankful for the Christian online writer's group that I facilitate the fourth Sunday of each month. Not only great writing partners but awesome prayer supporters as well! And I am grateful to be able to continue attending and also teaching at Oregon Christian Writers, Southwest Washington Writers Conference and West Coast Christian Writers.

For those curious about my writing process:

- I am a "pantser" not a "plotter". (I "fly by the seat of my pants".) Although I've written outlines for several books and/or chapter summaries, I never stick with them. Ugh! The story and characters take on a life of their own and my job becomes writing *their* story. I often think of what needs to happen next only after I'm done writing a certain section or chapter. Sometimes, I take notes on my phone in the middle of the night but there is no guarantee when I get to the computer that I will stick to what's on that list! This can have its downsides – and maybe explains why I wasn't so great in school until I got to college, where I got to finally write and write and write as a pantser, as long as I reached the end goal for that assignment.

- I write the story then re-read and edit what I wrote, always trying to catch passive voice, unnecessary lingo, head-hopping (changing point of view mid-scene – yes, even caught one of those on the final edit of this one), discrepancies in certain character's actions, tone, voice, funky plotlines, a loose end I didn't tie up, etc. I'm always the best editor of my work a day or so later – not the same day I wrote it initially.
- I turn it into Louise, my editor, who makes more suggestions.
- I accept or reject her suggestions, based on the situation, and sometimes add more in or subtract other things, re-reading again as I go.
- Cathie, my proofreader, reads through that copy when it's completed and makes additional suggestions and corrections.
- I read it again and accept or reject Cathie's suggestions and may make additional changes at that point.
- Once I format it into a final book format, I do at least two final readthroughs to catch any errors or omissions. I ended up doing third and fourth final readthrough this time but it's a good thing I did! Amazing what I caught. Ugh.

- I start all over with the next book!

Yes, writing a book is quite the process and takes many hours (although book 2 went much smoother and took less time than book 1!) And for those curious, the short eBooks I wrote about Rose and Penny were not edited by anyone but me. I think the difference of having a team became very evident to me when I read a review that said, **"I knew that after reading 'Penny' and 'Rose' that 'Innocent Lives' would be good, but I didn't realize *how good* it would be!"** (-dagaz98, Amazon Reviewer)

Having a team can make a great book into an excellent one and so THANK YOU, MY TEAM. You are invaluable to me.

As always, you can keep up with me on social media or on my website. I love connecting with my readers! *If you liked this book, I again ask you to consider leaving a review wherever you purchased it from or on GoodReads.com.* We authors are not playing games when we tell you how incredibly important great reviews are. THANK YOU!

Links:
Website: **www.juliebonnblank.com**
Facebook: **www.facebook.com/juliebonnblankauthor**
Instagram: **www.instagram.com/juliebonnblank**
Twitter: **www.twitter.com/juliebonnblank**
You Tube: **https://www.youtube.com/@juliebonnblank**

If you want to see my speaking schedule or listen to some of the podcasts and media I have been a guest on, please visit https://www.juliebonnblank.com/speaking/

As always, if you are suffering from abuse or have abuse to heal from, you are not alone! Please visit **www.abuserecovery.org** for some important resources (several articles also written by yours truly) and healing groups called "Her Journey" that were essential to my healing and thousands of others. You may call them at 503-846-9284 or 866-262-9284.

A Gift for You!

Don't forget! There is a two-in-one eBook boxed set for FREE for my readers. This is my THANKS for continuing to hang out with me. Just visit **www.innocentjourneys.com** to download them for no charge. You will also be added to my newsletter list which I currently email out to once a month or so.

Young Penny hides in cupboards to escape the bad man and especially his mean dog, Trigger. Despite this, Mike drags her out occasionally for domestic servitude and to her use as his punching bag.

But Penny has a secret, and a friend to help through the worst of times. What will happen when Mike discovers she's made a friend, and will Penny get out before his anger becomes deadly?

***

The streets become a refuge for Rose after her father leaves her home and her mom becomes the family drunk-passed out on the couch much of the time.

Her savior arrives in the form of Roman, who gives her a home and employment.

When she gets pregnant, his abuse takes a wicked turn. Will she get out in time to protect herself and her new baby?

MY READERS ROCK! I THANK YOU!

Made in the USA
Columbia, SC
01 January 2023